B

CANDYLAND

108658001

CANDYLAND

Evan Hunter & Ed McBain

COMPASS PRESS
★ OXFORD ★ MELBOURNE ★

Copyright © HUI Corp., 2001

First published in 2000 by Orion Publishing Group

Compass Press Large Print Book Series; an imprint of
ISIS Publishing Ltd, Great Britain, and Bolinda Press, Australia
Published in Large Print 2001 by ISIS Publishing Ltd,
7 Centremead, Osney Mead, Oxford OX2 0ES,
and Bolinda Publishing Pty Ltd,
17 Mohr Street, Tullamarine, Victoria 3043
by arrangement with Orion Publishing Group

**British Library Cataloguing in
Publication Data**
Hunter, Evan, 1926–
Candyland - Large print ed.
1. Suspense fiction
2. Large type books
I. Title II. McBain, Ed, 1926–
813.5'4 [F]

**Australian Cataloguing in
Publication Data**
Hunter, Evan (aka Ed McBain)
 1926–
Candyland: a novel in two parts /
 Evan Hunter
1. Large print books
2. Detective and mystery
I. McBain, Ed. II. Title
813.54

ISBN 0-7531-6508-2 (hb) ISBN 0-7531-6509-0 (pb)
(ISIS Publishing Ltd)
ISBN 1-74030-508-6 (hb) ISBN 1-74030-509-4 (pb)
(Bolinda Publishing Pty Ltd)

Printed and bound by Antony Rowe, Chippenham and Reading

Yet another time, always, this is for my wife—

DRAGICA DIMITRIJEVIĆ-HUNTER

The rain may never fall
Till after sundown

By eight, the morning fog
Must disappear . . .

Alan Jay Lerner and Frederick Lœwe, *Camelot*

The rain may never fall
till after sundown...

Evan Hunter

CHAPTER
ONE

The brunette is telling Ben that what he's done with the space is truly remarkable. She's a lawyer with the firm, and he can't possibly imagine her knowing anything at all about matters architectural, so he guesses she's flirting with him, although in an arcane legal sort of way.

The name of the law firm is Dowd, Dawson, Liepman and Loeb. It is on the thirty-sixth and thirty-seventh floors of the old Addison Building on Eighteenth Street and Ninth Avenue. The brunette is telling him that his multilevel concept echoes the very precepts of the law, exalted justice on high, abject supplicants below. Through the huge cathedral windows Ben designed for the eastern end of the space, he can see storm clouds gathering.

The brunette is drinking white wine. Ben is drinking a Perrier and lime. This is DDL&L's first party in their new offices. They have invited all their important clients as well as the architect and interior designer who together restructured and redecorated the two top floors of the building. It is now ten minutes past six on the twenty-first of July, a Wednesday. Ben flew in this morning and is scheduled to take the eight A.M. flight back to Los Angeles tomorrow. He listens to the brunette telling him how wonderful he is. She is full figured and wearing a very low cut red cocktail dress.

He looks out again at the threatening sky.

Ben's firm is called Ritter-Thorpe Associates. The company was Frank Ritter's before Ben became a partner, hence the top billing. There are seven architects altogether, but Frank and Ben are the only partners. Their receptionist, Agata, is a Chicano girl they hired straight out of a high school in the Venice ghetto. She greets him warmly in her accented English, and then puts him through to Frank who, she informs him, "hass joss return from a meeting."

"How'd it go?" Frank asks at once.

"Good," Ben says. "Lots of nice comments, half a dozen people asking for a card."

"Any mention of those windows that popped?"

"No, no. Why should there be? That was a long time ago, Frank."

"Only six months."

"Nobody mentioned it."

"You should have had a model made."

"Well . . ."

"Tested it in a wind tunnel."

"Spilled milk," Ben says. "Anyway, it worked out all . . ."

"We're lucky it happened when it did. Every window in the place could have blown out."

"Well, nobody mentioned it."

4

"Still," Frank says.

He's not too subtly suggesting that Ben's been letting too many details slip by nowadays. The air exchange for the storage room in the house in Santa Monica. The support for the free-standing staircase in the Malibu beach house. Minor details. Well, the windows popping out here in New York wasn't so minor, they were lucky nobody got hurt. But that was the structural engineer's fault, not Ben's. Still, the architect always takes the blame.

"Did anybody say when we can expect final payment?" Frank asks.

"I didn't bring it up."

"Big party, no check," Frank says.

"I'm sure it'll be coming soon."

"Unless they plan to bring up the windows again."

"I don't think so."

"We'll see," Frank says, and sighs. "When are you coming back?"

"I'm on the eight o'clock flight tomorrow morning."

"What time is it there, anyway?"

Ben looks at his watch.

"Five past seven."

"What are your plans?"

"Dinner. Sleep."

"Fly safely," Frank says, and hangs up.

Ben finds his airline ticket in his dispatch case, locates the phone number to call, and dials it. He knows it isn't necessary to reconfirm, but he wants to make sure he's on that flight. The woman he speaks to assures him that he is indeed confirmed for American's number 33, leaving Kennedy at eight A.M. tomorrow, non-stop to LAX.

"That's first class, correct?" he asks.

"First class, yes, Mr. Thorpe."

"Thank you," he says, and hangs up. He lifts the receiver again, waits for a dial tone, dials an 8 for long distance and then direct-dials his home number. It is ten past seven, which makes it ten past four in L.A. The phone keeps ringing. He hopes she's back from the hospital by now. Come on, he thinks, pick up the . . .

"Hello?"

"Grace?"

"Ben? What's the matter?"

"Nothing. I just got back to the hotel. My flight's okay for tomorrow morning, I just checked."

"Why wouldn't it be okay?"

"No reason. Well, it's raining here. Sometimes. . ."

"It's raining here, too."

"Sometimes rain can cause cancellations. Or delays. But everything seems to be all right. What I plan to do is leave the hotel at six-thirty tomorrow morn . . ."

"Isn't that early? For an eight A.M. flight?"

"Well, I like to get there a little early. I should be in L.A. at a quarter to eleven. Shall I come directly to the hospital, or what?"

"They want to do a bypass," Grace says.

6

"How does she look?"

"Gray. Tired. Sad. She's resting quietly now, but the pain was excruciating."

"I can imagine."

"I'm exhausted, Ben."

"I shouldn't have come East," he says.

"You didn't know this would happen."

"I should've come home the minute you called."

"Nonsense. It was important that you stay."

"I guess so. Anyway, I'll be home tomorrow."

"How did it go?"

"Oh, fine. The usual."

"Have you had dinner yet?"

"No, I just got back. I want to shower and change, then I'll go down."

"Where will you eat?"

"I thought Trattoria. It's right around the corner."

"Yes, it's good there."

"I want to get to bed early. It's been a busy day."

"Here, too."

"I'll call again when I'm back from dinner," he says.

"You don't have to, Ben."

"Well, I want to."

"I'll be here, but really, you don't have to."

"When will they do it, do you know?"

"Tomorrow morning. I think. It has something to do with all the numbers being right. I don't know what the hell they're talking about."

"I'll try you when I get back."

"Really, you don't have to."

"Well, whatever you say."

"Really."

"But call me if you need me, Grace."

"I will."

"Otherwise I'll talk to you tomorrow morning."

"I'll be leaving for the hospital early."

"Yes, but we're three hours . . ."

"Right, I forgot."

"In fact . . . well, let me see."

He hears her sighing on the other end of the line.

"You'll be asleep," he says. "We'll probably begin boarding around seven-thirty. That's only four-thirty, your time. Maybe I'd better call you when I get back from . . ."

"For Christ's sake, don't *worry* about it!" she snaps.

The line goes silent.

"Well . . . if I don't talk to you before then, I'll see you at the hospital."

"Fine."

"Call me if you need me, Grace."

"I will."

"Love you."

"Love you, too," she says, and hangs up.

Gently, he replaces the receiver on its cradle.

It is always "Call me if you need me, Grace."

In the twenty-two years they've been married, she has called him only once, and then to tell him that Margaret fell from a horse at camp. He travels a lot. There are always clients to confer with in St Louis or Chicago, sites to inspect in New Orleans or New

8

York, lectures to deliver in Omaha or Salt Lake City. He is Benjamin Thorpe, an important architect who is very much in demand.

It is still raining hard outside.

His daughter lives in Princeton, New Jersey, where her husband is a tenured professor of economics. Charles is perhaps the cheapest man in the United States of America, if not the entire world. It would never occur to him to make a long distance call to find out how Margaret's grandmother is doing out there in the wilds of Los Angeles. Nor would it ever occur to her to pick up the phone of her own volition, call Ben here, call her mother out there for a progress report.

This is now twenty past seven. His darling daughter has known since twelve noon that her grandmother had a heart attack early this morning L.A. time, and that her mother is frantic with worry. But she has not called since Ben spoke to her earlier today. Perhaps she's been too busy barbecuing hamburgers and hot dogs in her back yard.

He dials the New Jersey number now, hoping he won't get Charles the First, as he refers to him in private to Grace, the implied hope being that one of these days Margaret will move on to a second, more desirable mate. He is happy when his granddaughter picks up the phone.

"This is the Harris residence," she pipes in her three-year-old voice.

"Hi, Jenny," he says.

"Is this Grandpa?"

9

"This is Grandpa. Is this Jenny?"

"Hi, Grandpa. Are you watching television?"

"No. Are you?"

"They're still talking about John John."

"Yes, darling, I know."

"I want to go put flowers at his building."

"Maybe Mommy will take you."

"She says no. Will you take me, Grandpa?"

"I can't, honey. I have to go back to L.A."

"Ask her to take me, okay?" she says, and is suddenly gone. He waits. He does not like being a grandfather. He is only forty-three years old, and he blames his present premature senior-citizen status on his daughter, who married at the age of seventeen and delivered Jenny a scant ten months later. A man of forty-three — well, almost forty-four — should not be a grandfather. He does not enjoy being called Grandpa, or Gramps, or as Charles the First is fond of putting it, "Papa Ben." He is Benjamin Thorpe, Esquire, famous architect whose multilevel concept echoes the very precepts of the law, exalted justice on high, abject supplicants below — and not anybody's damn grandpa.

"Grandpa?"

"Yes, Jenny."

"She's coming. Ask her," she whispers, and puts down the phone with a clatter.

His daughter comes on, high-pitched and frantic as usual. He cannot imagine how he ever spawned such a nervous individual.

"She's dead, right?" she says at once.

10

"No, Margaret, she's not dead."

"Everybody's dying," she says. "Isn't it awful, what happened?"

"Honey, if Jenny wants to go put flowers . . ."

"I can't take her into the city just for that, Dad."

"It's important to her," he says.

"All the way down in TriBeCa, no less," she says, dismissing it. "What's Grandma's condition?"

"She's all right for now. They'll be doing . . ."

"What do you mean for now?"

"She's resting quietly. They'll be doing a bypass tomorrow morning. Provided the numbers are right."

"What numbers? Numbers?"

He sometimes wishes she'd gone to college instead of becoming an instant nervous mother. Why did she have to turn him into a grandfather so soon?

"They do various tests to determine whether it's all right to operate."

"What tests?"

"I don't know, I'm not a doctor, Margaret. They know what they're doing, they do a dozen bypasses every day of the week."

"Well, I hope so."

"Don't worry, she'll be all right."

"I hope so."

"She will."

There is a long silence on the line. He never seems to know what to say to his daughter these days. His own daughter.

"Why don't you call Mom?" he suggests.

"Maybe I will," she says.

Which means she won't.

"Well, I have to go now," he says.

"What time is your flight?"

"Eight tomorrow morning. Margaret?"

"Yes, Dad?"

"These things are important to children."

"I know, Dad, but . . ."

"I was only eight when his father got killed in Dallas. I still remember it."

"Charles doesn't think it's a good idea," she says.

"Well."

There is another long silence.

"Do you want to come here for dinner?" she asks.

"I thought I'd get something near the hotel."

"You're always welcome here," she says.

"Thank you, darling, but I really don't think so."

"Well . . . call me later, okay?" she says.

What the hell for? he wonders.

"I'll talk to you in the morning," he says.

"Dad?" she says. "Do you remember when you used to read to me on Christmas Eve?"

"Yes, darling."

"'Twas the night before Christmas.' Do you remember?"

"Yes," he says. "I remember."

"So do I," she says.

She sounds almost wistful.

His personal telephone directory is written in a code only he can understand. In order to decipher it, he depends largely on his own very good memory; he can

12

recall the plot, and also lines of dialogue, from every movie he's ever seen. He can tell you which movie won the Academy Award in 1946. He can tell you who said, "Beware, Saxon, lest you strike horse!"

Heather's last name is Epstein. She is a twenty-year-old architectural student whom he met in April, when he was doing a guest lecture at Cooper Union. Ben has her listed in his directory as Stein, Ephraim. Her area code is 212, of course, she lives right here in Manhattan. But to throw off the bloodhounds, whenever or if ever they decide to go sniffing through his book, he lists the area code as 516. So if anyone dials 516 and then the phone number in an attempt to get Ephraim Stein who is in reality Heather Epstein, he will instead get some stranger in Nassau County who never heard of Benjamin Thorpe.

He dials her number now.

Nine for a local call . . .

He has just come out of the shower, he is still wearing only a towel.

Two, six, oh . . .

Heather Epstein. Five-feet seven-inches tall, long blond hair, blue eyes, a wide-shouldered, big-breasted Jewish girl who knelt before him three hours after they met and asked him to touch her hair while she sucked his cock.

He feels himself becoming faintly tumescent under the towel.

The phone is ringing.

Once, twice . . .

"Hello?"

Her little girl voice.

"Heather?"

"Yes?"

She sounds sleepy. She always sounds sleepy. He visualizes her in a baby doll nightgown. Wide hips, full thighs, long splendid legs.

"It's Ben," he says. "Ben Thorpe."

At the lecture that night in April, she was wearing a long tan skirt, her beautiful legs came as a delightful surprise. Peach colored blouse, silken to the touch. That was the only time he went to bed with her, that one night here in New York. Ever since, it's been phone sex. She sometimes calls him collect at the office and says, "Hi, what are you doing?" Which means, "Would you like to jerk off with me?"

"Guess what?" he says now.

"What, Ben?"

"I'm here in New York."

"Oh?"

"Alone," he says.

There is a silence.

"I haven't heard from you in a while," she says.

"I've been very busy."

"I thought you'd forgotten all about me."

"How could I forget you?"

"How do you know I haven't got a boyfriend by now?"

"Have you?"

"How do you know I haven't?"

14

"I hope you haven't."

"Married man, can't ever see me unless he's in New York giving a guest lecture."

"I'm in New York now," he says.

"When did you get here?"

"I came in on the Red Eye this morning."

"So what took you so long to call?"

"I've been busy all day."

"You should have called earlier. I'm going to a party. I was just about to shower."

"I'm already showered," he says.

"So what would you like to do?" she asks, her voice lowering.

"What would *you* like to do?"

"What do you think I'd like to do?"

"I mean tonight. What would you like to do tonight? Heather, I'm here alone."

"What does that mean?" she asks.

"It means we can spend the night together. The way we did that other time."

"A hundred years ago."

"Only this past spring."

"A hundred years," she says, and hesitates. "Anyway, how do you know I want to spend the night with you?"

"Don't you?"

"Maybe. How do you know I haven't already made plans to spend the night with someone else?"

"I hope you haven't."

"Do you think I just sit around here waiting for you to call?"

"No, but . . ."

"Waiting for you to tell me to take off my panties?"

"Can you meet me?"

"Where?"

"Wherever you like. Trattoria dell'Arte? We can have dinner and then . . ."

"Where's that?"

"Right across the street from Carnegie Hall. Or would you rather I came downtown?"

There is another long silence.

Then she says, "I told you. I'm going to a party."

"Skip the party. We'll have our own party."

"I'll have my own party, anyway. You didn't think I was going alone, did you? Don't you think I have any friends?"

"I'm sure you do."

"Why don't you take your wife to Trattoria whatever?"

"She's in Los Angeles. That's what I'm trying to tell you, Heather. I'm alone. I want to see you. I want to spend the night with you."

He waits.

"I'm sorry," she says, "I've made other plans," and hangs up.

He looks at the phone receiver. He puts it back on the cradle. Rain is lashing the windows. I should have accepted whatever she was ready to give, he thinks.

*   *   *

16

He dresses casually but elegantly, a gray cashmere jacket, darker gray flannel trousers, a pale blue button-down shirt with a darker blue tie, blue socks and black shoes. He looks at himself in the mirror inside the closet door. Studies himself for several moments, and then shrugs. To tell the truth, he does not think of himself as particularly good looking. In a world of spectacularly handsome men sporting Calvin Klein jeans and bulging pectorals, he considers himself only so-so. Quite average, in fact. Five-feet ten-inches tall, a hundred and seventy pounds, eyes brown, nose a trifle too long for his face, hair dark, a totally average American male. Who are you? he wonders.

He goes to the mini bar, opens himself a Beefeater from one of the small bottles arrayed on the shelf, pours it over ice. He opens a small jar of olives, drops a pair into the gin. The olives slide down past the ice cubes. He holds the glass up to the light, shakes the cubes. Everything twinkles like silver and jade. Grace doesn't like him to drink gin. That's why he drinks it. Fuck you, Grace. Sitting in a black leather casy chair under a standing floor lamp, he sips his drink and leisurely consults his address book again. He can feel the brittle booze burning its way down to his gut, feel too a spreading anticipative warmth in his groin. He does not yet know who, but some woman somewhere will soon be offering him comfort.

Most of the listings are out-of-town numbers, the names changed so that they appear to be men's names. Sometimes, he transmogrifies the name so completely that even with his phenomenal memory, he cannot for the life of him decipher the code. The challenge to recall becomes even more difficult wherever he's substituted one city for another. Sarah Gillis, for example, who lives in Chicago, Illinois, where he spoke at the Art Institute on two separate occasions, is listed as Sam Dobie and her Chicago street address is listed properly, but he's displaced it to Atlanta, Georgia. Her true telephone number follows not the 312 Chicago area code but instead the 404 code for Atlanta. He remembers Sarah Gillis with considerable ease because *The Affairs of Dobie Gillis* was one of his favorite movies, and Sarah was an astonishingly agile and inventive bed partner for the entire three nights he was in Chicago the first time, and the full week he stayed the second time.

Sarah has long blond hair on her head and wild black hair on her crotch and her unshaven armpits. She is a librarian, go ask. He frequently calls her from the office, and she describes torrid sex scenes for him while they both masturbate. He visualizes her in the stacks, coming all over *Remembrance of Things Past*. He is constantly amazed by the number of desirable women who will readily take off their panties and fondle themselves for him on the telephone. He attributes this neither to his charm nor his appearance. He merely wishes he'd known all this when he was sixteen. He may call Sarah later tonight. He is thinking that tonight he may pull out all the stops. Even call Heather again in the middle of the night, get her to do herself for him in contrition for her abrupt behavior ten minutes ago. Tonight is going to be the X-rated version of *Home Alone*. Tonight is going to be *The Rains Came* in garter belt and open-crotch panties.

Samantha is a black girl he met in New Orleans. He can remember every detail of her face and her body, but not her last name. Face as perfectly sculpted as Nefertiti's, perky little breasts with stubby brown nipples, crinkly crisp cunt hair, they'd fucked the hours away on a rainy summer night while the funky sound of jazz floated up from Bourbon Street— Samantha what? Not that she would do him any good here in New York City on a stark and dormy night, not all the way down there in New Orleans. He keeps leafing through the pages of his little black book, which is in fact soft brown Italian leather, purchased at Gucci on Rodeo Drive. Soft Italian leather and something much harder, more insistently prominent in his English flannel trousers now. He sips at his gin. Drinking and sex go well together, he's discovered, the hell with Shakespeare's observation. He takes another sip, exclaims, "Beautiful," out loud, and keeps turning pages. He is leafing through the M's when he comes to Milton, David. Oh yes, he thinks, Millicent Davies, right here in New York City, although the area code listed in his book is 813. Yes. Dear, dark-eyed, dark-haired Millie. He takes another sip of the gin . . .

"Beautiful," he says again.

. . . and dials.

He gets a busy signal, hangs up, puts on the speaker phone—nobody home to eavesdrop, how nice—and hits the redial button. Still busy. He picks up a pencil, begins alternately doodling and hitting the redial button. Millie is a marathon talker. He looks at his watch. It is already five minutes to eight. Ahh, the phone is ringing now. Once, twice . . .

"Hello?"

"Millie?"

"Who's this?"

"Ben."

"Jesus, Ben, I've got a house full of people here!"

"I just wanted to . . ."

"I told you never to call me again! What the hell's wrong with you?"

And hangs up.

He looks at the receiver. He feels instant anger. What the hell's wrong with *me*? he thinks. What the hell's wrong with *you*? After everything we did together on the phone? All those times? You ungrateful bitch! he thinks, and slams the receiver down onto the cradle.

CHAPTER
TWO

He is not a man who frequents saloons as such, but he does enjoy sitting at restaurant bars — waiting for Grace, usually — or at hotel bars when he's alone in another town, as he is alone tonight. He sits alone on a stool toying with the olive in his second gin since sundown, listening to the heavy rain lashing the windows on the street side of the room, hearing the sound of the lounge piano smoothing the clatter of cocktail conversation.

Come to think of it, he cannot remember a single occasion when Grace was on time. He is usually early, Grace is invariably late. In fact, promptness is a habit with him, and he prides himself on arriving at any given destination some five or ten minutes before time, which isn't easy to do in Los Angeles, the goddamn freeways. He remembers, before they relocated out there from New York, they were dining one night with Frank and his wife, and he was selling them on L.A., bragging about how "convenient" the city was, explaining that here you were always only twenty minutes from wherever you wanted to go. Frank's wife, a bit in her cups, said, "Only problem is there's no place to go."

He sits alone.

The buzz in the lounge is all about the discovery of the three bodies some seven miles off Martha's Vineyard. Everyone is talking about the tragedy. It is now ten minutes past eight. The men and women sitting here drinking and chatting have already known for several hours that JFK, Jr. and his wife and sister-in-law are in fact dead. Ben can remember the day President Kennedy got killed—well, his eighth birthday, how could he forget? The grief in this room is almost palpable. Some of these people are perhaps guests here, some may later be dining in the hotel dining room, others may be moving on to other restaurants or bars, but there is a shared intimacy among these strangers joined in mutual sorrow.

There are only two women sitting at the bar.

He wonders if either of them is a hooker.

He has met hookers who tell you they assemble Ancient Sumerian artifacts at the local museum, hookers who say they sell real estate, hookers who claim they are here for the Philatelic Convention, hookers who look like kindergarten teachers from North Dakota. It is sometimes enormously difficult to distinguish a working girl from a so-called respectable woman. Actually, he never knows for sure until it gets down to the wire. Until the essential question comes from either him or her.

He looks at his watch.

There is time.

He doesn't have to leave for the airport till six-thirty in the morning. There is time to savor his

22

second drink tonight, and listen to the conversational hum, the spongy sound of cocktail lounge music, the rattle of cutlery in the adjacent dining room, where he may or may not be having dinner, if he has dinner at all tonight.

The woman sitting closest to him, a stool separating them, seems an unlikely candidate for a hooker, but he has been wrong before, and often. She looks to be in her late thirties, dressed to the nines, a possible sign that she's on the prowl, but then again she may be a Park Avenue divorcée who dresses for dinner and visits a different restaurant every night, stopping at various hotel bars for a drink beforehand. She is elegantly dressed in a gray tailored suit with a pink silk blouse, ruby and gold cufflinks showing at the wrists. She is smoking a cigarette and drinking what appears to be a Manhattan, a slice of orange and a maraschino cherry still floating in it.

She seems distressed about something. Sorrowful somehow. Taking occasional long drags of the cigarette, peering into her glass, seemingly unaware of anyone or anything around her. Sometimes they put on that act, to encourage conversation. Is anything wrong? you're supposed to ask. You seem sad, you're supposed to say. Oh, no, she'll answer, my mother just died five minutes ago, that's all. And one thing will lead to another until the essential question is asked by one or the other of you. He has asked and been asked the essential question many times in many different hotel bars.

The other woman at the bar tonight is sitting at the far end, closer to the service bar. She is a redhead in her mid-twenties, he guesses. She seems to know the bartender. At least, she is in occasional conversation with him, checking her watch every few minutes, as if she is expecting someone who's late. They sometimes do this. They'll sit at the bar, becoming more and more concerned when a phantom date doesn't arrive, making nervous chatter with the bartender because they're presumably embarrassed sitting here alone at a bar. You're supposed to make some comment about signals getting crossed, he probably went to the Plaza instead of the Peninsula or wherever, and she'll immediately correct the impression that she's waiting for a *man,* this is her *girlfriend* who works at the same bank she works at, over on Whatever Street, she's worried something might have happened to her.

She'll finally leave the bar to make a phone call, giving you an opportunity to look her over top to bottom and when she comes back she'll tell you Wouldn't you know it, her girlfriend's baby came down with double pneumonia, and she had to get the doctor, and there goes her dinner date, oh well. At this point, you're supposed to ask her if she'd like to join you for dinner, seeing as you're all alone in a big strange city and all. Or else you simply ask the essential question. Or wait for her to ask the essential question. Which, if she's a hooker, she will eventually ask unless she thinks you're a hotel detective or somebody on the Vice Squad. Some of them will ask

24

you straight out if you're a cop. That's the prelude to the essential question. Once she asks you if you're a cop, she's upstairs in your bed.

The redhead sitting there looking at her watch is dressed in a simple black dress, no jewelry except the watch, which is gold and expensive-looking. High-heeled black pumps, hair falling loose and sleek, she turns to glance toward the entrance door, her eyes grazing him in passing. If he were a betting man, he would put his money on her as the professional. In fact, the lady in the gray suit and pink blouse is already paying her check and preparing to leave, putting her cigarettes and lighter in her handbag, pushing her stool back — display of long legs as she does so — same sad look on her face, not a glance at anyone in the room as she moves away from the bar. She is either off to a costly dinner alone at Le Cirque, or — if she's a pro — she's decided there's nothing here for her and is moving on to another venue. If he'd been interested —

But there's so much time yet.

— he should have indicated at least some regard for her obvious sorrow, the poor woman's mother so freshly deceased and all. You choose or you lose is the name of the game at these hotel bars, and the lady in the pink blouse — if she's a pro — has obviously decided that he's already chosen the redhead and so she is now on her way to greener pastures, fuck you, mister.

The redhead has obviously reached the same conclusion: she herself is the chosen morsel from tonight's menu of *hors d'oeuvres,* no pun intended. The next time she turns to check the door for her girlfriend who is now so terribly tardy, she initiates the action, making eye contact and tossing a slight shrug in his direction. The shrug seems to say I really don't know what's wrong, do you? Where can she possibly be, do you think it's the rain that's keeping her, it doesn't look all that bad to me, does it to you? All of this in the simple shrug and the helpless eyes and the little girl moue. All of it saying Why don't you move over here, Big Boy, where we can discuss this?

He shrugs back.

She smiles.

Quite a dazzling smile.

Or—

She is probably waiting for her husband, who just flew in from Chicago, Ben hopes not. But that's it, of course. Her husband is right this minute rushing from La Guardia in a taxi, on his way to the hotel where he's supposed to meet her here in the bar because they have an eight o'clock dinner date.

He hesitates only a moment longer.

Then he picks up his drink, walks toward her . . .

She is still smiling.

. . . and sits on the stool next to hers.

"It must be the weather," he says.

"What do you mean?" she says.

He thinks at once he's made a mistake. She will signal to the bartender and complain that this man is making unwanted advances. But she is still smiling.

"I thought you might be waiting for someone . . ."

"No."

". . . and the weather . . ."

"No, I'm not. But thanks for your concern," she says, and flashes a quick appraising look before turning back to her drink.

He supposes that Grace would find what he's about to do quite disgusting. Is already doing, in fact, since the game has been afoot since the moment the girl made eye contact. Well, since long before then, actually. Afoot since he first decided how he would be spending this night alone in New York City. Afoot, in fact, since the very first time he'd ever placed his hand on a strange woman's silken thigh in a hotel lounge, on an airplane, at a dinner party, anywhere, everywhere, afoot for a long, long time now, my dear Watson.

If only you knew how much there is to be disgusted about, Grace.

If only you knew that an hour from now, a half-hour from now, ten minutes from now, I may very well be eating this young girl's pussy, would you then ask me if I'd used your goddamn sacrosanct towel or toothbrush? I mean, really, Grace, if a woman won't let you use her toothbrush, how can she even entertain the notion of sucking your cock?

Think about it, Grace.

If you ever think about such things.

"Isn't it awful what happened?" the redhead asks, turning to him again.

"Yes," he says. "Terrible."

"They found the bodies, you know."

"Yes."

"A tragedy," she says.

Shaking her head, eyes all wide in wonder and awe. Green eyes, he notices. Those cool and limpid green eyes. The Jimmy Dorsey orchestra. The Big Band sound. His father playing trumpet at more weddings and engagement parties and beer parties and bar mitzvahs and proms than Ben can count, most often with just four pieces, sometimes seven, less frequently with what his father used to call "a full orchestra," ten or twelve or fourteen pieces, like the time he played a gig—he called them gigs—up at Saranac Lakes in New York.

Weekend musician, he always pretended to be oh so hip, How you doin, man? he'd say to his own son. Called Ben "man." How you doin, man? Sported a little triangular beard under his lower lip, the tip pointing toward his chin, called the beard a "Dizzy kick," after Dizzy Gillespie, one of his idols. Told Ben it cushioned the mouthpiece, so how come Al Hirt didn't have one? Or Herb Alpert? Ben was growing up during the time of the Tijuana Brass and "Taste of Honey," Mama Cass and "California Dreamin'," The Rolling Stones, Jefferson Airplane, but his father's music drowned out the sounds Ben preferred. He couldn't count the number of times he'd heard his father blowing "Concerto for Cootie" or "Night in Tunisia" in the spare room of the old house in Mamaroneck, where he practiced every night of the week after he got home from his day job selling real estate.

"How'd you like that, Louise?" he would proudly ask Ben's mother, opening the spit valve on the horn, blowing moisture into a chamois cloth, which his mother found disgusting.

"Don't give up your day job, Henry," she would say, shooting him down, and wink at Ben, conspirators. Henry. A wimp's name, an accountant's name. Henry Thorpe Real Estate, it said on his stationery. But he called his band The Hank Thorpe Orchestra, even when it was just four pieces at an Irish wedding, and that's what it read on the business cards he handed out, *The Hank Thorpe Orchestra*, in delicate script lettering. His mother never stopped calling him Henry.

"Have you eaten here yet?" the redhead asks.

"I'm sorry?"

"The hotel dining room. Zagat says it's very good."

"No, I haven't."

"I thought . . . well, actually, I don't even know if you are, for that matter."

"Are what?" he asks.

"Staying here," she says. "At the hotel," she says.

"Yes, I am."

"Which is what I assumed. Which is why I asked if you'd eaten here yet."

There is still time to back away from this. He knows there is time. But in that instant, the redhead crosses her legs, and all at once there is a sleek expanse of naked white thigh below the suddenly higher hem of the already short black dress. His mouth goes dry. He tries not to appear too aware of her exposed thigh, but he is thinking she's not wearing pantyhose, maybe she isn't wearing panties, either, maybe she is naked under that short black dress. He pokes his forefinger into the gin, toys with the olive, finally grasps it between thumb and forefinger, and pops it into his mouth.

"What are you drinking?" he asks.

"Bourbon. Rocks."

"Would you care for another?"

"Are you having another?"

"I thought it might be a good idea."

"Then sure."

The dazzling smile again.

He signals to the bartender.

"Another round here," he says.

The bartender nods.

The bartenders all know who the hookers are. In most good hotels, the manager doesn't like hookers wandering in off the street, but for a slight weekly fee the bartender allows a select handful to solicit at the bar. He knows this for a fact because a bartender in St. Louis, where he was designing a synagogue four years ago, shared the information during the early hours of the morning, just before the bar closed. Of course, if anyone dared mention to the compassionate barkeep here in this fine hotel that at least in this one respect he is behaving suspiciously like a pimp, he would become highly offended, no

30

Eugene O'Neill character he, oh nossir. But, really, sir, isn't that what the situation here most closely resembles? You, sir, are something of a pimp, and I am something of a john, and this redhead sitting beside me with her legs recklessly crossed is most certainly something of a whore.

Or is she?

Before he asks the essential question—

In architecture, or at least in the kind of architecture he practices, the essential question is: Does it work? Does it work both functionally and esthetically? For him, for Benjamin Thorpe, AIA, that is all there is, and all there is to know. Will it delight the eye and will it not fall down around the ears? Does it work? The essential question in the game afoot here at the bar is quite similar to the question Ben asks himself each time he sits at his computer. Does it work? Or, to be more precise, does *she* work? Is she a working girl? Or is she, in reality, an innocent young thing who has wandered in out of the storm in search of an overpriced dinner here in the hotel restaurant?

"Cheers," he says, and raises the fresh drink the bartender has deposited before him without a word. The redhead raises her glass, too.

"Cheers," she responds, with a tone and a shrug that suggests she never expected to be sitting here sharing a drink with a delightful male companion on this otherwise distressing night.

It's unusual that a hooker will sit drinking hard liquor when she is trolling for a customer, or a client, or a patron, as he has been called variously by women from whom he's accepted comfort and solace hither and yon, one of whom called him a son of a bitch bastard, in fact—but that was another story. The redhead's drink looks genuinely alcoholic, though, so perhaps she isn't what she seems to be at all, but is indeed a sweet little naïf enjoying a pre-dinner drink in the cozy warmth of the hotel bar, it being so nasty and stormy and wet out there. Or perhaps she is, in fact, the slut he first took her for and still guesses she is, who's decided that old Ben here—who is forty-three, mind you, and incidentally beginning to feel these two and a bit more gins—is a sure thing, and so it's safe to have a drink in celebration of her catch. In which case, all that remains is for one or the other of them to ask the essential question.

"So what's your name?" she asks.

This is not the essential question.

Besides, it's been his experience that most respectable ladies—

Oh, listen, don't give me the Madonna and the whore bullshit, he thinks suddenly and fiercely. I'm not cruising the universe tonight because I think my mother was Hail Mary, full of grace, and all other women are harlots, I mean the hell with that shit. I am sitting here working this redhead because . . .

Well, who knows why I'm here?

It has nonetheless been my experience, he thinks, still annoyed without knowing quite why, that most respectable ladies as opposed to most whores will not immediately ask a man what his name is, preferring him to take the lead as they've been taught in proper finishing schools where they wear white gloves.

"Michael," he lies. "And yours?"

"Karen," she says, which is not the sort of name hookers normally choose for themselves. He has never in his life met a hooker with a name like Mary or Jane. Or Karen, for that matter. Kim seems to be the most common hooker's name, or for that matter the name of most common hookers.

Hello, Michael, I'm Kim.

Or Tiffany.

Tiffany is a good one.

Or Lauren.

He has met three hookers named Lauren, two of them in Miami.

"Do you live here in New York, Karen?"

"Oh yes," she says.

There is an almost playful manner about her now. Well, if not playful, at least more relaxed, more casual. It is as if now that the matter has been settled—although it really hasn't been settled since the essential question hasn't yet been spoken by either of them. But perhaps it's already been settled in her mind—I am a whore and you are a john— and so she can afford to be more, well, intimate, he guesses, swinging her stool around so that her knees are almost touching his, the skirt riding very high on her thighs now, her legs looking white and shiny and young and smooth and touchable in the pale blue spill from the lights behind the bar.

"Where do you live, Michael?"

"Los Angeles."

"Long way from home. How long will you be staying?"

"I'll be leaving tomorrow morning."

Across the room, the piano player is noodling a medley of what Grace calls "Old Fart Music," which is only the music Ben grew up with in the Mamaroneck house, the music he heard his father practicing at home every night, the music Ben heard him playing with his band and even his orchestra in various banquet halls and dance emporiums throughout Lower Westchester and the Bronx—but don't give up your day job, Henry. Which he finally did when he was sixty-three and suffered a heart attack that killed him, how you doin, man? Ben's daughter Margaret was sixteen at the time. She refused to go kiss him in his coffin. A year or so later, she met Charles the First and married him. Made me a grandfather, he thinks, isn't that odd? Until that time, my father was the grandfather. Now I'm the grandfather, and my father is dead. He used to play tunes for her on his mouthpiece. Just the mouthpiece, no horn attached to it. Blew actual tunes for her, delighting her. Used to call the trumpet his "ax." Let me go get my ax, man. Wouldn't go in to kiss her own grandfather. No wonder she won't call California to see how Grace's mother is doing.

"I love this tune, don't you?" Karen says.

The tune happens to be "I'll Walk Alone," a big hit for Harry James during World War II. If Karen is,

34

in fact, the twenty-three, twenty-four-year-old he guesses she is, she wasn't even born when Helen Forrest sang it. His father used to put a mute in the horn when he was playing this tune, the better to evoke a lovesick woman waiting for her man to come back from overseas. His father never stopped talking about the goddamn war. Guys who'd seen combat were supposed to be shy about it. Not his father. His father could remember all the fucking Nazis he'd ever killed, took pleasure in describing their demise right down to the surprised expressions on their faces when he shot them. Karen is swaying to the tune now, hugging herself, white breasts swelling in the low neckline of the black cocktail dress, all creamy white above and below, long shapely legs and firm young breasts, swaying in time to the music floating from the piano, sleek red hair framing an oval face, eyes closed. He feels an urge to kiss her while her eyes are closed, surprise her with a soft gentle kiss tasting of green olives and gin, but he doesn't because he's still not sure she's a prostitute, or perhaps he's still hoping she isn't a prostitute.

Once, when he tried to kiss a prostitute, she turned her face away and said, "What the hell are you looking for, mister? Love?"

The word "love" was almost contemptuous on her lips.

She almost spit out the word "love."

He had dressed silently and left her, shamed somehow.

35

Tipped her twenty dollars, he couldn't imagine why.

Most hookers will kiss, what the hell.

Karen opens her eyes.

"Do you like this tune, Michael?" she asks dreamily.

"My father used to play it."

"Is he a musician?"

"Was. He's dead."

"I'm sorry."

"Almost five years now," he says.

"And do you play, Michael?"

"I'm an architect," he says.

"I love architecture," she says.

They are sitting knee to knee now. Her eyes are so very green in the blue light.

He supposes it is time for the essential question.

"Are you a working girl?" he whispers.

"Yeah," she says, and pulls a face. "But I hate the job, truly."

He looks at her. This is the first time in all his experience that he's heard a hooker complain about the job. Is she planning to march for higher pay and shorter hours? Is he expected to show sympathy? Express compassionate understanding? Tell her not to worry, he'll be gentle? Or is she pretending ignorance of the code until she can make certain he's not a cop? Is she about to tell him she's a graphic artist or a social worker or an account executive at Merrill Lynch?

"I'm a phlebotomist," she says.

36

"Uh-huh," he says, and smiles conspiratorially. "And what's a . . . lobotomist, did you say?"

"Phlebotomist."

"Someone who grows exotic plants, right?"

The knowing smile still on his mouth.

"I draw blood," she says, and grimaces again.

"Ah. You're a nurse."

"No. I just draw blood. P-H-L, phlebotomy. It's from the Greek word for blood-letting."

"I see."

"Yes. But I'm not a nurse. I just go from floor to floor, taking blood. It's a part-time job. I start at five A.M. and I quit at nine. The hospital pays me thirty bucks an hour."

"I see. And which hospital would that be?"

"Memorial Sloan-Kettering?"

"Where's that?"

"On York Avenue? Near Sotheby's? Do you know it?"

"Uh-huh."

He is studying her more closely now. He has met hookers with enormously elaborate stories to tell until the essential question is asked. But he has already asked the essential question, and he is now getting an unexpected song and dance. If she's suspicious, she should be asking personal questions, fishing to learn if he's a cop before they strike a deal.

"I wear a white lab coat," she says, "and go from floor to floor with my little cart and syringes. Some contrast between that and your basic black, huh?"

She nods, grins, happy with herself, happy with the way she looks in black, flaunting it a bit, is she a hooker or isn't she? He really doesn't have time to chat up a twenty-three-year-old girl, this is not *The Dating Game*, this is a mature man alone in the city of New York, very far from home. Is she or ain't she? Does she or doesn't she?

"What do you do when you're not at the hospital?" he asks.

Lead into it that way. What do you do when you're wearing your basic black cocktail dress without panties perhaps, sitting at a hotel bar, flashing legs that won't quit, what do you do at night, what are you doing this very night, and how much do you charge?

"Make rounds," she says. "Take lessons."

"Rounds?"

"I'm an actress."

"Have I seen you in anything?"

"Everyone always asks that."

"I'll bet."

"Do you ever go to any Off-Off productions? When you're here in New York? Off-Off Broadway?"

"No, I'm sorry, I don't."

"Then you haven't seen me in anything."

"So as I understand this, you draw blood from five A.M. to nine A.M. . . . ."

"Yes."

"And then you make rounds and take lessons."

"Right."

"What kind of lessons?"

"Acting. Singing. What do you do?"

"I told you. I'm an architect."

"Cause I thought maybe you were a district attorney, all these questions."

"I'm sorry, I didn't mean to be nosey."

"Or a casting director."

"I'm sorry, really."

"Not that I mind. In fact, it's kind of nice to have a man take such interest in what I do."

"I'm sure there are many men . . ."

"Oh sure, zillions."

". . . who take interest in what you do."

"You want to know something?" she says, and leans closer to him, and puts her hand on his arm. "In this city, most interesting men you meet are either married or gay, that's the God's honest truth."

"I'm sure you don't have any trouble at all."

"Right, no trouble at all."

"A beautiful young girl like you . . ."

"Oh sure, seventeen, right."

"Well, how old are you?" he asks.

"Oh dear," she says.

"I know a person's not supposed to ask . . ."

"I'm twenty-five."

"No."

"Yeah."

The phlebotomist grimace again.

"You don't look at all like twenty-five."

"Twenty-nine? Thirty? Don't tell me. Forty?"

"I honestly thought twenty-three."

"Well, thanks. Twenty-three. Boy. How old are you?"

"Forty-three," he says.

"My *father's* forty-three!" she says, and bursts out laughing. "Excuse me," she says, covering her mouth, "oh, Jesus, I'm sorry."

"Your father can't be forty-three."

"But he *is!*" she says, still finding it funny, reaching for a paper napkin on the bar, dabbing at her eyes with it.

"If you're twenty-five, how can your father . . .?"

"He got married when he was seventeen."

"That's very young."

"Well, he's still very young."

"Oh, sure, make amends," he says, smiling.

"Well, he *is.* Forty-three is *very* young."

"But I remind you of him, huh?"

"Not at all!" she says, and bursts out laughing again. "I mean it. You definitely do not remind me of my father! Did I say you reminded me of him?"

"Well, I mention I'm forty-three and next thing you know your father's in the conver . . ."

"*Stop* it!" she says. "Would I be sitting here flirting with you if you reminded me of my father?"

"Are you flirting with me?"

"Well, what do you think all this leg show is about?" she says, and kicks up her legs, and then hooks the rung of the stool with her heels again.

"They're very beautiful," he says.

"Thank you, I know," she says. "My best feature actually."

She shows them again, hands flat on her thighs, toes pointed, looking at them admiringly. Brings them back, hooks the bar stool rung again. Looks at him. Serious look now. Almost a solemn look. Green eyes steady.

"So?" she says.

This has turned into a different sort of game.

He would have preferred her to be a hooker. There is no uncertainty about hookers. You determine the playing field, and play the game, and that is that. With a respectable woman, you have to take time. True enough, he has all the time in the world—well, at least till six-thirty tomorrow morning. But, yes, he has the time. He's just not sure he has the energy. Once upon a time, he had the energy. Once upon a time, long ago, he thought it was all about love. Now he realizes it is only about fucking. That is somewhat sad, he supposes.

"You don't really want to eat here in the dining room, do you?" he asks.

"I am hungry," she says.

"I know, but the dining room?"

"Too stuffy, huh?"

"Very."

"Then where?"

"Where would you like to go?"

"You're the man."

He looks at her.

Almost says How about my room?

Hesitates.

Again almost says it.

How about my room?

Karen?

Would you like to come to my room?

"There's a very good Italian restaurant right around the corner," he says.

"You twisted my arm," she says.

CHAPTER
THREE

He asks for a corner booth and a waiter immediately leads them to one. He watches her walking ahead of him, and cannot detect a panty line, which ordinarily he finds very sexy, except when he's entertaining thoughts of Irish nakedness under the dress. He does not know whether or not she is in fact Irish—well, the red hair and the green eyes—any more than he knows for sure that she isn't wearing panties under the black dress. He likes to think she's Irish. He likes to think he can slide his hand up under the dress and discover her open and exposed. He is beginning to like the idea that she's not a whore, though she probably is.

The normally packed restaurant is virtually empty. Perhaps this is because it's still raining. Or perhaps it's because the rain has done nothing to cool the steaming streets and people would rather stay home in this ridiculous heat. Or perhaps it's because this is July and many New Yorkers are in the Hamptons or on the Vincyard. Or perhaps it's simply because JFK, Jr. was a New Yorker and the locals are staying home out of respect. Whatever the reason, he is grateful. The booth is cramped and intimate. He can feel her thigh alongside his on the leatherette seat, can feel the occasional glancing touch of her knee under the table.

Once, in Seattle, he picked up a girl in the hotel bar, and when they got to his room, she asked if he would mind her ordering something from room service since she hadn't eaten since breakfast and was truly very hungry. They had already negotiated five hundred for the night, and he didn't think another fifty or so for a sandwich and a beer would destroy him. Instead, the girl ordered one of the pricier items on the menu—duck à l'orange, if he now remembers correctly—and then went to sleep immediately afterward, still wearing all her clothes. It was raining, as he recalls. Well, it's always raining in Seattle. Grace called while the girl was still asleep on his bed. He had by then taken off her panties and unbuttoned her blouse, the girl snoring right through it. That was the time Margaret was thrown from a horse at camp. She was eleven, hated camp. She still hated everything. He hopes Grace will not call tonight.

He feels relatively certain that Karen will be sharing his bed tonight, and he does not want Grace interrupting with news that someone else has fallen from a horse. Her mother dying would be the only reason she'd call, he figures, so he hopes her mother doesn't die. Aside from the fact that she's a very nice lady whom he likes a lot, he doesn't want her spoiling his night with Karen. He has already convinced himself that he has never known a girl as desirable as this one in his entire lifetime. He knows for certain now—or guesses he knows for certain—that she is not wearing panties under the black dress. As they study the menu, her thigh warm against his, he fantasizes raising the dress above her hips to discover no panties—he was right!—and a flaming red bush. He visualizes himself dropping to his knees before her. Her head is thrown back, her hands are holding the bunched dress above her hips, her legs are widespread. She moans. He feels her legs beginning to buckle. She screams.

"Tell me what's good here," she says.

He recommends the linguini puttanesca.

"It means whore-style," he says, testing her.

"Yes, I know," she says, and their eyes meet and lock, and he thinks This girl is definitely a hooker, what's *wrong* with you? In which case, why hasn't she told me how much she wants for the night? Or is she going to eat a good dinner and then go to sleep like the one in Seattle, who finally woke up at midnight? By which time, he had fucked her twice, feeling somewhat like a necrophiliac each time. Rain pouring down outside. Yawning, she asked him if it would be all right if she went home now. He told her Sure, go ahead. Now, ten years later, he still doesn't know if she was a hooker or just some kind of hippie who'd swallowed a handful of whatever it was before he picked her up in the bar. No more than he knows if this redheaded Irish girl who's not wearing panties under her black dress is a hooker or just somebody hungry who's come in out of the rain.

She orders the veal parmigiana.

He orders spaghetti with tomato sauce and basil.

"Shall I order a bottle of wine?" he asks.

"I'll be useless," she says, and again their eyes lock. "Can I just have a glass?"

"Red? White?"

"Red, please."

He orders two glasses of the better Merlot. They sit sipping the wine, the restaurant inordinately still.

"So how often do you come to New York?" she asks.

"Every six months or so."

"That's not a lot."

"Sometimes more often. I was here just this past April, for example. It depends," he says.

"Do you travel a lot?"

"Most of our work is in California. But, yes, we have clients all over the United States. And, of course, there are lectures. I do a lot of lectures."

"Are you famous?"

"No. I'm just a good architect, I guess."

"Would I know you?"

"I doubt it."

"Michael what?"

"Thorpe."

He figures that's safe. Michael Thorpe. Relatively safe.

"Where do you lecture, Michael?"

"Schools."

"Here in the East?"

"Well, on the East Coast, yes. New York, of course. Boston. Lots of colleges in Boston."

46

"That's not far, Boston."

"Washington, D.C. Atlanta. Miami. We have several clients in Miami."

"So you're away from home quite a lot, actually."

"Well, I wouldn't say a lot. But I do my fair share of traveling, yes."

"Are you married, Michael?" she asks.

He hesitates. He does not want to lose her. Losing her now would be altogether too crushing to bear.

"Yes," he says. "I'm married."

"How long?"

"Twenty-two years," he says.

"Any children?"

"A daughter."

"How old?"

"Twenty-one. She lives in Princeton."

He knows he's made a mistake, he should have lied. He has found in the past that talking about his daughter is a definite turnoff to girls scarcely older than she is. Not hookers. Hookers don't care if you're single, married, separated, divorced, remarried, redivorced, whatever, hookers simply do not give a damn. But Karen is not a hooker, and he cannot imagine having been so unbelievably stupid as to tell her he's married with a twenty-one-year-old daughter in Princeton, has he completely lost his mind? An incredibly beautiful Irish girl *sans culottes* drops into his lap—or almost into his lap, they are sitting that close on the banquette—and he tells her his life history? Why didn't he also mention his three-year-old granddaughter? Put the icing on the cake, why not?

47

"Is the wine all right?" he asks, clumsily changing the subject, and she says, "Yes, yummy," but she seems suddenly distant and thoughtful, and he knows he will lose her in the next twenty seconds unless he does some very fancy footwork. "Do you feel moved by his death?" he asks, changing the subject yet another time to something that's on the lips of everyone tonight, anyway, the death of John F. Kennedy, Jr., even the waiter commented on it when he brought their wine.

"Kennedy, you mean?"

"Yes."

"Not very," she says.

Still distant. Aloof almost.

I've lost her for sure, he thinks.

"His father got killed on my eighth birthday," he tells her, and she immediately says, "I wasn't even *born*," and rolls her eyes, which causes him to think he's just made a worse mistake than talking about his twenty-one-year-old daughter in Princeton, New Jersey. He remembers his mother keeping him home from school to celebrate his birthday. November twenty-third. He remembers her taking him into the city. All the women were crying over the President. Just thinking about it upsets him, somehow, all these years later. It was a mistake to mention the President, anyway, because she wasn't even born then, rolling her eyes that way, sitting there so still and silent now, the hell with her, he thinks. She reaches for her wine glass, sips at the Merlot. Picks up her knife, cuts into the veal. He knows he's already lost her, easy come, easy go, the hell with her. She looks up from her plate, turns to him, nods.

"Married, huh?" she says.

"Married," he repeats, and nods ruefully, trying to put a lighter spin on it, but he knows it's already over and done with.

She lifts the glass of wine, sips at it.

"So what do we do now?" she asks.

"What would you like to do?"

"Give it a shot," she says, and smiles.

He feels the soaring joy he knows when the roof goes on. That is when he knows it's going to be a building. Something that started in his mind, something he transferred to paper, has miraculously turned into walls and a roof. He has that same feeling of accomplishment now. Not satisfaction; that will come later. But fulfillment nonetheless. A secure knowledge that his efforts at the bar earlier and now during dinner have miraculously resulted in a promise of gratification from this beautiful young redhead at his side. He almost winks at the waiter on the way out.

"Do you think I could have another drink?" she asks.

"Of course," he says, and goes immediately to the mini bar. "Bourbon on the rocks, right?" he says, pleased that he remembers. "Wild Turkey okay?" he asks, rummaging through the bottles on the rack inside the refrigerator door.

"Yes, fine. Thank you."

The ice bucket on the counter above the mini bar is empty. He goes to the phone, asks room service to send up some ice, please, and then goes to where she is sitting, and leans over her, searching for her lips. She turns away.

"There's something I have to tell you," she says.

She's a hooker, he thinks. She is going to tell me this will cost five bills. She is going to pull one of those little credit-card machines out of her handbag, the way a hooker in San Diego did one night.

"What is it?" he asks.

What were you expecting, he thinks. A virgin? *What the hell are you looking for, mister? Love?*

"Wait till after the ice comes," she says.

The bellhop arrives some five minutes later with a plastic bag of ice that costs Ben a dollar tip. The bellhop glances at Karen where she is sitting in an easy chair near the television set, her long splendid legs crossed, the black skirt high on her thighs. He glances admiringly at Ben as he leaves the room. Ben closes and locks the door. He carries a glass over from the bar counter, shakes ice cubes into it, unscrews the cap on the bourbon, and pours.

"Aren't you drinking?" she asks.

"I don't think so," he says.

He carries the glass to her. Hands it to her. He almost asks Okay, how much? She takes the glass, nods thanks, and sips at the bourbon.

"I lied to you," she says.

She is going to tell him she's not really a phlebotomist. She is going to tell him she arrived here in New York from Minnesota last winter, got off the bus at the Port Authority Bus Terminal, hungry and cold, and was offered solace and cheer from a black pimp wearing a black leather coat. She is going to tell him she's a good girl who got trapped in evil ways but who wants nothing more than to go home to her rheumatic old mother and crippled younger sister in Moose River Falls. She is going to say she's saving every penny so she can go home, which is why she's asking seven bills for the night instead of the customary five, because she has to hold back a deuce for her pimp, you see, honey? Around the world, no holds barred, no questions asked, what do you say, honey?

He says nothing. He knows what's coming. The rest is all a matter of negotiation.

"Remember when you said it was probably the weather? And I said, No, I wasn't waiting for anyone? Remember? I was lying. Actually, I was waiting for a blind date. He never showed. Would you mind if I take off my shoes?" she asks, and then slips out of them, and pulls her legs up under her, making herself comfortable, the skirt riding higher on her thighs. He wonders again if she's wearing panties. "The way it works," she says, "before you actually meet, you talk on the phone. He must have called me every day last week. We had these long meaningful conversations on the phone. Finally, we arranged to meet for a drink. The way it works, if the drink goes okay, you usually move on to dinner. I waited a full hour. I never wait for *anybody* that long."

"I'm glad you did."

"Me, too. I was sitting there feeling sorry for myself when you walked in." She sips at the Wild Turkey. "I love bourbon," she says, "even though it gives me a head in the morning. I don't know why. Nothing but bourbon ever gives me a head." She takes another sip. "You thought I was a hooker, didn't you?" she says.

He hesitates. He still doesn't know if this is some sort of game. You thought I was a hooker, didn't you? And then: Well, you were *right,* baby! Five hundred for the night, how's that sound?

"Yes," he says. "I thought you were a hooker."

"I can see where you got that idea."

"But you're not."

"I'm not. Relax."

"Okay."

"We'll give it a shot, okay?"

"Sounds good to me."

"I know you're married, but you won't have to worry about me calling your wife in Los Angeles and telling her I just slit my wrists, this won't be anything like that."

"I'm glad to hear that."

"When you first told me, I thought just my luck, a married man. I don't have much luck with men, you know. Well, my blind date tonight, for example."

"Maybe he was gay."

"Maybe, but I doubt it. I lived with a gay guy for six months. *He* was a prize, believe me," she says, and rolls her eyes. "But back there in the restaurant, I began thinking . . ."

52

"I was wondering what you were thinking."

"Yeah, I could sense the panic. I was thinking this might turn out to be a good thing for both of us."

"I think it could."

"I'm sure it could. You only come East every now and then, which means I'd still have my freedom..."

"Of course you would."

"And *you* won't have to worry about me getting all clingy and weepy. I could see you whenever you're in town, or even come to meet you in Boston or Atlanta, Washington, wherever you said ..."

"Washington, yes."

"Wherever you'll be," she says, and sips at the bourbon again, and lowers her eyes. "If you think you might like that," she says.

"I think I might like that very much," he says.

"Well, good. I think I might like that very much, too."

"I will have that drink, after all," he says, which line he guesses he has heard in about two hundred movies. Though not as often as the most frequently used five words in the history of film, which, once he knew what they were, ruined one out of every two movies he went to see. He is tempted to reveal the five words to her now, in exchange for what she's promised will be a long and mutually satisfying relationship, but maybe he'll save them till tomorrow morning when they're on the way to the airport together, the sweet redheaded Irish girl accompanying her lover to bid him a fond farewell till next time. Walking toward the bar, he shakes his head in what he hopes will express to her his amazement and delight at having found this cuddly little darling now sitting there curled up with her skirt so high he feels if he drops to his knees before her, he'll know in an instant if she's naked under it. Just a single glance will tell him. Grinning like a schoolboy, he finds another little gin bottle, and pours it in a glass over ice. He raises the glass.

"I'm happy you're here," he says.

"I am, too," she says.

What goes around comes around, he thinks. Earlier tonight, he was sitting here thumbing through his little black book and sipping a Beefeater, and here it is almost ten o'clock, and he's still sipping a Beefeater, although no longer searching for a bed partner because it seems he has had the extreme good fortune of finding one who's looking for a good steady fuck, no strings attached.

"The thing is I feel I really know you," she says. "I feel we're so alike in so many respects, don't you? I know that's ridiculous, I mean, what've we spent together, an hour, two hours? But don't you feel this affinity? I know I do. You're a dear sweet gentle person, Michael, and I really do want to make love with you. I visualize something very good for both of us here. In the future, too. For a long time to come. And I won't call your wife, you don't have to worry about that."

"I know you won't," he says, and goes to her where she's sitting, and leans over her, and kisses her gently on the lips. Gently, he takes her hands, lifts

54

her out of the chair, holds her against him, kisses her again, gently. Rigid cock in his pants notwithstanding, he will treat her gently. He will be kind and gentle and tender and loving, and she will nevermore think about the blind date who stood her up tonight. Tonight, he will be her friend and her lover both, and she will leave this room eternally grateful to the masked man from California.

But meanwhile, he has to pee.

"Why don't you make yourself comfortable?" he says, which he is certain is a line from another thousand movies he's seen. "I won't be a minute." He's heard that one before, too. She smiles somewhat wanly, nods, and watches him as he goes toward the bathroom door, and opens it, and walks inside. There is a fierce urgency to his need. If he does not pee within the next ten seconds, he feels he will explode. He loosens his belt and unzips and lets his trousers fall to his ankles. Forcibly angling his stiff cock down toward the bowl, he waits for the stream to start, the flow inhibited by his erection—God, how he wants to fuck this girl! Like a sputtering spigot after the water has been turned off for a while, the urine trickles and spits from his shaft, and then at last gushes forth in a strong steady stream. He closes his eyes and throws his head back. He does not want to lose the hard-on. He knows this is not an early-morning piss hard-on, but he's fearful the reaction may be the same, you pee and it's gone. He wants to come to her stiff and eager and obliging.

He washes his hands, and brushes his teeth, takes off all his clothes and folds them neatly on the hamper top. Removing the white bathrobe from its hook on the bathroom door, he puts it on, and ties the belt at his waist. He looks at himself in the mirror over the sink. Who are you? he wonders again, and opens the door.

"I hope I haven't . . ." he says, and realizes the room is empty.

But no.

But yes.

His eyes cut around the room fitfully. To the chair she was sitting in. The chair is empty. To the dresser where she'd placed her handbag. The bag is gone. To the door where her open blue umbrella was on the floor drying. The umbrella is gone.

"Karen?" he says.

Is she hiding somewhere? In the closet perhaps? Is she playing a game? Find the phlebotomist and she is yours? He goes to the closet door, opens it. Hanging on the rod are the trousers and jacket he will wear on the plane tomorrow morning. There is nothing else in the closet. So where is she? Come on, he thinks. This isn't funny anymore. Really.

"Karen?" he says again, and goes immediately to the window, and pats down the drapes hanging on each side. There is no one behind the drapes. Rain slithers down the windows. He stands there looking out blankly at the shimmering lights of New York. Where else can she be? If there was a fire escape, she might be outside on that. But there is no fire escape. So where?

"Karen?" he says, but he has already given up hope, the way the searchers for John John and his party gave up all hope long before they found the bodies. Well, wait, she might be under the bed. He knows damn well she won't be under the bed but he gets down on his hands and knees and looks anyway. Of course not. He pushes himself to his feet, goes to the entrance door, opens it, and looks out into the corridor.

"Karen?" he calls, softly.

He can hear the elevator down the hall, humming down the shaft. He wonders if he should race down the steps, try to catch her before she leaves the hotel, visualizes himself bursting into the lobby in a bathrobe, and abandons the idea at once. Should he call the front desk, ask one of the clerks there to stop her before she hits the revolving doors? For what purpose? She's gone.

He closes the door.

"She's gone," he says aloud, sounding surprised even though he's known it for the past five minutes.

He was in the bathroom too long, that was it. He shouldn't have given her all that time to change her mind. Why had he afforded her an opportunity to panic? To escape? Goddamn it, how could he have been so fucking stupid? He can just imagine her sitting here in the easy chair, sipping at her bourbon, going over her present situation, *I don't have much luck with men, you know*, wondering if old Michael here who has a wife in Los Angeles and a twenty-one-year-old daughter in Princeton, New Jersey, is really the right man to *change* that situation. What is she getting herself into here? What was she even thinking? And finally—ta-*ra*! The five most famous words in the history of motion pictures, racing through her mind and propelling her out of that chair and out of the room and down the hallway and into the elevator: *Let's get out of here!*

I'd have preferred your not having discovered those words on your own, he thinks. I'd have preferred whispering them in your ear as part of our afterplay, Oh, just a clever little observation of mine, Karen, based upon having watched hundreds upon hundreds of movies, listen for them the next time you go see one. I would much have preferred that, Karen, couldn't you at least have given me a chance? I'm not a bad person, really.

It is ten-thirty.

Three hours earlier in Los Angeles.

Should he call home and tell Grace he's back from dinner and is going to bed? Clear the decks for whatever the night might still hold in store? He's got eight hours before he has to leave for the airport. He can sleep on the plane. Karen, I'm sorry to have lost you, he thinks, but there's always another streetcar.

He picks up the phone, hits 8 for a long distance line, then dials 1, and 310 and then his home number. Grace's voice on the answering machine picks up on the fourth ring. "Hello, you've reached Grace and Ben

Thorpe, neither of us is able to come to the phone just now, but if you'll leave a message we'll get back to you as soon as we can. Thanks."

"Honey," he says, "this is Ben, I just got back from dinner and a nightcap downstairs, and I'm going straight to bed. I won't be talking to you again before I leave, but I'll see you tomorrow. I hope Mom's okay. Tell her I love her. You, too."

He hangs up.

So what now? he wonders.

Do I get dressed again and go down to the bar? Really have the nightcap I mentioned to Grace on the answering machine? See who else might be sitting there having a nightcap? See who or even whom of the female persuasion might be patrolling the night in search of company? What time does the bar close? he wonders. He picks up the phone, dials 0, waits.

"Good evening, Mr Thorpe," a woman says.

He visualizes her sitting with earphones on her head. Is she Lily Tomlin or Judy Holliday?

"Good evening," he says. "Is the bar still open?"

"Which one?" she asks.

"How many are there?" he says.

"There's the lounge bar and the roof bar," she says. "Both close at midnight."

Then why'd you ask me which one? he wonders.

"Thank you," he says.

"Goodnight, sir," she says, though it was "Good evening" a minute ago.

He is beginning to feel irritable. He supposes that achieving erection and then losing erection so abruptly is not too good for equanimity. He wonders idly how Bob Dole manages mood swings within the parameters of erectile dysfunction and popping Viagra pills. He wonders where Karen is now. Is she sitting downstairs at the bar again? Or perhaps up on the roof at the other bar? Crossing her legs and searching for yet another dear sweet gentle person whose room she can enter and evacuate in a similar hurry? He really regrets her leaving. Now he will wonder forever if she was truly naked under that black dress. He had wanted her so very much. Truly. He sighs heavily, picks up the phone again, dials 0 again.

"Good evening, Mr Thorpe."

Same girl again. "Goodnight" has become "Good evening" again. A switch hitter. She sounds Puerto Rican.

"Good evening," he says. "Is the gift shop still open?"

"No, sir, they close at ten."

He looks at his watch.

"Is there anywhere else I can get a magazine?" he says.

He is tempted to ask if she's wearing panties.

He is tempted to tell her he's sitting here at the phone wearing nothing but an open robe. *The Open Robe* by Seymour Hare, he thinks.

"There's a newsstand on Fifty-seventh and Sixth," she says.

"Are you Puerto Rican?" he asks.

"Dominican, sir," she says.

"What's your name?"

"Maria Teresa."

"Thank you, Maria Teresa. Goodnight."

"Goodnight, Mr Thorpe."

Little flirtatious lilt to her voice there?

Smiling, he replaces the receiver on the cradle, and goes into the bathroom for his clothes.

He is dressed again and about to leave the room, actually has his hand on the doorknob, when the telephone rings, startling him. Can it be Maria Teresa calling back to say she quits work in a little while, does he want her to come up to the room and discuss hot tamales? He virtually bounds across the room, yanks the receiver from its cradle.

"Hello?"

"Ben? You weren't asleep, were you?'

Grace.

"No, no." Instant recovery. Not Maria Teresa, after all. Grace. Calling from California. Her mother is dead. What else can it be? "What time is it?" he asks. He knows very well what time it is. If he doesn't hurry downstairs, even the newsstand might be closed. "It isn't your mother, is it?" he asks.

"No, she's all right. They'll be doing it early tomorrow morning. Are you in bed?"

"Yes," he lies.

"I'm sorry. I shouldn't be calling."

"What is it, Grace?"

"You told me you'd be going to sleep. It could have waited till you got home."

"That's okay, I wasn't asleep yet."

"But if the restaurant's still open, you might want to go there."

"Grace, I have no idea what you're . . ."

"You left your credit card," she says.

"What?"

"At the restaurant."

"I left my . . ."

"MasterCard called here just a few minutes ago. The person I spoke to said you'd left your card at Trattoria dell'Arte . . . is that where you had dinner?"

"Yes?"

"Said you'd charged a hundred and five dollars and sixty cents there—and left your card behind. They're holding it there for you. I don't know how late they'll be open. What'd you eat?"

"What?"

"That cost a hundred and five dollars and sixty cents?"

There is a silence on the line.

"Ben?"

"I had a few drinks before dinner," he says.

"I still don't see . . ."

"And a bottle of wine with the meal."

"You drank a whole bottle of wine?"

"There was nothing by the glass. Nothing I liked."

"But a whole bottle?"

"Well, I didn't drink *all* of it, Grace."

"After two drinks?"

"I had a long, hard day, Grace. I really don't see anything too terrible about a grown man . . ."

"It just seems like a lot of money."

"It *is* a lot of money. New York is an expensive town. Trattoria is an expensive restaurant. I earned two hundred thousand dollars *designing* that fucking building, so I think I'm entitled to a lousy . . ."

"Ben? Lower your voice, please."

There is a long silence.

In even, measured tones he hopes are conveying weariness, impatience, and not a little annoyance, he says, "I had a couple of drinks. I had spaghetti with tomato sauce and basil to start. I had the veal parmigiana as . . ."

"You don't have to tell me everything you ate, Ben. I'm just calling to say you left your card there."

"Thank you, I appreciate that," he says.

You're full of shit, he thinks.

"What kind of wine was it?"

"A French Merlot."

"How much did it cost?"

"I have no idea. I would guess forty or fifty dollars."

"I hope you enjoyed it," she says.

Another silence.

"I guess now I'll have to dress and go down for the card," he says.

"Call first," she suggests. "Make sure they're still open."

"I'm sure they're still open. They get a big after-dinner crowd."

"Then you're safe," she says.

"I'll let you know how I make out."

"You don't have to. I know you're tired. Get some sleep. Anyway, I'm going out to dinner."

"Oh? Who with?"

"Whom," she corrects automatically. "Sue Ellen."

"Give her my love."

"I'm sure she sends *her* love, too. Good night, Ben."

"Love ya," he says.

But she is already gone.

Well, he thinks, what the hell was *that* all about?

Little bit of Sherlock Holmes out there in Topanga Canyon? Is she now calling a liquor store to check on the price of a French Merlot? Is she calling Trattoria dell'Arte to ask if Mr. Thorpe was there alone tonight? Will she call him back to say she now knows he was dining with a redhead, what's wrong with you, Ben, is something *wrong* with you? What is wrong with me is that I have a suspicious controlling wife who never wants to make love and who thinks I am fucking every other woman on the planet, including Sue Ellen Pearson, *I'm sure she sends* her *love, too*, my ass! I have never so much as blinked at Sue Ellen Pearson, try Rachel Fein instead, whose fine ass I have groped at many a country club dance, try *her*, why don't you? You have no goddamn reason to believe I wasn't dining alone tonight, having a couple of drinks and a good bottle of French wine, no reason at all. What's wrong with *me*? What the hell is wrong with *you*? What the hell is wrong with a woman who when she sees you walking into a bedroom preceded by a foot-long flagpole will smile like a virgin cheerleader and turn her head away? What's wrong with a woman who, when you're fucking her, *if* you're fucking her—

He would never dream of saying he *fucks* Grace, oh no. Every other woman in the world he knows or has known says, "Come on, baby, *fuck* me!" Grace says, "*Give* it to me!" As if she is actually going to take possession of it, slicing it off and putting it in her box of keepsakes on top of the faded love letters he wrote her while he was at Yale and she was at Radcliffe, and the gold pocket watch her grandmother left her when she died, which had previously belonged to Grace's adored grandfather in Kansas—well, he can't blame Kansas for Grace. Her father moved the family to Massachusetts when Grace was still a child, so he can't blame Kansas for whoever or whatever she is. He can only blame Grace for that.

He never has to fantasize in bed with any woman but Grace. Every other woman is here and now, to have, to hold, to fuck. With Grace, he fantasizes blondes and brunettes and redheads galore, in various postures and poses, alone or in pairs or in threes. Grace's hair is a blondish-brown these days, a cross between what Clairol calls "Twilight Brown" and "Moonlit Brown," lighter than her natural color, which is what people not in the Hair Trade might call "Mousy Brown."

Mousy brown was the color of her hair when he met her at a football game in New Haven, the girls having been trained down from Boston to cheer on the Crimson Tide, Ben not caring who won either way, sports never having been his particular cup of tea.

She was quite the most beautiful girl he had ever seen in his life.

What happened? he wonders now.

Where did you disappear to, Grace?

He's half-tempted to call her back, ask her why the third degree on a goddamn bottle of red wine when her bills from shopping Rodeo Drive come to thousands of dollars each and every month.

The newsstand.

He throws on a lightweight raincoat, checks the room one last time—

For what? Does he still think Karen might be hiding in here someplace?

—and closes the door behind him.

The newsstand is festooned with magazines like *Oui* and *Hustler* and *Juggs* and *Marquis* but he buys only *New York* and *Penthouse*. To the reader not looking for whore-house ads, *New York* appears eminently respectable. *Penthouse* is more problematic. It does not quite wallow in the gutter the way *Hustler* does, but neither is it as reputable as the dowager *Playboy*. Nonetheless, to ensure his veneer of proper gentleman out for a late-night stroll—which he is, after all, isn't he?—he carries the magazines with the cover of *New York* facing out, hiding *Penthouse* beneath it. He walks back to the restaurant in a slow drizzle that does nothing to dissipate the oppressive heat.

His MasterCard is waiting at the hostess's console. A pretty blonde tells him she's sorry for the inconvenience, and he assures her it wasn't a problem. He accepts the card, and momentarily places the two magazines on the console, wondering if the blonde can tell *Penthouse* is hidden beneath *New York*. But she pays no attention to the magazines. Instead, she watches him as he puts the credit card back into his wallet, as if making certain he won't leave it behind again.

"Well, goodnight," he says, picking up the magazines. "Thank you."

"Come again, sir," she says.

Come again, hc thinks.

Does she know to what purpose he'll be putting the magazines?

He smiles at her.

"Sir?" she asks, puzzled.

He is staring at her now.

Still smiling.

"Was there something else, sir?" she asks.

"What did you have in mind?" he says, and is instantly sorry. The puzzled look on her face becomes annoyance and then brief anger and then something like revulsion. She turns away from the podium, recedes into the depths of the restaurant. He feels suddenly embarrassed. He ducks his head, and hurries out into the humid mist.

This is a summer night, and the weather isn't truly rotten enough to keep people indoors. He knows without question that half the women out here on the street tonight are prostitutes. The problem is determining who is and who isn't. It's exactly like the two women sitting at the hotel bar tonight. His chances were fifty-fifty back then, and he's sure his chances would be fifty-fifty out here on the street as well. Stop some woman, any woman, ask her if she'd like to come back to the hotel with him, he'd either get his face slapped or she'd say, "Sure, honey, it'll cost you a deuce." He has never tested this theory, but he's sure that would be the case. He's similarly convinced that if he approached any shopgirl in any city in America, and asked her if her passport was in order, she would immediately answer, "Where you taking me, honey?" He feels he knows this for a fact.

He has known a great many women in his lifetime, you see. He won't even try counting them all. He started to do that once, and first found himself getting excited by the various memories, and next feeling guilty as hell when he realized the magnitude of his trangressions—well, perhaps that's too harsh a word, he thinks. No one's committing any crimes here. Flirting with women isn't a goddamn crime, is it? Well, it's more than flirting, actually. Even so, using a word like "transgression" for something that's essentially a habit—well, it's more than a habit. Well, a bad habit, all right? Well, more than that, too. What he does is . . . well . . . foolish. And reckless. And dangerous, too, he knows that. He knows that if it became known, for example . . . if a client telephoned California, for example, and said he'd seen Ben with a woman not his wife, a woman who looked like a whore, for example . . . well, that could lead to trouble. Very serious trouble. Not that Karen looked like a whore. But even someone who looked like a nice girl. Even someone like that. Someone who looked like Karen, in fact. If someone spotted him with someone like Karen, this could become a problem. His behavior, if it became known, could become a problem. Because, let's face it, behavior of that sort was simply foolish and reckless and dangerous. He knows that. He doesn't care what Grace might think, he's long ago stopped caring what Miss Kansas City might think, she already holds him in such low esteem, anyway, so who gives a damn? But he doesn't want his colleagues and peers to learn that when he's out of town on architectural matters, he's also out of town on certain other matters. He does not wish this rumor to gain credibility in the profession—or is a rumor still a rumor when it's true?

It is true that he seeks women.

Constantly. This is an undeniable fact, Grace, step to the head of the fucking class! To Ben, the world is an immense chocolate shop brimming with confectionery delights. The trick is in knowing which delectable sweet to select, which dark candy to sample. In the bar tonight, he made the wrong choice, settling for a goddamn phlebotomist when he could have had the melancholy pro in the pearl gray suit. But, oh, he has been so deliciously on the nose in the past. Oh, he has been so goddamn lucky in the past. He can remember different women in different situations as if he were meeting them for the very first time right this instant—but, look, I don't want to count them, he thinks, I really don't want to start feeling guilty all over again! I feel guilty enough after each time, anyway, I don't have to relive the fucking guilt now, do I? Okay?

There is something enormously romantic about the soft drizzle, the wet pavements and streets, the muted shine of the street lamps glowing through the mist. He suddenly misses Karen with a poignancy he hasn't known since he was a teenager, when girls became suddenly available but oddly unattainable. Along Sixth Avenue, there are lights burning in apartment buildings above the closed and shuttered shops. He visualizes women in those apartments, behind the drawn yellow shades, women disrobing, women in their tubs, women powdering themselves, women touching themselves, their nippled breasts, their crisp pubic hair, their dark hidden—

Stop it, he thinks.

And hurries back to the hotel.

CHAPTER
FOUR

Glancing into the lounge, just in case—

There are no women sitting at the bar, and only one woman sitting alone at a table, but he has never been bold enough to simply walk up to someone at a *table* and say "Mind if I join you?" Besides, she is a woman in her early fifties, he guesses, and he is not quite that desperate tonight, though once at the Bel Air in Los Angeles, sitting at the bar and waiting for a client to arrive, he struck up a conversation with a not unattractive woman who told him she would be celebrating her sixtieth birthday the following week (Oh my, really? I never would have guessed!) and one thing led to another until he mentioned he lived in L.A. and had never seen any of the rooms in this hotel. Which naturally prompted her to ask if he'd like to take a peek at *her* room, and five minutes later she was on her bed with her panties off and his cock in her mouth while he rejoiced in praise of older women—but not tonight. Tonight, the night is still young.

He wonders if she should call Heather again. Heather Epstein, listed in his little Gucci book under Stein, Ephraim. See if she's back from her party yet, what time is it, anyway? He looks at his watch. It's a little past eleven, she might be home, who knows? Give her a dingle, see if she'd like to pop by, renew old times, old glories, who knows? He is feeling suddenly secure again, in possession of *Penthouse* and *New York* as well, his insurance policies if all else fails. He opens his dispatch case, finds his soft brown leather address book, and is scanning the S's when the phone rings, almost scaring him out of his wits.

Grace again?

For Christ's sake, what . . . ?

He picks up the receiver.

"Hello?"

Trying to sound half-asleep in case it's his wife waking him up again. In his mind, she has already woken him up once tonight. And now again. When she knows he has to leave the hotel at six-thirty. What the hell is it now, Grace?

"Michael?"

A woman's voice.

"Who's this?" he says.

"Karen," she says, sobbing. "Please forgive me. I'm not a cock tease, Michael, really. I never have been."

"You're forgiven," he says.

You only broke my heart, he thinks.

Which he knows isn't true at all.

"I don't know what got into me," she says.

Certainly not me, he thinks.

"Please stop crying," he says. "I forgive you. There's nothing to be upset about."

"But there is."

"No, forget it, really."

"I walked out on you."

"That's okay. Don't worry about it."

She keeps sobbing into the phone. He feels helpless. He stands holding the receiver, listening to her sobbing.

"Michael?" she says.

"Yes, Karen."

"Do you really forgive me?"

"I do. I really do."

Her sobbing is gentler now.

"You're a very nice man, Michael."

He hears her blowing her nose.

"I shouldn't have left," she says. "I freaked out, is all."

"We all . . ."

"But it won't happen again. I promise you. Michael?"

"Yes, Karen?"

"I haven't been to bed with anyone since last Christmas."

He doesn't know what to say. He says nothing.

"Michael?"

"Yes, Karen."

"This was the gay boyfriend I was telling you about? He brought home two Butch friends on Christmas Eve, watched while they both did me.

It wasn't rape, exactly, but it was horrible. I left on Christmas Day." She is silent for several moments. At last, she says, "I'm sorry, forgive me. I know I've got to get over this."

"There's nothing to forgive," he says.

"I let them do it," she says.

"Well, you mustn't . . ."

"It makes me so ashamed."

"No, no, don't be."

"You're a very nice man, Michael. I don't want to cause you any kind of trouble."

"I know you don't."

"It was horrible," she says. "I'll never forget it. But I have to get over it, I know I do. I really used to enjoy sex, I mean it. A *lot*," she says. "I have to get over this, Michael, or I'll never forgive myself. Do you understand what I'm saying?"

"Of course I do."

"Would you like to come here, Michael? I'm downtown on Greenwich Avenue. I'm in bed already, I'll be waiting for you."

He visualizes her naked in bed, red hair fanned on the pillow. Green eyes smoldering. Remembers wanting to slide his hand up her leg to her naked pussy under the short black dress. Visualizes wild red hair at the joining of her legs. Imagines licking her there. He looks at his watch. It is ten minutes past eleven. He does not like the thought of venturing out into New York City at this hour of the night—well, it isn't really that late. But still. New York. And she lives all the way downtown in the

Village, Greenwich Avenue, she said, homosexuals cruising the night down there, he's not sure he wants to go all the way down there. In fact, all at once, he's not sure about *any* of this.

Girl walks out on him for no good reason except that two big fags fucked her in the ass last Christmas, does that excuse her abrupt departure? We're *all* of us rape victims, he thinks, one way or another, honey, so don't come begging mercy for what was done to you last Christmas, okay? In some venues, that just won't wash. We *all* had something done to us last Christmas or the Christmas before that or Christ knows which Christmas? All at once, this girl seems to have too many ghosts of Christmas Past bugging her. And Ben's not sure he wants anything to do with any of them.

"I'd love to come down there," he says, "but I'm expecting a phone call."

"What?" she says.

"From my wife."

"Oh."

"She said she might call."

"Turn off your phone. Say you're about to go to sleep."

"I am about to go to sleep, that's another thing. I have to catch an early plane."

"Come here instead. Turn off your phone and come here. You could even call her from here. She won't know where you are. If your phone's turned off, she won't know."

"Well, she might say it's an emergency."

"You can tell the operator no emergencies."

"Well, her mother's in the hospital. There really might be an emergency."

"Give me another chance, Michael," she says. "Please. I don't know what possessed me. I just got so frightened all at once, the thought of actually *doing* it scared me half to death. Please come here, Michael," she says. "Come to me, okay? We'll start all over again. It'll be a beginning, Michael. I'll see you whenever you come East, I'll never bother you, I promise you, I'll never call your wife or anything, I just want you to make love to me. Please, Michael, can you please . . .?"

He places his forefinger on the cradle rest bar.

Hears a dial tone and puts the receiver back on the cradle.

His heart is pounding.

He stands with his hand pressing down on the receiver, finalizing the act, shutting this suddenly dangerous woman out of his room, out of his life. I won't call your wife, indeed, you don't have to worry.

He goes to the mini bar.

Cracks open a bottle of gin, pours it into a short glass. The ice bucket is empty.

He looks at the phone as if suspecting she's still lurking inside there someplace, ready to spring out at him again.

He takes a long swallow of gin.

He feels a bit calmer now, God, that was close.

But suppose she calls again?

He picks up the receiver, dials the 0.

"Good evening, Mr Thorpe."

"Good evening," he says. "Is this Maria Teresa?"

"No, sir, this is Elizabeth."

"Elizabeth, no further phone calls tonight," he says.

"Including emergencies?"

"Everything. No calls. None."

"We'll just take messages then, sir."

"Yes. Take messages. Thank you, Elizabeth."

"Did you wish to leave a wake up call, sir?"

"Yes. Five-thirty, please."

"No calls till five-thirty, yes, sir. Goodnight, sir. Sleep well."

He finishes the drink.

Looks at his watch.

It is now eleven-thirty. But he can sleep on the plane. He finds Heather's number in his book, dials a 9 to get out of the hotel and then the seven digits and waits while it rings on the other end, twice, three times, four, five, again, again, and is about to hang up when —

"Hello?"

The girlish voice, always sounding a bit sleepy.

"Heather?"

"Yes?"

He visualizes the long blond hair and blue eyes, the wide hips and long splendid legs. He wonders what she's wearing.

"It's me," he says. "Ben. How was your party?"

"Took you long enough to call again," she says.

"I didn't think you'd be home yet."

"I just got here," she says.

"So how are you?"

"Same as I was before."

"Want to come here?"

"Nope."

"Why not?"

"Cause I've got somebody with me."

"No, you haven't."

"Yes, I have."

"You don't sound as if someone's with you."

"She's right in the other room. We're watching television."

"Oh?" he says.

There is a silence on the line.

"Why don't you bring her with you?" he says.

"What do you mean? There?"

"Sure."

"You've got to be kidding."

"Or I can come there."

"You'd like that, wouldn't you?"

"I think I might. How about you?"

"I'm not into that sort of thing."

"What sort of thing?"

"Whatever it is you're thinking."

"What do you think I'm thinking?"

"Whatever. Anyway, it's late."

"Only eleven-thirty."

"Five. And it's raining."

"What sort of thing, Heather?"

"A three-way. Whatever."

"Might be fun."

"For you maybe, sure. Anyway, we're not coming there, so forget it."

"I'll come there then, how's that?"

"I told you no."

"Why not?"

"What is it with you?" she asks.

"I just want to see you."

"You should have called before you got to New York."

"I know I should have. I'm sorry about that, Heather. Really."

"Sure."

Pouting.

"Anyway, I'm here now, and you're home from your party . . . so why don't you ask your friend if she'd like me to come over?"

"I don't have to ask her. I know what she'll say."

"She might surprise you."

"I don't think so."

"What's her name?"

"Lois."

"Lois what?"

"Ford."

"Like the car?"

"Uh-huh, like the car."

"Ask her, go ahcad."

"No. She's watching television."

"What's she watching?"

"Something about Kennedy."

"Go ask her if she'd like to come here."

"No. Anyway, I don't want to come there."

"Then let me come . . ."

"No."

There is another silence.

"How was the party?" he asks.

"Fine."

"What'd you wear?"

"My green dress. You don't know it."

"Are you still wearing it?"

"Ben," she says, "nothing's going to happen here, okay?"

"I just want to know . . ."

"Goodnight, Ben," she says, and hangs up.

He feels angry and embarrassed and ashamed. He feels like calling her back and asking her just who the hell she thinks she is, a twenty-year-old twerp who was cleaning board erasers when he gave his lecture at Cooper this spring, how does she dare treat him this way? Does she know there's a girl downtown on Greenwich Avenue — a multiple sodomy victim, no less — who practically begged him to come fuck her, does she know that? If he had her number, he would call her right this minute and tell her he was on the way and she'd welcome him with open arms. Does she know there are girls he talks to on the telephone who aren't so goddamn coy about telling him what they're wearing or even not wearing, as the case might be? Does she know, for example, that Karen downtown isn't wearing a goddamn thing right this goddamn minute? Why didn't he get her telephone number? Why'd he hang up on her?

He goes angrily to the television set, snaps it on, clicking the remote past channels busy with news of the burial at sea, witnesses for the hundredth time since the plane went down, the black-and-white image of John John saluting his father's coffin as it rolls by, keeps clicking the remote until he comes to a leased access channel where commercials for escort services provide telephone numbers a person can call if he desires instant company. Beautiful busty white girls look ecstatically orgasmic as they fondle breasts or coddle pussies. Black girls lick their lips and show glistening teeth and pink vulvas. Slitty-eyed Asian girls adjust gartered silk stockings as they step out of limousines. Gay guys stroke cocks the size of telephone poles. There is something here for everyone, a cornucopia of promised pleasure just a phone call away. In fact, if these commercials were a bit longer and a bit more explicit, a man could satisfy himself with no trouble at all. But they are designed to inspire telephone calls, and he's afraid they might send him a dog instead of one of the sleek beauties displaying their wares onscreen. He has never called any of the services advertising on television, but some of the creatures the Yellow Pages loosed on the night were truly horrific to behold.

What do you look like? you asked on the phone, when they called your room some ten minutes after you rang the service. They sometimes phoned from a town half an hour away, who the hell wanted to wait that long to satisfy an urge? Though in all truth, it

81

never was an urge as such. In fact, he thought about sex all the time. Well, most of the time. No, all the time. Well, most men thought about sex, didn't they? Most of the time.

I'm blond, they'd say, or brunette or redheaded or My hair is green, one of them said, which was tempting, but he visualized some sort of junkie who looked like a parrot, and promptly called another service. They'd tell you how tall they were, and how much they weighed, and usually they were telling the truth, because they didn't want to describe themselves as five-nine and weighing a hundred and ten, and then show up in your doorway looking like a fire hydrant. This was one occupation where it was okay to ask a prospective employee if she was black, though you could usually tell by their voices on the phone. Sometimes, you could even tell a Chinese girl by her voice on the phone. Anyway, most of the services asked flat out what kind of girl you preferred, White, Black, Latino, Asian, you pays your money and you takes your choice. It always amazes Ben that politicians get all exercised by dirty movies or television shows, and local watchdog groups take *Catcher in the Rye* off library shelves when you can go to any city in the United States of America and find hundreds of advertisements for escort services or massage parlors right in the goddamn Yellow Pages.

If the girl sounded okay on the phone, you asked how long it would take to get there because you didn't want to call at say, ten, and have somebody rapping on your door at midnight, which one girl did one night, told him she was right around the corner in a bar, when actually she was coming in all the way from Waukegan. To Chicago, this was. He'd been asleep when she tap-tap-tapped discreetly on the door, only two hours later than when she said she'd be there. A fright. A total horror. Grinning foolishly, badly in need of dental work, apologizing for what she called her "tardiness," a skinny-legged black girl in a sleeveless pink dress, track marks up and down her left arm, a hooker from Central Casting if ever there was one, he hoped she hadn't stopped at the front desk to announce herself. He told her she was too late, told her he was already asleep, told her he had to catch a plane early the next morning, and she said, "I can do deep throat, honey," and he was instantly hard.

He clicks to the music video channel, catches Madonna repeatedly thrusting her crotch into his face. Do any of these rock singers—excuse me, *artists*. They call themselves performing artists nowadays. Do these performing *artists* realize that after ten minutes of watching them grinding their hips and fondling their tits and licking their lips and slitting their eyes and otherwise *performing* on videos that have nothing whatever to do with the songs they're singing, any red-blooded American male out here might easily be persuaded to a performance of his own, in his fist? Does Madonna realize that hundreds of boys and men are out here jerking off to her gyrations right this instant? He supposes she does. Or maybe not. In any case, he doesn't choose to fuck the screen image of

Madonna or any of the other dry-humping performing artists, or even any of the soft-focus, soft-porn movie queens in the so-called adult flicks the hotel provides on a pay-per-view basis. He truly wishes he could at least talk to Heather and her girlfriend Lois like the car, doesn't anyone want to talk anymore? He's not even angry at her anymore—what the hell, she's just a kid. Get both of them talking on extensions, have them tell him what they're wearing, lead them through the paces, but that doesn't seem to be in the cards tonight, does it? Well, there's always *Penthouse*. That's why he bought the magazine in the first place.

He has never called any of these magazine phone-sex numbers, but there's always a first time, and tonight seems as good a time as any, given the lack of amateur talent available. He fans through the magazine to the 800 and 900 numbers at the back of the book. There is no question here about what is being sold. He is glad he's not blind because the photographs are explicit and in full color, goodlooking men or women or both exposing themselves or each other in poses designed to encourage and entice, the more the merrier, Ben thinks. The last several digits of the telephone numbers spell out words like DICK and CUMM and PUSS and PINK and SEXY and PETT and LICK and WETT and HEAD and WILD and LEGS and COCK and STUD and SUCK and BUTT and DEEP and FUCK and other subtle variations on the theme. The headlines range from the maudlin: LONELY? CALL

ME NOW! to the boastful: SIMPLY THE BEST LIP SERVICE to the quasi-medical: MASTURBATE? ORGASM IN 30 SECONDS! to the confessional: I ADORE GIVING HEAD to the imperious: CUM FILL BOTH MY HOLES or SPREAD MY LEGS WIDE or GIVE IT TO ME! (does Grace have a phone-sex line?) to the merely didactic: ASS FUCKING or SWEET ACHING SNATCH or DILDO FUCKING or TEENAGE TARTS or HOT COCKS HERE or QUICKIE BLOWJOBS or HORNY LOCAL HARLOTS.

Ben chooses a service that shows a color photograph of two scowling young girls sitting spreadlegged with shaved pussies. The headline over the photo reads FILTHY YOUNG COCKSUCKERS and the 900 number ends in the word SUCK. He dials a 9, which he supposes will get him out of the hotel, and then a 1 and the 900 number ending in SUCK, visualizing his call going out into the wild blue yonder to where a middle-aged farmer's wife will be sitting in a XXX-rated flour sack on the front porch of a ramshackle house, shucking sweet peas while she talks dirty to him. Instead, he gets a very proper male voice on a recorded message that informs him he cannot dial 900 numbers from the room, so much for that.

He wonders if he should try Heather again, beg her pardon for having committed the unpardonable sin of not having called her from California the moment he knew he'd be in New York, ask her if he could just talk to Lois Ford for a minute, maybe she might understand the possibilities of—no, the hell with it. There are girls galore here at the back of the book, all of them with 800 numbers to call, all of them patently more receptive than Heather or her pal. In a wild swing away from his first choice, he settles on a service with a headline reading SEX SLAVES! DAY AND NIGHT!, and listing an 800 number ending in the word LASH. He dials a 9 again, gets a dial tone, dials a 1 and then 800 and then the first three digits and the word LASH and to and behold he gets a human female voice, albeit not a live one.

"You have reached the Sex Slave line," the voice intones, "where young girls ache to satisfy your every need. You may charge this call to any major credit card or direct-bill it to your telephone number. Please stay on the line for our next available . . ."

Wait a minute, he thinks, and hangs up.

Does that mean I can direct-bill it to the *hotel's* number? Because I certainly don't want an item called SEX SLAVES INTERNATIONAL to appear on any of my credit cards, and I don't want an 800 number ending with the word LASH to appear on my next telephone . . .

Well, wait a minute.

L-A-S-H translates as 5-2-7-4. If that appears on the phone bill, no one's going to raise an eyebrow. But there'll also be a date alongside the number, won't there? And Grace might wonder why he called an 800 number on the night he was in New York, not that he gives a damn what she wonders. Still, she's already grilled him about a non-existent bottle

86

of fifty-dollar wine, whatever he said it had cost. What'll she do if she gets her hands on an 800 number charged to the home phone? In fact, will these Sex Slave people even be willing to charge it to a number he isn't calling from, without first checking with that number? It all sounds suddenly too risky. He picks up the receiver, and dials "0" for Operator, intending to ask whether he can bill charges from an 800 number to the hotel here, and then realizes that this is like telling her he'll be dialing out for phone sex. He puts the receiver back on the cradle.

Nothing's ever simple, he thinks.

He sits in the comfortable chair under the glow of the floor lamp, and opens *New York* magazine in his lap. He has used this magazine before. There are no booby traps awaiting him here. He would have preferred not leaving the room again tonight, but it's still early . . .

A glance at his watch tells him it's eleven forty-five.

. . . and he'd rather venture into the rain than go to bed with this cramped and somehow ugly feeling still inside him. He skips past the ads listed under the heading MASSAGE / THERAPEUTIC. All too often, these are legitimate practitioners catering to jocks with pulled muscles or strained tendons, although some of the ads sound highly suspect.

Like:

Heavenly Hands. Private. In/Out. Complete Bodywork.

Or:

Magic Touch. Personal and Private. Sensual Therapy.

But why waste time and why take chances offending someone who may indeed be a licensed therapist? Instead, he flips past BOATS AND YACHTS and NEW YORK KIDS (do pedophiles skim the ads under this heading in vain?) and SUMMER ENTERTAINING and INTERIORS AND EXTERIORS and comes to the heading MARKET-PLACE, which is an apt description for what he hopes to find listed there. Skipping the sub-headings for APPLIANCES and ASTROLOGY and CLEANING SERVICE and LIMOUSINE SERVICE and PETS, he comes to a heading in bolder, larger, blue type: **ROLE PLAY**.

SUTTON PLACE BLACK BEAUTY
WILD AND UNINHIBITED
TENDER BUT NOT

MISTRESS VERONIKA
DECADENT CHARM WITH
A SLAVIC TOUCH

He has often been tempted to visit a dominatrix, but he has never followed through on the impulse. And yet, he finds exciting and seductive all these ads that promise **Creole Role Play** or LADY HELEN — BEHAVIOR THERAPY or *STRICT SISTERS* or *ASIAN FANTASY BONDS* — but all of these possible delights are listed under the

88

"Role Play" heading and he does not wish to submit himself to anyone who wants him to crawl on his belly and lick her shoes or her asshole, not tonight, not after having narrowly scored with Karen. He turns the page somewhat reluctantly, flips back again for a final glance, his eye scanning the listings until it lights on:

SENSUOUS MISTRESS AND MAIDENS TRAINING FOR DISCERNING MEN

Attracted, but afraid to call, fearful the phone will be answered by a fierce woman who will belittle him or demean him, insist that he control himself or pay attention, he almost breathes a sigh of relief as he turns the page again and comes to the next heading, again in larger blue type: **MASSAGE**.

Here, now, is the true marketplace. Here is *New York* magazine's own little open air meat market, beef on the rack, juicy cuts of tender-loin or porterhouse, how would you like your cunt, sir — your *cut*, excuse me — medium, well done, or rare? He is tempted to open *Penthouse*, allow his eyes to sample pages of pink lips and rosy nipples, permit his glance to alternate between the open crotches there and the open invitations here. But he resists the bait, so close at hand, stays with the printed ads instead, at least a hundred of them on the page, it seems, so many treats and so little time, his plane leaves at eight in the morning. Idly, he wonders what such an ad costs. He wonders, too, if the people

89

busily running around New York padlocking sex shops in decent neighborhoods know that in equally decent neighborhoods all over the city there are hookers galore who advertise their wares in *New York* magazine, do they know this? Do they realize that there are lonely men like me who look through these ads in the hope —

Well, I'm not lonely.

I have a wife in Los Angeles. A daughter in Princeton, New Jersey.

I'm not lonely.

And anyway, there's, nothing wrong with looking through a magazine.

If there's nothing wrong with placing the ad in the first place (in a respectable magazine like *New York*, no less!) then there's nothing wrong with a person *glancing* through the goddamn ads, is there?

He glances through them now.

Here is a veritable grab bag of unsorted, unalphabetized pleasures, all of them but a single telephone call and a taxi ride — or perhaps even a short stroll — away from the hotel. He looks at his watch. It is six minutes to twelve, but most of the services listed here are available around the clock. He knows. He has called as early as ten in the morning or as late as three A.M. They are always figuratively and literally wide open. No padlocks here, Your Honor. Here instead are all the "sensual," "hidden," "elegant," "extraordinary," "pure," "classy," "incredible," "smooth," "professional," "discreet," "silky," "exotic," "satisfying," "luxurious," "affordable," "sweet," "soothing," "private," "unforgettable," "magical," "superb," and "exceptional"—

Take a deep breath, Ben.

. . . "escapes," "body rubs," "delights," "colonics," "relaxations," "synchronizations," "body scrubs," and good old "massages," either "Shiatsu," "Swedish," or "Mongolian"—

Another deep breath.

. . . administered by a "Southern belle," a "Viennese lady," a "skillful French masseuse," a "classy Russian masseuse," "a professional masseuse from Japan," a "California model," a "mature woman," an "ebony goddess," a "refined woman," a "China doll," a "British lady," a "sophisticated beauty," a "Boston girl on summer break," a "sensitive Swede," and "3 Asian Lovelies . . ."

A yet deeper breath.

. . . with names like Margo, Claudette, Bridget, Patricia (and Friends), Millicent, Sandrine, Ruriko, Stefanie, Maria, Helena (and Hildy), Bedelia, Darlene, Katie, and Natasha from Kiev.

He wonders if Maria is Puerto Rican.

He can remember fucking a Puerto Rican girl in San Juan.

She told him she had two little girls in nursery school.

It occurs to him that his keenest memories are of sex.

It further occurs to him that perhaps all of his memories are of sex. Well no, he thinks. He can certainly remember . . .

Well, yes.

Well.

He doesn't like to believe this about himself. Someone secretly pre-occupied with . . .

Well, there's nothing secret about this, there's nothing furtive about remembering pleasant episodes or events that were frankly sexual in content . . .

Well, unpleasant sometimes, too, he supposes, but nothing in life is without its darker side. The point is, a healthy interest in sex is not what anyone might consider perverse. If his mind occasionally wanders down the garden path, what's so terribly wrong about that? He's a forty-three-year-old man who finds women attractive, is that so difficult to understand? Thinking about sex, recalling sex, dreaming about sex, searching for sex isn't something to be ashamed of, or even embarrassed about, or even anything to worry about, for Christ's sake! It isn't as if his constant . . .

Well, it isn't constant, come on.

His *occasional* sexual "associations," he would call them, are something every man in the world experiences at least as often as he does — and perhaps women, too, they think about sex, too, don't kid yourself, all the time probably, it takes two to tango, honey. Finding the opposite sex attractive is something wonderful and strange, *vive la différence!* Besides, he's in complete control of the situation, thank you very much, Grace. This isn't some kind of adolescent habit like, well, masturbation. This isn't a habit at all, when one examines it. Finding women attractive is not the same as smoking two packs of cigarettes a day or drinking six martinis before breakfast or shooting dope in your arm. Habits are something a person tries to kick. Habits are something bad. Since when did fucking beautiful women become undesirable? I'm not some perpetual adolescent trapped in a monkey-spanking time warp! I am Benjamin J. Thorpe—gentleman. Is what Karen called me. A gentle man.

He goes down the columns of ads again.

Something called XS Salon catches his eye.

Just those words. XS Salon. And a phone number.

He likes the pun on the word "Excess." He is in the mood for excess tonight. He likes the dyslextic quality of the "XS" ellipsis, which he imagines to be "sex" spelled backwards with a missing "e." "Salon" is exotically French with a Sunday afternoon literary feel to it. Hoping some black guy in his undershorts won't be answering phones for a stable of junkie hookers who make outcalls only—he is not in the mood for any more surprises tonight—he dials the listed number and waits. His heart is pounding.

"XS Salon, good evening."

A young girl's voice. Breathy. Inviting.

"Hello," he says. "I'm calling about your ad."

"Yes, sir, where did you see it?"

"*New York* magazine?"

"Yes, sir?"

"Where are you located?"

"In the East Seventies."

"And where?"

"Third Avenue."

"Your ad didn't . . . uh . . . say very much. I was wondering . . ."

Always the difficult part. On the phone, you can't come right out and ask if this is a . . . er . . . whore house? Everything on the phone is in code. On the phone, he sometimes feels like a spy.

"I was wondering if you can tell me a little about yourself," he says. "What kind of a salon are you?"

They're listed under "massage," but he doesn't want to get there and have someone offer him a haircut and a manicure.

"We're massage," she says.

"Full body rub?"

"Full body rub, yes, sir."

Meaning hand jobs.

"Complete satisfaction?"

"Complete, yes, sir."

Meaning they'll jerk you off till you come. No squeeze and tease.

"What do you charge?" he asks.

"A hundred dollars for the hour massage, sir. Sixty for the half-hour."

"How about gratuities?"

"Strictly between you and the girls, sir."

Meaning they'll fuck or suck if the price is right.

"How many girls do you have there?"

"There's usually a nice selection, sir."

"How many?"

"Usually from six to ten girls, sir. Depending on the hour."

Meaning it's a full-scale brothel.

"How many girls do you have there right now?"

"I believe there are seven, sir. I haven't been downstairs in a while."

"Okay," he says.

"Sir?"

"Can I have the address there, please?"

"Did you wish to make an appointment, sir?"

"Yes, I think so. What's the address?"

"I'll need your name, please."

"Michael," he says.

"Have you ever been here before, Michael?"

"No, never."

He almost says *That's why I need the fucking address*, hmm?

"Just a moment, please," she says.

He waits. Is she running the name through a computer, to make sure they don't have a Michael who's a serial murderer or a rapist, a Michael . . .

"Have you got a pencil, Michael?"

Apparently he's passed the security check.

"Yes," he says, "go ahead."

She gives him the address. He writes it down on a pad that has the hotel's name across its top in script lettering, using a hotel pen stamped with the hotel's name on its barrel.

"When you get here," she says, "ring the bell for apartment B for Beautiful, do you have that, Michael?"

"Yes," he says.

"B for Beautiful," she repeats. "Can you remember that, Michael?"

"I'll try," he says drily, but she misses the sarcasm.

"When do you think you'll be here, Michael?"

"Ten, fifteen minutes. If I can find a cab."

"It's raining, yes," she agrees. "Well, we'll see you when we see you. You didn't have anyone special in mind, right?"

"I've never been there," he says.

"Right," she says. "Okay, we'll be looking for you, Michael."

"See you," he says, and hangs up.

He almost decides to go straight to bed, the hell with this. It's raining outside, it's already a quarter past twelve, and he has to leave the hotel at six-thirty in the morning, the hell with this. But he goes to the door instead, and out into the hallway, and into the elevator, and down to the lobby and out into the night.

CHAPTER
FIVE

The building is on Third Avenue and Seventy-fourth Street, a four-story, red-brick tenement squatting between a Korean grocery and a bar called The Shamrock, how original. As he steps into the bar, he feels as if he is in some sort of trance . . . well, not a trance, certainly, no one has hypnotized him. But he knows he's performed this same action before, in cities stranger to him than New York is, and he recognizes that he is now following the same compulsive . . . well, not compulsive, he can go back to the hotel room anytime he wishes, there's nothing *compulsive* about what he's doing now. You start thinking compulsive, you automatically think obsessive, and then you've got someone who's being led around the universe by his dick.

He admits that he enjoys women, perhaps enjoys them a bit too much for his own good, but to say that first stopping for a drink is part of a customary delaying tactic . . . well, that would be jinxing it somehow. He wants a drink because he's excited. He doesn't want to walk into a whore house advertising his need. One look at the bulge in his trousers and all at once a girl with a sixth-grade education will think she's superior to a Yale graduate. He doesn't want a chorus of whores stroking crossed fingers and chanting "Shame, shame, everybody knows your name."

The drink is a way of cooling his ardor somewhat, and not any part of a ritual he's developed over the years, although he recognizes it as something he does habitually before going to any of these places he picks from a magazine or the Yellow Pages. This isn't some kind of voodoo ceremony here; it's just something he does as a matter of course. In fact, when he thinks about it, it seems to him that whiskey is somehow part of it all, at least when he's doing what he's doing tonight. He has identified his quarry in the pages of *New York* magazine, has made initial contact over the phone, has tracked the beast to its lair, so to speak, here on the Upper East Side, and is now ready to pounce upon it—but not before he has a soothing little drink in an amiable little pub here on Third Avenue.

The bar is, in fact, rather cozy, with a great deal of mahogany and brass, and black leather booths with green-shaded lamps hanging over wooden tables. He checks it out for women, because he always does this, even when he's not looking for anything. Two girls are sitting drinking alone in one of the booths, heads almost touching over the table as they exchange secrets about men, that's all girls talk about when they're alone together. Otherwise, there isn't a woman in the place, nor does he need one. He's already made arrangements, they're expecting him next door at any moment—but they'll have to wait.

He hangs his raincoat on a peg just inside the entrance door, takes a stool at the bar where he can watch the coat, and asks the bartender for a Beefeater martini on the rocks, couple of olives, please. The bartender mixes his drink, and brings it over, and then says, "Hell of a thing about Kennedy, ain't it?"

"Terrible," Ben agrees, and wonders why he didn't cry when he heard the news earlier tonight. He realizes he didn't cry when Robert Kennedy got killed, either, and he wonders now if he cried when the President got killed. Well, there was so much confusion that day, his eighth birthday and all. But did he cry? He can't remember crying.

The bartender is in his early fifties, Ben guesses, a reddish-blond Irishman wearing a green vest open over a white shirt with the sleeves rolled up over muscular forearms. One of the men sitting at the bar is wearing a brown suit, brown shoes, a button-down shirt with a striped brown-and-gold tie. He looks as if he came here directly from work and has been sitting here since. A bottle of Amstel beer sits on the bartop in front of him. The other man at the bar is in his mid-sixties, Ben guesses, wearing a blue cotton cardigan with a shawl collar, a bluish-green plaid shirt, blue cotton trousers, and white sneakers. He has a white mustache and green eyes, and he looks as if he just came off a sailboat. He is drinking something brownish in a glass brimming with ice cubes. He takes a sip of his drink, and scoops up a handful of peanuts.

The man in the brown suit pours beer from the Amstel bottle and says, "It's the curse of the Kennedys. First the President, then his brother, and now the son. It's a curse, is what it is."

"I remember just where I was when the President got killed," the bartender says.

"So do I," the man with the mustache says.

"Everyone does," the man in the brown suit says.

"I was fifteen years old," the bartender says. "I used to work delivering groceries. I remember I knocked on the door to this apartment, and an old lady opens the door and tells me she just heard on the radio that JFK had got shot. I'll never forget that minute as long as I live. We both started crying like babies."

Ben tries to remember if he cried. All he can remember is that it was his eighth birthday.

"I was just coming in off the road," the man with the mustache says. "I used to sell books for a living, my territory was the New England states. I walked in the front door and my wife was in tears. I thought something had happened to one of the kids. I burst out crying when she told me it was Kennedy. I don't know if it was relief or what. Later, I felt guilty, I don't know why."

"It was my eighth birthday," Ben says, and almost adds *I felt guilty, too* —and wonders why.

"My wife and I were in California," the man in the brown suit says. "We'd gone out for my parents' fiftieth wedding anniversary. My sisters were there, too, the whole family had come from all over the country to celebrate. My parents almost called it off. They should have. Nobody wanted to dance, believe me."

"I'll never forget what Moynihan said," the bartender says. "Senator Moynihan? This woman was telling him they'd never laugh again. And he said, 'Oh, we'll laugh again, Mary. It's just that we'll never be young again.'"

"He was right," the man with the mustache says. "We lost our innocence that day."

Ben nods silently.

But he can't remember crying.

Sipping at the martini, he begins anticipating what lies just ahead, savoring the gin and vermouth, savoring as well the secret he harbors here among these hearty men drinking and smoking on a rainy night. Keeping the secret is almost as exciting as the anticipation of the illicit adventure that awaits him just next door. He asks for his tab at last, leaves a good tip on the bartop, bids the other men goodnight, and puts on his raincoat. It is twelve-forty-two on his watch.

If only you knew where *I'm* going, he thinks, and smiles secretly, and steps out into the rain again.

He looks up and down the street before he steps into the shallow doorway. A row of bells beckons, but only one has a nameplate under it, the letter B in outline, filled in with a red marker. B for Beautiful, he thinks, and rings the buzzer. He knows there is a surveillance camera over the door, he spotted it before he stepped

101

close to the rack of bells. He knows he is being observed now. Perhaps by the same girl who answered the phone. He waits. He rings again. He feels exposed here, huddled in the doorway, his back to the street, the rain falling behind him. He rings yet a third time.

"Yes?"

A girl's voice, but not the same one who was on the phone.

"It's Michael," he says.

"Do you have an appointment, Michael?"

"I called a few minutes ago."

Longer ago than that, actually.

"Come on in, Michael, we're on the first floor."

He hears a buzzer, twists the knob, gratefully steps into a small foyer with cracked black-and-white tile underfoot, a row of mailboxes on his right, none of them bearing a name. He resists the temptation to look out into the street, see if anyone spotted him coming in. There is an inside door as well, glass panel on its upper half. It opens to his touch the moment he twists the knob. A row of wooden steps leads upward at a sharp angle. A bulb shaded with a frosted globe hangs on a wall to his right. He glances past the steps, suddenly fearful someone may be lurking there in the hallway, sees only a shadowed gloom, and hurries up to the first-floor landing. A door without any marking on it is at the top of the steps. He walks past it, turning right, past the steps he just climbed, past a wooden banister and railings that define a narrow hallway smelling of Lysol, and comes directly to a door at the far end, a brass letter

B hanging on it. There is no bell button set into the doorjamb. He knocks on the door. A voice inside says, "Yes?" A girl's voice. She is looking out at him through the peephole.

"It's Michael," he says.

"Just a second, Michael."

The door opens a crack, held by a night chain. He sees a partial face and figure in the narrow crack of the open door. There is a red light in the area immediately behind the girl. He smells incense burning.

"Open your coat, Michael."

"What?"

"Your coat. Unbutton your coat. Hold it open for me, please."

He does as he is told. Unbuttons the raincoat for her. Holds it open like a flasher.

"Turn around, please, Michael."

He turns around, back to the door.

"Raise the coat, please."

He pulls the coat up over his hips, as if he's beaming a moon.

"Face me again, please, Michael."

He is thinking What the hell.

"Sorry, Michael. We have to do this."

He faces the door again.

"Pull up your pants legs, please."

He realizes she's looking for a weapon.

He pulls up first one trouser leg and then the other.

"Okay," she says, "thanks."

And the chain comes off.

And the door opens wide.

"Sorry," she says, "we were held up last week."

A dazzling smile.

"Come in, Michael. Please."

Hesitantly, he steps into the small entryway. He is thinking he doesn't want to be anyplace that gets held up. He doesn't need cops, and he doesn't need crooks, either. He's a respectable architect. He stands there feeling clumsy and somewhat foolish and not a little frightened as the girl brushes past him to put the chain on the door again. He smells the heady aroma of powder and perfume, hears the rustle of satin or silk, feels the merest touch of her breasts as she squeezes past him. And then the chain is in place again, and the door is double-locked, and he is here, he is home, he is safe. She is wearing a flimsy black wrapper over red bra and panties, a red garter belt, black nylons. Her blond hair is frizzed. Her lipstick looks shiny and wet. She seems bursting out of her skimpy lingerie, a buxom bawd standing some five-feet eight-inches tall in black, ankle-strapped sandals with stiletto heels. She is somewhere in her late twenties, he supposes, a girl with an obliging smile, generous hips, and cushiony white breasts.

"Well, come in, come in," she says. "Let me take your coat."

He still feels clumsy and awkward, certain he is blushing, the girl standing behind him half-naked, breasts behind him, close to him, almost touching

104

him again, helping him out of his coat. There is the murmur of voices from the adjoining room. Another girl suddenly laughs, is she laughing at him? Something is going to happen here, he doesn't know what. He knows exactly what, and yet he doesn't really know. He feels this way each time he's with another strange woman, or women, a tight, flushed, clogged feeling that is exciting but embarrassing at the same time, he can't imagine why. It's as if he's in a movie theater watching a particularly thrilling scene that's making him feel ashamed somehow, but he can't do anything to change the scene or affect its outcome. Nor can he leave the theater until the movie is finished. He can only sit there watching the movie, helplessly enthralled. It is like that each time.

"Girls," she says, "this is Michael."

There are not the seven girls he was promised on the telephone. There are, instead, only three in this "nice selection." Four including the frizzed blonde who did the security check and who is now leading him into the room. Even in the dim red light, he can tell that none of these girls are racehorses. In fact, he dismisses two of them at once.

One is an Irish-looking girl, freckle faced, too fat for his taste. Reddish hair and very dark eyes, perhaps thirty years old or so, flopped sloppily on a velvet thrift-shop couch that once must have adorned the living room of an old Romanian lady who fell upon bad times. She is wearing white silk tap pants printed with oversized red hearts. No bra. Red garter belt with opaque, patterned white stockings. Red sequined pumps, like Dorothy's in *The Wizard of Oz*—but this ain't Kansas, Toto.

"Alice, this is Michael," the blonde says.

"Hello, Michael," she says, and smiles.

The second reject is introduced as Fatima.

She is very tall and slender, with pale good looks that seem to indicate Mediterranean or Near Eastern origin. She wears a silk robe patterned in a floral design and hanging open over black, elastic-topped stockings, black high-heeled shoes—and nothing else. Crisp black pubic hair at the joining of her legs hints fierce sexuality. But the look in her pale blue eyes is hollow and somewhat frightening.

The third girl has possibilities.

There is the long leggy look of a thirteen-year-old about her, though she is surely older than that. Tiny cupcake breasts under a short, sheer, white, baby doll nightgown encourage the image of precocious teeny-bopper. She is wearing high-heeled, white satin slippers with puffy white pom-poms. No panties. Long blond hair on her head. Blond hair shaved close below. Lounging in a doorway that leads to the further reaches of the apartment, an amber light glowing somewhere behind her, she throws Ben a sultry look when she is introduced as Heidi. She could be sucking her thumb as easily as his cock. He is tempted. But there is something frightening about her—he cannot imagine what.

Perhaps the single gold tooth in the corner of her mouth.

Perhaps the wise eyes.

"And you are?" he says to the tall, frizzed blonde who let him into the apartment.

"Cindy," she says. "See anything you like?"

"Yes," he says. "You."

She looks surprised.

"How long did you have in mind?" she asks.

"An hour," he says.

She looks at him again. Appraisingly this time.

"Heidi?" she says. "Wanna take the door?"

Heidi gives him a petulant look to chastise him for his inferior choice, and then walks coltishly to a high stool in the little shelved alcove just inside the entrance door. She climbs onto the stool. Behind her, the red light glows and a wispy trail of smoke rises from the incense burner. A telephone on the shelf above the burner begins ringing. Heidi picks up the receiver. "Heidi," she says, and listens. "She's going upstairs with a client," she says, "I'm on the door." She listens again. "Okay," she says, "I'll watch for him." Ben immediately figures someone else has called the number in *New York* magazine, or wherever else it may be floating around out there, to make an appointment with one of the nice selection of beauties here in this room. He hopes he does not run into whomever Heidi will be watching for, the next man who will be submitted to an anterior, posterior, and lower extremity search in the narrow hallway smelling of Lysol. He thinks for a moment—but only for a moment—that he ought to get out of here. But Cindy—all hip, strut, and insinuation—is already walking toward the amber light beckoning from the room beyond. Uncertain he's following, she glances back over her shoulder, raises an inquisitive eyebrow, and asks, "Coming?"

He is certain now that the blonde in the restaurant fully intended "Come again, sir" exactly the way he'd heard it.

Ben has been in whore houses all over the United States. He has visited one in the upstairs room of a go-go joint in San Francisco, another in a store-front massage parlor in Washington, D.C., yet another in a rickety wooden shack near the Mississippi River, others in a two-story building on the Houston waterfront, and a high-rise on Lake Michigan, he has visited all these at one time or another in his lifetime. He prefers to use the word "visited" instead of "frequented," a more heavily freighted word. "Frequented" might imply that he's been to the same whore house more than once, which is not the case, except on a few occasions he's already forgotten. It's a matter of semantics, he supposes. An occasional "visit" to a different location whenever he's footloose in a strange town and can't raise an old friend on the phone or meet a willing partner in the hotel bar is not the same thing, for example, as Simenon strolling down into the village each and every day of his life to "frequent" the local whores when he wasn't being seductive with his own daughter who wore his wedding band, for Christ's sake! Ben has never given Margaret a ring in his lifetime. Nor has he ever behaved in anything but a circumspect manner with his daughter, who is just a little younger than Cindy here, but nowhere near as invitingly juicy. He suddenly wonders if the man on the phone just now, the one Heidi will be watching for, the one probably speeding breathlessly crosstown in a taxi through the rain, could possibly be Charles the First, wouldn't *that* be something! Run into his own son-in-law here in an Upper East Side whore house? Talk about worst fears realized. Charles the First with his meager dick in his hand, Ben feels certain.

He does not know where Cindy is leading him. He is usually good at assembling in his head complete structures by viewing merely disparate parts. But he suspects the original architecture in this old building has been altered in recent years, interior walls, ceilings and stairwells restructured to accommodate a previously unanticipated use. He feels as if he is being led through dim, labyrinthine corridors in an old fortress, up secret staircases to the king's chambers or perhaps to a tower room where prisoners hang in chains on dripping stone walls—*Yonder lies d'castle of my fodder d'caliph.* There is the caustic scent of Lysol again. He suspects they have come several flights up and have now exited into the same interior stairwell space again, coming down a banistered corridor similar to the corridor two or three floors below, where Charles the First might at this very moment be knocking on a door identical to the one here, save for the brass letter B for Beautiful, God forbid.

Cindy has a key to the door.

Voilà!

She pulls it from the cleft between her ample breasts, glances back at him once again, smiling, and inserts it into the keyway in the door. He wonders if all these minutes climbing and strolling and now waiting for Cindy to unlock the door here will be deducted from the hour for which he'll soon be shelling out a hundred bucks minimum. He hopes not. He doesn't wish to get into an accounting dispute with a common whore who will then undoubtedly have to check with the high command on the other end of the phone, the person or persons screening any potential "client" (as Heidi had called him not a few moments before), the keepers of the gate who'd asked her to "watch" for any arriving Peter, Paul, or Charles—bite your tongue.

Cindy flings the door open, flicks a light switch, and steps aside to let him pass. He is aware again of her truly extraordinary breasts, creamy white and soft in the red bra, a Wonderbra, no doubt, otherwise she's all the more wonderful. As he moves past her, the scent of her perfume wafts about him, not quite "Sweet Gardenia and Lace" but not "Cheap Pussy and Piss," either, more a blend of "Girl Next Door" and "Femme Fatale." Grace never wears perfume. Never. She prides herself on smelling of good clean soap. Has it ever occurred to her, he wonders, that a man might sometimes prefer a woman who smells cheap? A woman who reeks of sex, has that ever occurred to you, Grace?

110

There is a king-sized bed in a room the size of his own vast living room back in Topanga Canyon. The room here appears even larger because it is virtually unfurnished. There is the bed, a pair of night tables flanking it, a lamp on each table, a painting of a nude above the bed, a single wooden straight-backed chair at the foot of the bed—and that is it. Minimalist design, he thinks. The painting looks as if someone purchased it at one of those store-front galleries that sell genuine Rembrandts for thirty dollars apiece, you see them all up and down Broadway, Gypsy Girl lying voluptuously on an inexpertly rendered, fringed red velvet throw, one leg outstretched, the other bent at the knee, breasts tipped with bursting nipples, secret smile on her face, at least she's wearing golden earrings, so who knows? Cheap. The painting is cheap, and the room is cheap and the frizzed blonde in the Victoria's Secret lingerie is cheap. And *you* are cheap for being here, he thinks. In which case, don't fucking smell of *soap* all the time!

"So," Cindy says, "you want to make yourself comfortable?"

She says this not because she's trying to be seductive but only because, if he's a cop, she wants him naked before she asks for money. In that way, he will have already compromised his position. Legally. He will have engaged in something called entrapment, which for some legal reason will cause a judge to throw the case out of court. Entrapment was explained to him a long time ago by a hooker who

111

used to be a police officer before she realized there was better money to be made out of uniform. Though why prostitutes, trapped or otherwise, should be dragged into court in the first place is another thing Ben can't quite understand. This isn't somebody sniffing his life up his nose or drinking it into the gutter. This is a productive human being satisfying a perfectly normal and natural urge, which thank God there are women like Cindy willing to satisfy, however cheap they may seem to some.

Still fully dressed—or at least more fully dressed than the girl in the painting over the bed—she watches him as he takes off his clothes. This is a little embarrassing because he is already faintly tumescent, and he doesn't want her to think he's some horny jerk who wandered in off the street, but at the same time he wants her to know she's going to get fucked within an inch of her life, wants her to see the weapon he's still got hidden in his pants because he's removing first his jacket and then his shirt and tie and shoes and socks, and now his trousers, and now—here it comes, sweetheart, shield your eyes, you are about to witness a rod of such astonishing magnitude and dimension that it will forever change your perceptions of width, length, and girth! Are you ready? Get set . . .

He takes off his undershorts.

"Nice," she says. "Very nice, Michael. Impressive."

Which they always say in one way or another. My, what a huge cock! Boy, are you endowed! You don't plan to stick that thing in *me*, do you? He knows they're exaggerating. Well, lying, in fact. He's not really that big. He's not some black guy with a dong like Godzilla's, which is what occasional hookers have told him black guys possess, intimately sharing racial sex secrets with him after they've been in bed together for ten minutes and know each other like good old home boys from the hood. He knows these girls are being paid to tell him how wonderful and manly and sexy and exciting he is. He knows this. But he smiles modestly anyway, and feels himself growing perceptibly larger as she studies his cock with all the solemnity and professional aplomb of a urologist.

"Uh . . . I hate to ask you this, Michael," she says, tearing her eyes away, "but the basic massage is a hundred bucks."

"Okay," he says.

"Could I have it now, please?" she says, and pulls a girlish face. "I know, it's tawdry," she says, "but I do have to ask."

He takes out his wallet. Finds two fifties. Hands them to her.

"Thanks," she says. "I'm sorry."

She does seem genuinely sorry, but he knows that's an act, too. This is all a performance here. This is a movie. They are both performers in a movie about a man and a woman in a whore house. Except that it is all real. He sits on the edge of the bed, studying her ass and her legs as she stands on tip toe to reach for a handbag on the top shelf of the closet on the wall beside the bed. She takes down the

113

handbag, opens it. A black handbag. To match the stiletto-heeled, ankle-strapped black shoes. She puts the hundred bucks inside the bag. Isn't she afraid he might steal it? Didn't she tell him they were held up here only last week?

"O-kay," she says, and snaps the bag shut, and puts it back on the shelf, and slides the closet door closed, and turns to him. "I don't usually do this, you know," she says.

I'll bet, he thinks.

"I'm usually on the door," she says. "I sort of greet people."

"How come I'm so lucky?" he asks.

Please don't tell me I'm gentle, he thinks. I've already been there tonight.

"Is that meant to be sarcastic?" she asks.

But she's smiling.

"No, not at all. I'm curious."

"I don't know," she says, and shrugs. "Change of pace." She takes off the black wrapper, drapes it over the back of the chair, and moves to where he's sitting on the bed. "Want to kiss these?" she asks, and leans over to offer her breasts, squeezing them together with her hands. He finds the clasp at the back of the bra. Unfastens it. Her breasts fall free. He kisses her nipples.

"Mmmm," she says, faking enjoyment.

Or maybe not.

He tries to kiss her mouth.

She turns her face away.

"Uh-uh," she says.

"Why not?"

"I hardly know you."

"I'm hoping we'll get to know each other better."

"Even if we do."

"What I'm thinking . . ."

"Yes, tell me, Michael, what are you thinking?"

"I'm thinking we should go beyond the basic massage," he says.

"Where*ever* we go, we go *safe*," she says, and to emphasize the point, she opens the drawer in the end table on the right hand side of the bed, and takes out a box of lamb's skin rubbers.

"We don't need those," he says.

"Oh, that's what *you* think," she says.

"I got tested just last week," he lies.

"Mm-huh, and I suppose you've got the signed papers with you, right?"

"No, but you can trust me."

"Oh, I feel certain," she says.

"I've never had a venereal disease in my life."

"Me, neither," she says. "And I don't want one now."

"Here's what I'm thinking," he says.

"If you're thinking no rubber, think again."

She smiles to show him she's still a genial whore. But she shakes her frizzed blond head at the same time, to let him know she's dead serious about safe sex. He smiles secretly, wisely, raises one eyebrow. The knowing look is to tell her that every hooker has her price, dear, a theory he is about to put to the test. But the box of condoms is still in her hands, so

115

maybe he's wrong. In fact, she's now tearing off the cellophane wrapper.

"I'm thinking you should bring in the Arabian girl," he says.

"Oh, is that what you're thinking, Michael?"

"I'm thinking all three of us should forget about tomorrow," he says. "That's what I'm thinking."

"But how *much* are you thinking, Michael?"

Shaking one of the small blue plastic containers out of the package now, bringing it to her mouth, ripping the blue plastic seal with her teeth.

"How much do you think would be fair?" he asks.

She spits out blue plastic, and then, surprisingly, puts the box and the single condom down on the end table. She comes to where he is still sitting on the edge of the bed, steps between his legs, puts her hands on his shoulders, his cock standing stiff between them. She glances down at it. Her look is almost proprietary. She looks up again. Her eyes meet his. They are the deepest blue. He notices this for the first time. She is really a very beautiful girl.

"For what you have in mind," she says slowly, carefully, balancing time and demand like an accountant in a button factory, "me and Fatima, the busiest time of the night . . . I'd say a thousand flat."

"I'm not talking about a month in Europe," he says, and smiles again.

"You're talking about sticking that big hard cock in both of us bareback, is what you're talking about," she says, and glances down at it again. He is outrageously hard now. He reaches behind her to cup

116

her buttocks. She presses his face between her breasts. She lets him finger her asshole. She grabs his hair and pulls his face away from her.

"What do you say?" she says. "Both of us. A thousand flat."

"For how long?"

She still has his hair gripped in her hand.

"Whatever you want to do," she says, avoiding the question. "However you choose to do it."

"Six hundred," he says, bargaining. "For however long I need."

He is breathless in her grip.

"Six hundred for an hour," she says. "Me and Fatima, okay? Both of us."

Helpless in her grip.

"Yes," he says. "Okay."

"Let me go get her," she says, and releases his hair, and drops suddenly to her knees before him. She gives his cock a swift wet lick, her tongue lashing out and back into her mouth again, and then she rises, and for a moment stands tall and splendid before him, a frizzed blond goddess. Then she slides open the closet door and takes her handbag down from the shelf. Lifting the sheer black wrapper from where it is draped over the chair, she slips into it, and glances slyly at his cock. Grinning, she says, "Don't let that thing go down," and spins away from him and leaves the room.

He wonders how long it will take for her to get back here with Fatima. Suppose Fatima is right this minute in another room in the building with the guy

Heidi said she'd be watching out for? Otherwise engaged, as one might say. Suppose he has to wait till Fatima is finished with this guy, whoever he may be, until she can come in here with Cindy? He doesn't like the idea of her coming to him fresh from some other guy. Maybe he should have asked for Heidi instead, no, the gold tooth. Besides, by now she may be with some other guy, too, leaving the fat freckled babe to guard the sacred portals. He knows he's not the only man these girls see, but he likes to think of himself as such. The sultan calling for one or another of his harem girls. The eunuchs outside watching but not allowed to touch. All the girls belonging to him and him alone. Oh sure. He knows this is nonsense. But it's a nice fantasy. Moreover, he knows it's a fantasy. Knows this entire scene here, this scenario, this lavish production that's about to cost him an additional six hundred bucks is a figment of the imagination, a dream concocted—or about to be concocted—by himself and the two girls scurrying down the hall toward him this very moment, he wishes. Maybe he should have asked for Heidi, if it's going to take Fatima so long to get her ass in here for their big spectacular dream sequence.

He can just imagine Grace being picked for a spontaneous three-way dream sequence like this one. Grace, there's some guy upstairs wants both of us, go put on your garter belt! With Grace, you have to "plan" everything. She's like the commanding general of some vast army about to invade the European continent, she has all these complicated "plans" to make. She's the same way about sex, too, she has to "plan for it. Nothing is spontaneous with Grace. In the morning, she doesn't feel clean enough for sex because she hasn't bathed yet. At night, she feels too clean for sex because she takes three baths every single day of the year—not showers, *baths*—and at night, when you roll over against her with a hard-on, she tells you she just took a bath and doesn't want to get "messy." Grace Howell Thorpe is the cleanest woman on the face of the—

The door opens suddenly, startling him.

Cindy comes into the room first.

"I hope you waited for us," she says, pretending to scold him. "Six hundred, please," she says, "I hate to ask," and extends her hand to him, palm upward. He slides down to the end of the bed, and reaches for his trousers where they're draped over the seat of the chair. He removes from his wallet six hundred-dollar bills, and hands them over to Cindy. "Let me take this downstairs," she says. "You two get started, I'll be right back." She licks her lips, winks at him, and leaves the room again. He wonders how long she'll be gone this time. He wonders whether all this coming and going is on the clock. Wonders if he'll get time off for good behavior.

"So I hear you have some ideas," Fatima says, sitting beside him on the bed.

She is not smiling. She sits on her heels beside him on the bed, hands flat on her thighs, studying him with those pale blue eyes of hers. He feels

119

himself growing hot under her steady gaze. He feels himself growing hard.

"I hear you want to forget tomorrow," she murmurs, and nods at his cock.

The nod frightens him.

"*I* have some ideas," she says.

He is angry with his cock for betraying him, annoyed at himself for not being more in control of his emotions, sitting here ridiculously and visibly hard under Fatima's steady gaze, exposed to her view, vulnerable to whatever ideas she may be entertaining. He thinks he knows what those ideas might be. He has met this woman in fantasies on one or two occasions before in his lifetime, three or four, has met Fatima during half a dozen daydreams, a dozen perhaps. He knows what vile and unspeakable acts she might ask him to perform, knows that if he allows this dumb fucking rigid cock of his to control him, he'll do whatever she orders him to do, right this minute, now. What's wrong with me? he wonders. What the hell is wrong with me?

She is rising to her knees on the bed now, her hands moving from her thighs to her crotch, her fingers spreading her lips for him. He has imagined this dark and merciless gaze before.

"So how about it?" Fatima asks. "You want to lick my cunt?"

Above the bed, the Gypsy Girl smiles lewd approval.

"Let's wait for Cindy," he says.

120

"Sure," she says, and sits beside him again, and casually takes his cock in her hand. "Where you from, Michael?" she asks. Stroking him. Casually.

"Los Angeles."

"Nobody's from Los Angeles."

"You mean originally? Mamaroneck."

"Is that your real name? Michael?"

"Sure."

"Sure," she says. "The way mine is Fatima."

He's tempted to ask what her real name is.

"What do you do, Michael?" she says.

"I'm an insurance adjuster," he says.

"Yeah?"

"Yeah. Marine insurance. There are lots of boaters in L.A. Lots of boating accidents, too."

"I'll bet. So what do you do, you investigate boating accidents?"

"Yes."

"You're full of shit," she says.

"I know," he says, and smiles.

She does not return the smile. He notices that she never smiles.

"Okay," she says, "so don't tell me."

"I'm an architect," he says.

"Okay, that's possible," she says.

"It's true."

"So what do you design?"

"Houses, churches, buildings."

"Yeah?"

"Yeah."

"You married, Michael?"

"Yes."

"You got kids?"

"One. A daughter."

"How old?"

"Twenty-one."

"You ain't that old yourself.!

"Ho-ho," he says.

"Ho-ho," she echoes.

But does not smile.

"That why you like fucking young girls, Michael?" she says.

He looks at her.

"Cause you got a twenty-one-year-old daughter?"

He does not answer her for a moment.

Then he says, quite seriously, "I don't know why I fuck young girls."

Or older girls, too, he thinks. Or mature women. Or even a sixty-year-old grandmother one time at the Bel Air in Los Angeles.

Her thighs are very white above the black elastic-topped stockings. There is a purple bruise on her right thigh. He wonders if she has a pimp who beats her. He didn't think these places were run by pimps. The Mafia, he thinks. He imagines the Mafia running weekly ads in *New York* magazine. She keeps stroking him almost idly.

"What's your real name?" he asks.

"Why? You wanna get married?" she says. But does not smile. Josie, okay?" she says.

"Should I call you Josie?"

"No. Here, I'm Fatima."

"What do you do when you're *not* here, Fatima?"

"Why? You wanna go out sometime?"

"I'm just curious."

"You wanna go out with a whore, Michael? Is that it? Take me to dinner? Take me to the movies?"

"Is that how you see yourself?"

"No, I see myself as a brain surgeon."

"Where'd you get the name Fatima?"

"Who knows? Where'd you get the name Michael?"

"My best friend's name was Michael."

"Did he die or something?"

"No, no. I knew him when I was six."

"Fatima suits me, don't you think?"

"It's more exotic."

"Like me, right?"

"You do look exotic."

"I know. People think I'm from Morocco."

"I thought Arabian or something."

"You know where I really come from?"

"Where?"

"Brooklyn. I was born in Brooklyn. How old are you, Michael?"

"Forty-three."

"You don't need Viagra, though, do you?"

"Not yet."

"All you need is a young girl, right?"

"Not necessarily."

"How old do you think I am, Michael?"

"I have no idea."

"I'm not as young as your daughter, that's for sure. But how old do you think I am? Seriously."

"Tell me."

"I'm thirty-two."

"You look much younger."

"I know."

"You really do."

"It's because I'm so thin."

"You are thin, yes, but . . ."

"I'm *too* thin, right?"

"No, I wouldn't say that."

"My tits are okay, though, don't you think?" she says, and drops his cock suddenly, and cups both firm breasts, and looks down at them. "For someone as thin as I am? I mean, they're proportionately right for my body, don't you think?"

"Yes, they're very attractive."

"And my nipples are *great*," she says. "I really have terrific nipples." She suddenly releases her breasts, shrugs, grabs his cock again. "What's *your* real name, Michael?"

"Well, I don't think we really want to get into that, do we?"

"What *do* we really want to get into, Michael? Tell me what you'd like to do when Cindy gets back."

"Well, we'll just have to figure that out, won't we?"

"Cause zee clock she will be ticking, *comprende, amigo*?"

"Where is she, anyway?"

"She'll be back. Let's just keep this nice and hard for her, okay? How come you picked the name of a six-year-old friend?" she asks.

124

"He was seven."

"Are you still friends?"

"I haven't seen him since I grew up."

"But you use his name."

"Sometimes."

"When you come to places like this, huh?"

"I guess."

"That's very interesting," she says. "Lie down on the couch and tell me about it." She is not smiling, she never smiles. "I'll sit on your face while you talk. Would you like me to sit on your face, Michael?"

"Well . . ."

"While Cindy blows you?"

"I don't know. Maybe."

"I taste of cinnamon wine, Michael," she says, and licks her lips.

"Really? What's cinnamon wine taste like?"

"Like me," she says. "Or would you rather fuck me in the ass? A hundred-dollar tip and you can stick this big thing in my ass, Michael, would you like that? Do you like to fuck young girls in the ass, Michael?"

The door opens suddenly, and Cindy rushes into the room, seemingly out of breath. "Big crowd downstairs, all at once," she explains. "We'd better get started here." She glances at his cock in Fatima's hand, nods appreciatively, and says, "Not bad for a beginner." He doesn't know if she's talking about him or Fatima, who now slides off the bed, her pale blue eyes searching his as if confirming a pact they've already made. She turns away at once, removes the peony-patterned robe, and tosses it over the back of the chair. Cindy glances at him more intimately than Fatima did, seeming to measure his cock with her eyes. She tosses her own sheer black robe over Fatima's. As if by signal—but he has seen none—the girls move to either side of the bed, Rockettes performing a rehearsed maneuver, blond hair and black, bookends in reverse. Cindy wriggles her red panties down over her knees, steps out of them, leaves them on the floor. Both girls stand akimbo, legs widespread in frank and open invitation.

Cindy is the heftier of the two, the more *zoftig*, the one he imagined would now call the tune and lead the band. But when she sits beside him and reaches for his cock, Fatima brushes her hand aside in silent reprimand. Their eyes lock, deep cobalt and pallid sapphire. The look they exchange is intimate and female, dark and savage, electrifying but frightening.

Fatima insinuates herself beside him on the bed, swings her knees up, black elastic-topped stockings, black high-heeled ankle-strapped sandals. The lifeless blue eyes flick his cock, as if drawn to it against her will. Cindy watches her, deep blue eyes learning; she is usually on the door, she is the one who sort of greets. Without warning, Fatima seizes him. He catches his breath sharply, caught in her grip, tight in her grip. She does not move her hand. She simply holds him firmly, staring at his cock as if unaware of the person attached to it, cognizant only of the

126

clogged and aching member in her hand. Without glancing at Cindy, she says, "Suck it."

The trick now is to maintain control.

It is easy enough to let oneself go, he can do that anytime. Instead, one must hold oneself back to the very last moment, stay in charge here—though it is Fatima who is truly in charge, one hand guiding Cindy's blonde and bobbing head, the other cold-bloodedly clutching his cock in a Mediterranean death grip. In a day and age of indiscriminate sex promising dread disease and certain death, he is uniformly amazed by the heedless abandon of most women he encounters—well, his own recklessness, too, for that matter. As he mentioned to Cindy earlier, he has never had a venereal disease in his life. Considering how sexually active he is, although he guesses other men are just as active, he is surprised but nonetheless grateful. He has never had gonorrhea, nor syphilis, nor even herpes. He knows he will never contract AIDS, either. He simply knows this. He is immune. He believes he is immune.

Cindy works him with excruciating precision, Fatima's left hand resting on top of her bobbing head. On her pinky, Fatima wears a ring with a ruby-colored stone. Her fingernails are painted to match the stone. Her lipstick is the same color. She holds his cock excruciatingly tight, as if trying to choke off the blood supply. Each time Cindy's mouth lowers around him, her lips touch Fatima's clenched right fist. Fatima will not allow him to escape the deliberate rise and fall of Cindy's blond head and

127

soft methodical mouth. Occasionally, Cindy's eyes raise to meet his, a whore's trick. Occasionally, she smiles around his cock, another whore's trick. Fatima watches her as she works, her hand unrelievedly tight around him. Then suddenly, as if jealous or unexpectedly aroused, she says, "Me, bitch!" and grabs Cindy by the hair, yanking her head away from him and off of him. His cock feels suddenly wet and cold, but only for an instant.

Fatima's mouth engorges him, savagely hot, as tight and insistent as her encircling hand had been, her ferocious lips demanding instant submission. He says, "Careful," and tries to stop this surprise assault on his hoarded treasure, his hands coming up to her face, his back arching in contradiction, cock eagerly thrusting to meet her determined plunge. She brushes his hands away, her descent resolute, her murderous intent acidly clear.

"Give it to her, baby," he hears Cindy say.

He knows that within an instant he will surrender totally, he will shatter and burst, he will be punished.

"Oh, please," he says.

Fatima's mouth relents.

"No, don't," he says. "Stop," he explains.

His cock stands rigid and throbbing between them.

"Come on, sweetheart," Fatima says, "let it go."

"Let it go," Cindy echoes. "Give it to her."

Give it to me, Grace says.

Fatima takes him in her hand again. Straddling him, sitting back on her heels, she holds his cock stiff at the joining of her legs, as if it is her own

128

cock springing from her tangled black crotch, sitting back on the black high-heeled sandals, legs bent. Strict black stockings and bruised white thigh promise further mischief from her; she will punish him cruelly, she will keep him enslaved forever, she will never let him go. But instead she becomes surprisingly kind, coaxing him with soft murmuring sounds, all cooing vowels and childish lisps.

"Yes, baby," she whispers. "Yes."

"I have to," he says, pleading with her now.

"Yes," she whispers, "I know, baby."

"I really have to," he says.

"Yes, come for me," she whispers.

"I will," he says.

"So do it."

"I will."

The room becomes intensely silent. Fatima's hand glides smoothly, gently, encircling him, encouraging him, persuading him. Like a patient predator, Cindy watches. In the near-dark, he can hear her harsh breathing.

"Honey, you got a problem here?" she asks.

"You been drinking, honey?" Fatima says.

"I'm fine," he says, "please don't stop."

"Cause we ain't got all night here, you know," Cindy says.

"What?" he says.

"Your hour's almost up," Fatima says.

"You've got ten minutes, honey," Cindy says, and lowers her mouth onto him.

"Ten minutes? How . . .?"

"Tick-tock," Fatima says.

"You said however long . . ."

"We said an hour," Fatima says. "Do him deep," she advises Cindy.

There is a desperation to their efforts now. He senses that Cindy doesn't want to fail at this, she takes pride in her blowjobs. Neither of them wishes to fail, there is a certain sense of professional pride these girls take in their work, he senses this about them, and respects this about them. They are really trying quite hard to give him the "complete satisfaction" the XS spokesperson promised him on the phone, Fatima fingering his asshole now while Cindy labors above him, her mouth descending deep and deeper, her hand tight on his shaft, both girls sweaty and serious and industrious and infinitely patient, but zee clock she is ticking, *comprende, amigo,* and he can't imagine what the hell is wrong with him. This has never happened to him before in his lifetime, well, maybe with Grace, but never with girls he has known, women he has known, never!

"Last chance saloon," Fatima says.

"Just give me another minute."

"You've got about five," Cindy murmurs around his cock.

"Tick-tock," Fatima says again.

He can't believe he agreed to a mere hour for six hundred dollars! Was he out of his mind? Was he drunk? He knows he hasn't drunk too much. He's drunk far more than this on occasions too numerous to count, and has later come two, three times in a

130

night, well, twice anyway, so what the hell is it? How much has he drunk tonight, anyway? There was the gin in his room, and then the one at the bar with the redhead, whatever her name was — was it two at the bar?

"That's the way, honey."

"Keep that big cock working, Michael."

"Oh yes, baby."

"Shove it deep in her mouth!"

Cindy's mouth is hungry on his cock. Fatima's middle finger is urgent in his asshole.

"Let's see that juice, babe."

"Give it up, honey."

"Shoot all over her stockings."

"Come on, honey."

"Come on, Michael, what the fuck's *wrong* with you?"

There is a moment when he feels he will come, knows he will come. The moment hangs in silence. A knock sounds on the door, urgent, demanding.

"Time," someone outside calls.

He hears high-heeled shoes scurrying down the hall, hears another knock on another door, hears the word "Time" again, distantly. The girls are suddenly off the bed, scrambling off the bed. He is alone on the bed, lying on his back, alone on the bed, looking up at the Gypsy Girl lying voluptuously on the inexpertly rendered, fringed red velvet throw, one leg outstretched, the other bent at the knee, breasts tipped with bursting nipples, secret smile on her

131

face. She knows he could not come, did not come. Time, he thinks.

Cindy puts on her black peignoir. Like a butterfly, she flits toward the door, opens it, and is gone without a word. Fatima pulls on the peony-patterned wrapper, picks up her shoes and stockings. "Get dressed, Michael," she says. "Somebody'll come up to take you down." Barefooted, she pads to the door, reaches for the knob with her free hand, turns to him. For a moment, she seems about to say something more. Instead, she nods wearily, opens the door, and then closes it softly behind her.

He listens to her bare footfalls going down the hall. He looks at his watch. It is ten minutes past two. Was it really an hour? He can't believe it was really an hour. And even if it was, couldn't they have given him a few extra minutes? For six hundred bucks? Psychiatrists get less than that, for Christ's sake! All he'd needed was a few extra minutes. Was that a lot of time to ask? Angrily, he begins dressing.

There is another knock on the door. Soft this time. Discreet. A gentle rapping.

"Come in," he says, but the door is already opening. He's never seen the girl who stands there, tentatively peering in at him. She was not one of the "nice selection" presented to him when he arrived. Is she part of a new shift? Or had she been with a customer? She looks Hispanic, wearing a green silk wrapper belted at the waist, high-heeled shoes, of course, curly black hair trimmed close to her head, large brown eyes, pouty mouth painted red. He is still sitting on the bed, putting on his socks and loafers.

"I'm supposed to take you down," she says. No accent. Maybe she isn't Hispanic. Or maybe she was born here. Maybe she's from Brooklyn, like Fatima, who looks like she's from Morocco.

"In a minute," he says.

She waits impatiently in the doorway, leaning against the doorjamb, hand on her hip. He slips into the other loafer, rises, says, "Okay," and follows her out. As they head down the stairs, he says, "I didn't see you before."

"I was busy," she says.

"I have a raincoat," he says.

She turns to look at him. She appears angry but he figures she's only puzzled.

"Downstairs," he says. "Cindy took my raincoat to hang up."

"Okay, we'll get it."

He follows behind her, watching the movement of her ass under the green silk.

"What's your name?" he asks her.

She turns to look at him again.

"Blanca," she says. "Why?"

"What are you doing now, Blanca?" he asks.

"What do you mean?"

"Are you busy now?"

She looks him over, hands on her ample hips.

"What'd you have in mind?"

Appraising him. Eyes gliding down to the front of his trousers, coming up to meet his again.

"What I have in mind is a secret room with a narrow bed and a little blue light," he says.

"All that, huh?" she says, and smiles.

"All that."

"I don't know about the little blue light," she says. "You got a hundred bucks for me?"

"I've got time left on my hour."

"Time, I see," she says, and nods. "I didn't know we gave chits for time here."

"Check it with Cindy and Fatima. They'll tell you."

"They're with clients right now. Also, it's not the girls who keep time," Blanca says. "It's the manager. He just sends one of us around to knock on doors."

"So let me talk to the manager," he says.

"I don't know if he's available right now. We got kind of busy all at once." She looks him over again. "Whyn't you just slip me an ace, I'll find a bed someplace, take care of you real quick."

"Let me talk to the manager first, okay?"

"Whatever, I'll see if he's around," she says. "What kind of coat did you say?"

"A raincoat. Tell him I've got time coming."

"He'll want to hear that, all right. Wait here," she says, and uses a key to open the door with the hanging letter B on it. There is the glow of the red light as the door opens. Heidi flits by in her sheer white baby doll nightgown just as the door closes again. He waits in the hallway, eager to talk to the manager, eager to straighten this out. He has a seven-hundred-dollar investment here already, and even a small portion of that should buy the twenty minutes or so he needs with Blanca.

The door opens.

"You want to come inside a minute?" she says. "I don't know which one is yours."

He steps inside, and is suddenly awash in red light and the cloying scent of incense. Only Heidi in her white baby doll nightgown is in the room now, lying in deep uffish thought on the velvet thrift-shop sofa earlier occupied by fat Irish Alice in her *Wizard of Oz* slippers—though she too seems to be otherwise engaged just now, *We got kind of busy all at once.* Blanca leads him to a closet where there are three almost identical raincoats hanging on a pipe rod. He would be hard pressed himself to tell which one is his, were it not for a small stain on the right sleeve, which he spots at once. He has been telling Grace about that stain for months now. Grace does not like taking things to the dry cleaners. Grace does not like doing anything in this fucking world but take three baths a day and polish her fingernails and toenails. That is what Grace likes to do.

"This one's mine," he says, and takes the coat off its wire hanger.

"You still here?" Heidi says, and grins at him, the gold tooth in her mouth flashing.

"I'm waiting to talk to the manager," he says.

"I'll go get him," Blanca says. "We got a room with a little blue light, Heidi?"

"You want a little blue light?" Heidi asks him.

"How about *both* of you and a little blue light?" he says. "I've got plenty of time coming."

"He thinks he has time coming," Blanca says.

"No kidding?" Heidi says, and grins as if she's just heard something very comical. "You really think so, Michael?"

"That's what he told me," Blanca says, and goes out of the room, presumably to search for the manager.

He looks over at Heidi, who is now lying on the couch. White baby doll nightgown. Long blond hair. No underpants. Shaved close below. He says nothing for several moments, just keeps looking at her. She smiles at him again, the gold tooth flashing.

"What time do you quit here?" he asks at last.

"Around three-thirty, four o'clock," she says. "Why?"

"I was thinking after we get this time business straightened out . . ."

"The time business, right."

"After you and me and Blanca find that room with the little blue light . . ."

"Oh, sure, the blue light."

"You might want to come back to the hotel with me."

"Gee, a hotel," she says, and rolls her eyes in mock wonder.

"It's not far from here, Fifty-sixth and Sixth," he says. "What do you think?"

"I think it's not allowed, is what I think. But let's talk about that later, okay?" she says and

136

raises her eyebrows to indicate someone is standing behind him.

"Sir?" a voice says, and he turns to see a very large black man in blue jeans and a white tank top shirt standing near the telephone just inside the entrance door. "You wished to see me, sir?"

"Are you the manager?"

"I am. Is there some kind of problem, sir?"

"No problem at all," Ben says. "Whoever I spoke to on the telephone . . ."

"Yes, sir?"

". . .promised complete satisfaction. Well, I just now . . ."

"So what's the problem, sir?"

"I just now paid Cindy and Fatima a hundred dollars for the basic massage, *plus* an additional six hundred for . . ."

"Tell me what's bothering you, sir."

"What's bothering me is I think I have some time coming," Ben says. "To honor the basic contract."

"Which contract is that, sir?"

"Complete satisfaction," he says.

"From what I understand, sir, the girls spent a full hour with you . . ."

"That's debatable. In any case, our understanding . . ."

"Maybe next time you shouldn't drink so much."

"What?" Ben says.

"They told me you'd been drinking."

"Told you I'd been *drinking*?"

"Yes, and don't yell, sir."

"I gave them six hundred bucks," he says, lowering his voice. "What do they mean I was drinking? *Seven* hundred bucks. I can't believe this! Seven hundred bucks and they say I was *drinking*."

"Please don't yell, sir."

"No, wait a minute," he says, "don't go telling me not to . . ."

"Sir, we have . . ."

"If anything, I drink only in moderation . . ."

"We have other customers here, sir. I'm asking you to . . ."

"Maybe you ought to ask little Josie from Brooklyn if she and her blonde partner with the big tits aren't *themselves* responsible for what happened, hmm?"

"Watch the language, sir."

"Or is it easier to blame the whole fucking disaster . . ."

"Sir, I'm warning you . . ."

". . . on a social drink I shared in a bar next door to a fucking *whore* house!"

"That's it, let's go," the man says, and shoves him toward the entrance door, and then opens the door and shoves him again, this time out into the hallway, where he shoves him yet another time, toward the stairs leading down to the street. Flailing backward toward the gaping steps, Ben loses his balance, reaches out to the black man for purchase. He feels the top step sliding away under his heel, grabs more frantically for the black man's support, the open maw of the stairwell behind him—and feels himself going over.

He knows better than to try to stop his downward tumble by sticking out a hand, that's a sure way to break a wrist or an arm. He's positive he'll break something anyway, a leg, his head, something. The steps are sharp and cruel and unforgiving, each angular joining of riser and tread unyielding. He jounces in punishing collision to the bottom of the stairway, and lies there breathless. He touches his nose, wondering if it's broken, it hurts so goddamn much. Above him, he can hear the black man thundering down the steps. The narrow entrance cubicle inside the frosted glass door is perhaps six feet square. The black man looms over him, reaches down for him, twists his hands into Ben's coat lapels . . .

"Hey, watch it," Ben says.

. . . yanks him to his feet, nods as if confirming that he is about to hurt Ben very badly, and then frees his right hand and smashes his fist into Ben's mouth.

The entryway is a limiting arena at best, confining to say the least when a man who appears to be seven feet tall with muscles everywhere and jailhouse tattoos all over his arms is throwing Ben from wall to wall when he isn't trying to batter him senseless. "You want to have some fun here?" he keeps saying over and again, "You want to have some fun, Whitey?" Ben is bleeding from the nose and the mouth. The black man keeps hitting him, mostly in the face because he knows this is where his blows are most visibly punishing, blood spurting, cuts

139

opening, but he punches him brutally in the chest as well, and both arms, and the midsection, and the gut too because there is no referee here to warn about hitting below the belt, there is only a savage black man inexplicably enraged who is trying to teach Ben some kind of lesson here for having broken some kind of rules Ben didn't even know existed, when all he'd wanted to do was have a little fun here, "You want to have some fun here, Whitey?"

He is virtually senseless when the black man opens first the frosted glass inner door, and then the entrance door and drags Ben out onto the sidewalk and props him up with his left hand and punches him full in the face again with his right.

"Goodnight, Whitey," he says, and throws him into the gutter.

CHAPTER
SIX

His legs are on the sidewalk, the rest of him is in the gutter. It is raining very hard now. Rain riddles the puddle in which he is lying, he will drown. He will die in a New York gutter, his face broken and bleeding, there will be headlines. Bits of flotsam float past his face in the gutter, he will choke, he will drown. A dog has shit in the gutter, the feces lies in a puddle close to Ben's face, it is a shame the people in this city do not obey the law.

I once had a dog, he thinks.

Or perhaps says.

"I once had a dog," he tells everyone or no one.

"Well, well, what've we got here?" someone asks.

A man's voice.

"He drunk?"

Another man.

"Got the shit beat out of him, looks like."

"Roll him over."

Hands on him.

The rain falls steadily onto his face and the front of the light raincoat. His hair is wet and hanging in strings on his forehead. The coat is drenched through to the jacket and shirt underneath. He doesn't know

141

whether it's blood or water running down his face into the puddle in the gutter smelling of dog shit. He keeps his eyes squinched tight against the rain battering his face.

"Travelers checks ain't no fuckin good to us," one of the men says.

"There's cash, too," the other one says.

"How much?"

"Three hundred, looks like."

"Credit cards, too."

"Take "em. We'll fly ourselves to Paris."

Both men laugh.

His wallet splashes into the puddle.

One of the men kicks him in the head.

And then they are gone. And now there is only the sound of the rain beating down around him. He hopes a car won't come too close to the curb and squash his head flat into the asphalt. He hopes a cop won't find him and arrest him, lying in the gutter this way. He wonders if they took his driver's license. He doesn't want anyone to know who he is, lying in the gutter this way. He is Benjamin Thorpe, Fellow of the American Institute of Architects, but he doesn't want anyone to know who he is.

"Oh man," he hears someone say.

A woman's voice.

"You okay?"

He is not okay. He hurts everywhere, and he suspects he is bleeding from his nose or his mouth or both. He is definitely not okay. He shakes his head. Tries to shake it. Glances upward and to his right.

142

Sees high-heeled purple shoes, brown naked legs, a short purple leather skirt.

"You okay?" she says again.

She is kneeling beside him now. Shiny knees, purple leather skirt.

"Look what they done to you," she says.

She is lifting his head out of the gutter.

"Jesus," she whispers.

He can hear the sound of the rain everywhere around them.

"Listen," she says, "I got to call an ambulance, you hear?"

He shakes his head.

No.

No ambulance.

"You need a doctor, man."

Shakes his head again.

No.

"You're hurt real bad, man."

"No doctor," he says. "Go away. Leave me alone."

"You wanted or something?"

He doesn't understand her.

"You hear me? Are the cops looking for you?"

"No," he says. His lips hurt when he talks.

"Then let me call an ambulance."

"No."

"I ain't gonna stand all night here in the rain with you."

"That's okay," he says.

"No, it ain't okay."

"It's okay, you can go. Thanks. You can go."

"Why you being so obstinate?"

The word "obstinate" amuses him somehow. He starts to laugh, spits up something he suspects is blood, begins coughing.

"Oh shit," she says, and sighs heavily. "Come on," she says. "Get up. Get out the gutter, man, what's wrong with you? This wallet yours?"

"Yes."

She picks up the wallet, drops it in a purple leather tote, slings the bag over her shoulder again. He feels her hands under his arms, big hands, strong hands. Standing spread-legged, bracing herself on her high heels, she hoists him to his feet.

"Ow," he says.

"Yeah, Ow," she says. "Go tell a doctor Ow, you in such pain."

"Look," he says, "I think I can manage alone."

"Oh sure."

"No, really . . ."

"You cain't hardly stand up," she says, and waves her free arm at a taxi. She helps him into the cab, and then slides in beside him. He feels somewhat nauseous. He hopes he won't vomit here in the cab. The cab rolls through the sodden night, tires whispering against wet asphalt, windshield wipers snicking at the rain. Ben closes his eyes. Darkness rolls over him. He rests his head on her shoulder. She pats his hand. He wonders why.

"It's on the left," he hears her say. "Next door the laundromat."

144

The driver pulls the cab over to the curb. The woman takes Ben's wallet from her tote, opens the bill compartment.

"They cleaned you out," she says, and hands the wallet to him. Reaching into the tote again, she takes another wallet from it, opens it familiarly, hands the driver a ten-dollar bill, waits for change, and then tips him. Ben is on the curb side, he slides out first, puts his wallet into the right hand pocket of his trousers. He knows they haven't cleaned him out completely because he heard them talking about travelers checks being no good to them, but he doesn't want to look now, not with the rain coming down so heavily. He'd run for her building if he knew which one it was, but there are doors on either side of the laundromat. There are still people in there doing their laundry. He wonders what time it is. He stands swaying on the sidewalk in the rain, fearful he will lose his balance and tumble into the gutter again. The taxi pulls away from the curb, tires spreading a canopy of water. The woman comes to him, takes him by the elbow, and leads him to the doorway on the left of the laundromat.

He closes his eyes and leans against the doorjamb as she fumbles for keys inside the tote. "Don't nod out on me now," she says, and he hears the click of a key being inserted in the keyway, and then feels her arm around his waist again. He opens his eyes. She has pushed open the door and is helping him into a vestibule the size of the one where he was beaten. There is an inner door here as well, etched glass with a crack running diagonally across its face. She inserts another key and then—her arm still around him—helps him inside and toward a narrow flight of steps leading upward at a precarious angle. He remembers his mad tumble down the steps at the XS Salon.

"You okay?" she says.

"Mm."

"Stay with it."

"Okay."

His lip is swollen. Something has crusted under his nose, either blood or snot or both. He feels completely disoriented. He knows he should not be here, but he also knows he cannot allow himself to enter a hospital. He can barely see through his left eye. His entire face throbs with pain. He knows that if she loosens her grip around his waist, he will fall and possibly hurt himself even further. But he can't go to a hospital where they will ask him what his name is, ask him where he lives, ask if there is anyone they should contact, anyplace he should be. The truth is he does not know *where* he should be. And here is as good a place as any. He suddenly wants to cry.

"Careful," she says.

Side by side, as if joined at the hip, they move down the third-floor corridor to a door at the far end. Bracing him against her, she inserts a key, shoves open the door, and half-carries, half-drags him into the apartment. She eases him onto a sofa, and moves away from him to turn on a light. He winces against the sudden glare.

She is wearing a blond wig, cut in bangs on her forehead, falling straight and loose to her shoulders. She is wearing a little red monkey fur jacket over the purple leather skirt and a shiny purple blouse. She has thick lips and a flat nose, dark brown eyes lidded with purple mascara that glitters. She is a woman in her thirties, he supposes. He closes his eyes again. She helps him out of the soaking wet raincoat. He feels her easing his sodden loafers and wet socks off his feet. Something lands on the sofa beside him. He pulls back his hand, opens his eyes wide, turns his head, almost screams aloud when he sees a pair of yellow eyes staring back at him.

"Juss my cat," she says.

Her cat is a huge tabby, all black and gray, with eyes the size of quarters, sniffing around him, whiskers bristling. He is afraid the cat will bite him. Or claw him. Or whatever it is cats do to strangers. But he is purring loudly. Or she. Or it. Whatever it is, Ben wishes he had never allowed this blond black woman to take him here, wherever here is. What is he doing here, anyway, sharing a sofa with a cat the size of a young lion? He shifts his weight, trying to move away from the creature. But the cat nuzzles his arm and his hip, and the blond black woman says, "He's very friendly, ain't you, honey?" He gives the cat a dirty look intended to state unequivocally that he does not choose to be friends with a cat, not this cat or any other cat in the world.

She is unloosening his belt now.

"Lift," she says.

He raises his hips, and she pulls his pants down over his ass and lowers them past his knees and ankles, and tosses them onto an easy chair alongside the couch. The cat is still nuzzling him. He doesn't wish to appear rude because the cat's mistress did, after all, pull him out of the gutter and is now treating him with more gentleness than he's known all night long, but he truly does not like cats, nor dogs, for that matter, nor—Jesus Christ what is that in the corner! He sits up with a start because the first thing that registers is a sense of spectral whiteness, and then he hears a croaking sound like that of a witch, and then sees a distinct flutter of whiteness, and he realizes all at once that there's yet another living creature in this apartment even before she says, "Juss my bird."

He does not like birds, either.

"All you need to start your own ho house," she says, "is a little pussy and a cockatoo."

She grins broadly.

"You get it?" she says.

She has very white teeth.

"I get it," he says. His lips still hurt when he tries to talk.

She yanks off his undershorts and tosses them onto the trousers. He is too aware of this sudden menagerie everywhere around him to feel any embarrassment, even though the woman must think his cock looks shriveled and wet and limp, which it is. He suddenly hurts all over again, especially in the groin because he possibly aggravated something when he jumped up a moment ago. He is now fearful the cat will jump onto his naked lap in a further display of good fellowship. Or perhaps the white bird will fly into his face. Or worse, mistake his little boy's pee-pee—which it has suddenly become—for a white worm instead of a grown man's cock. Or maybe there's also a pimp on the premises because all he needs now is for yet another angry black man to throw him down the stairs again. He almost asks her whether she has an angry pimp who calls non-African-American clients "Whitey" and throws them down the stairs. He does not want to meet any more macho muscle men tonight. He does not want yet another gallant musketeer imagining a princess in a baby doll nightgown was insulted by his bad language when all he wanted to do was explain that he had some time coming. But she is busy loosening his tie and unbuttoning his shirt, and he doesn't wish to seem ungrateful for her hospitality and concern, any tart in a storm, he thinks. Her fingers move swiftly and expertly. She has undoubtedly unbuttoned many a man's shirt in her career as Hooker With a Heart of Gold. He still has one eye on the cat and another on the bird in the corner, who, he now realizes, is in fact a cockatoo. She has taken off the tie and shirt now, and tossed them onto the rest of his clothes so that they form a forlorn little heap on the easy chair.

"You smell like a toilet bowl," she says.

"Thanks," he says, and winces because his mouth and his left eye both hurt when he talks.

"Let's get you cleaned up," she says, and offers her hand to him. He takes it, allows her to pull him off the couch and onto his feet to the accompaniment of a sudden chorus of screeches from the white bird on its perch. The cat leaps off the couch, begins trailing Ben as if he's a long-lost, newly discovered master, following him over what Ben now sees is a worn Persian rug, toward an open door beyond which is a small bathroom. There is a smelly red plastic litter box just inside the door, and then a standing sink with a mirror over it, and then an old-fashioned claw-footed bathtub.

The face in the mirror startles him.

His left eye is swollen almost shut, encircled with puffy flesh bruised yellow and purple and blue. There is a cut on his right cheek and blood crusted inside his nose and under it. His upper lip is swollen and cracked. There is a black gap at the front of his mouth where two teeth have been knocked out.

He stands looking at himself.

Who are you? he wonders.

Jesus, who the hell are you?

"Something, huh?" she says.

As she turns on the faucets in the tub, he keeps staring at himself in the mirror. The cat rubs against his leg. In the other room, he can hear the cockatoo screaming. Steam begins filling the bathroom. The face of the stranger in the mirror begins to cloud over. He wants to cry again.

*　　*　　*

She soaps him gently. The water turns pinkish when she sponges away his blood stains, gently patting, lightly rubbing.

"What's your name?" she asks.

He almost says Michael.

"Ben," he says.

"You really lost this one, Ben."

"Mm."

"How many was they?"

He shakes his head.

"Beat you up, took all yo money. You had a big night, Ben."

She sponges him in silence for several moments. She has rolled up the sleeves of the purple silk blouse. Her arms are round and firm and brown. There is a small tattoo near her left wrist. Some kind of bird. Or insect. He can't quite make it out.

"Where was you, to run into such types?" she asks.

He closes his eyes.

"Mm-huh," she says knowingly. "You here visiting New York, Ben?"

He nods.

"Out havin youself a good time?"

He says nothing. Keeps his eyes closed.

"You got nothin to hide from me, Ben," she says. "I been hookin since I was sixteen."

He still says nothing.

"You goan drown here if I leave you alone a minute?"

He shakes his head.

"You need me, just yell."

He nods. In the other room, the cockatoo shrieks to welcome her arrival. He lies in the warm water, his eyes closed, feeling every aching muscle and bone where the steps and the black man punished him. Steam rises everywhere around him. He feels himself relaxing.

He dozes.

"You bout ready to come out?" she asks, startling him.

He opens his eyes.

She is holding a large white beach towel in her widespread arms. He climbs out of the tub, and she enfolds him in the towel like one of the children in Fellini's $8\frac{1}{2}$. He closes his eyes again.

"Just so we understand each other," she says, rubbing him, patting him dry, "if you plan on having any sex here, it'll coss you a hundred bucks."

"I don't have a hundred bucks," he says.

"You have five hundred," she says. "In travelers checks."

"I see."

"That's right," she says. "I looked thu your wallet. Just in case."

"I see," he says again.

"Cause I figure you for a man familiar with the ways of the world," she explains.

"Uh-huh."

"All I'm sayin is the tub and a cup of coffee's on me. But if you're lookin for anythin else, it'll coss you. You unnerstan whut I'm sayin?"

152

"Okay."

"Does that mean you're interested?"

"It means I understand what you're saying."

"Let me see I can find something for you to put on," she says, and leaves him wrapped in the towel and goes out into the other room again. The cockatoo does his little song and dance again, it's an act they have. Somehow, he feels a bit disappointed in her, he doesn't know why. He looks at himself in the mirror again. There is not appreciable improvement over what he saw the last time around. He wonders how he can go back to Los Angeles looking like this. He lifts his wrist to see what time it is, but his watch is gone. He tries to remember whether he took it off before getting into the tub, but he wouldn't have because it's a waterproof Rolex he bought on Rodeo Drive, did those sons of bitches take his watch, too? But he didn't hear them saying anything about a watch, could they have missed the watch? The dial is black, could they have missed it in the dark? Or did Little Miss Peek-In-the-Wallet here remove it from his wrist while she was undressing him, and pop it in her sugar bowl, he will have to ask her. You didn't happen to see a little Rolex worth close to five grand, did you? I wouldn't ask, but it has sentimental value. I bought it for myself the first time I had a house in *Architectural Digest*, you see, so if you happen to know where it is, I really would appreciate having it back, together with that cup of coffee you promised.

"Try these," she says, and hands him a cleanly pressed blue denim shirt, a pair of Jockey shorts smelling of soap, and a pair of faded blue jeans washed and pressed. He thinks these may be clothes that belong to her pimp. He can visualize her pimp strutting around the apartment in them. He can visualize her pimp coming home sometime later to find Ben sitting in his favorite chair, wearing his nice pimp blue jeans and shirt. Ben's every instinct tells him to get the hell out of here as soon as he can, go back to the hotel, explain to the night clerk that he just got hit by a bus, pack his bag, pay his bill, and go straight to the airport.

"Coffee?" she calls. "Yes? No?"

"Yes, please."

The clothes fit him a trifle snugly, but that's only because he had a few drinks and a big dinner, otherwise he can match his physique against any pimp's in the world. He comes out of the bathroom and into what he now sees is a small living room furnished like a Turkish bordello, with the patterned rug on the floor, and the cockatoo perch in the corner, and mirrored throw pillows everywhere, and beaded curtains on one door leading to what he guesses is the bedroom, and beaded curtains on another door leading to what he can see is the kitchen, the woman standing there at the stove, looking at a coffee pot. He parts the curtains. She has taken off the silk blouse and is now wearing only the purple leather skirt, the matching heels, and a black bra. There is another tattoo, he notices, near the bra strap on her right shoulder, which he recognizes as a larger version of the one near her wrist. He tries to remember what you call these things, James Bond had one in bed with him one time, didn't he, these brown *insects*, he guesses they are—*scorpions!* A blue scorpion near her wrist, a red one on her shoulder. There is something enormously intimate about seeing her this way. As if he has caught her quite by accident, surprising her only partially dressed this way—although she doesn't seem a bit surprised as she turns from the stove and smiles.

"Be hot in just a second," she says. "I don't have decaf, is regular okay?"

"Sure. Uh, you didn't happen to see my watch anywhere, did you?" he asks.

"On the counter near the lamp," she says. "How do you take it?"

"Light. One sugar."

He spots his watch on the counter, moves toward it, and backs away when the cockatoo starts shrieking at him.

"Just tell him to shut up," she says.

He picks up the watch, gingerly, and backs away from the perch. He snaps the watch on, and rolls up the cuffs on the blue denim shirt. In the pimp threads, he feels almost pimpish himself. Puts on a pimp strut. Goes into the kitchen. Pats the woman on the ass where she stands at the stove.

"Hey," she says. "That could start the meter running."

"Would you like to start the meter running?" he asks playfully.

"Depends on you," she says, and shrugs.

"You take travelers checks?"

"I even take green stamps," she says, and grins. "You get it?" she says.

"I get it," he says, and pats her on the ass again.

"Hey, I'm serious," she says. "You want to start foolin around here, it's the bread up front."

"I may want to start fooling around, who knows?" he says. "But let's have the coffee first, okay?"

He likes the idea of having coffee with her. There's something very intimate about the idea. He even likes the idea of her calling it "fooling around" now that she's in her bra cooking at the stove, instead of what Fatima had called it, "fucking." Or *would you rather fuck me in the ass?* Sounding exactly like a hooker. Well, this one's a hooker, too, no matter how daintily demure she may sound. She's made that quite plain, she's been a hooker since she was sixteen, and what is she now? Thirty-five? Thirty-six? Even her age is comforting somehow. There's something very comforting and intimate and warm about a thirty-six-year-old woman standing in her bra, in her own kitchen, waiting for the coffee to heat up, while he watches her. Unembarrassed while he watches her. Comfortable with him standing there watching her in her bra and her short skirt. He suddenly feels very much better than he did an hour or so ago. He looks at his watch.

"You got a taxi waiting?" she asks.

"No, no, I just wanted to make sure . . ."

"There's still time," she says.

Her eyes meet his.

"It's almost three," he says.

"Plenty of time yet."

Their eyes hold.

"What's your name," he asks.

"Lokatia," she says.

"You don't have a pimp who's going to beat me up, do you, Lokatia?"

"I used to have one," she says. "Who used to beat *me* up. This is ready," she says, and takes the pot off the stove. She pours coffee for each of them into two large mugs, adds sugar and milk to his, leaves her own black. Steam rises from the mugs as they drink.

"What do you mean used to have one?"

"I stabbed him."

He looks at her.

"I killed him," she says. Her eyes hold his. "I done six years in jail for manslaughter," she says. "He's the one put the red tattoo on me. His brother gave me the blue one. You don't want to hear this shit," she says.

"I do."

"Nah, come on. Drink your coffee."

"Tell me."

"Nah. Stabbing people is boring," she says, and smiles.

Her teeth look very white against the deep brown of her face. She is wearing the blond wig, but it does nothing to disguise her essential blackness. This lady is black, he thinks, no question about it, this lady is virtually African. Her lips are thick, her nose is flat, her eyes are a very dark brown, with that somewhat moist look you sometimes saw on very black people, as if they were still crying over centuries of slavery.

"You mind if I take this off?" she asks, and walks out of the kitchen. He follows her into the living room, and past the bird perch—the damn cockatoo squawking again—and through the beaded curtains, a light snapping on to reveal a small bedroom with drawn Venetian blinds, a queen-sized bed, more mirrored pillows on it, red velvet curtains, and a gilt-framed mirror over a dresser with a wig stand on it.

"Who invited you in here?" she asks, but she is merely pretending annoyance, arching an eyebrow, turning to the mirror and saying to her own image, "Cain't a lady have no privacy these days." Totally ignoring him, she begins removing bobby pins from under the wig someplace, her fingers probing, until at last she lifts the wig off her head and settles it gently on its stand.

"You didn't really stab anyone, did you?" he says.

"I wish."

She has a rat tail comb in her hand now, and is picking at her nappy black hair with it. She looks at him in the mirror.

"How old are you, Ben?" she asks.

"Forty-three. I'll be forty-four in November."

"You look older."

"Gee, thanks."

158

"All battered up, I mean. You know they's two teeth missing the front of your mouth?"

"I know."

"You could maybe ask for them for Christmas," she says, and grins like a little girl. "You get it?"

"I get it," he says.

"You upset I said you look older?"

"No."

"Don't be. I'm forty."

"I'm just wondering how I can explain it."

"You could say you fell out a third-floor window."

"I could."

"You married, Ben?"

"Yes."

"How long you been doing this, Ben?"

"Doing what?"

"I think you know doing what."

"Too long," he says.

"You care what she thinks?"

"Not really."

"Then fuck it. Tell her the truth."

"That'd be the end."

"Maybe it's already the end."

He looks at her.

Maybe it is, he thinks.

There is a very long silence.

He thinks maybe he should go. He almost looks at his watch again, but that would be rude. The silence lengthens. She puts down the comb, and looks at herself in the mirror. "I really *must* have a shower," she says, "fore the Board of Health closes me down. You mind bein alone for a few minutes?"

"Maybe I should go," he says.

"What's your hurry? I won't be but a minute."

"I have a plane to catch."

"What time's your plane?

"Eight."

"There's time."

"Well."

"Stay," she says. "Ain't no hurry." She takes his hand. "Come," she says, and leads him through the beaded curtains back into the living room again. "Shut up, Whitey," she says to the squawking cockatoo. "Nothin personal," she explains. "It's just cause he so damn white. You like Sinatra?" she asks, moving around the small living room while she speaks. "Let me put on some music." Opening one side of a long cabinet to reveal a CD player and a stack of discs. "Would you like a drink?" Opening another door, behind which Ben sees an array of liquor bottles and glasses. "Fix yourself a drink, okay? The cat's name is Francis, you get it?" Kneeling at the CD player, short purple leather skirt and shiny knees, long legs and ankle-strapped pumps. "Make yourself comfortable," she says. Fiddling with the player. "Five minutes," she says, "I promise," and Sinatra's lush voice floods the room.

She is gone.

He sits alone. Hearing Sinatra. Hearing his father's golden horn. Hearing the sound of the shower behind the closed bathroom door. He can leave now. Pull a

Karen on her. Split while she's in the bathroom. Take a taxi back to the hotel, what time is it, anyway? He looks at his watch. It is nine minutes past three. Grace will be angry, of course. He will go home to Los Angeles with his face looking like a club fighter's, and he will explain to Grace that he was walking back from the restaurant where he'd gone to pick up his credit card, just walking back through the rain minding his own business when these two big black guys attacked him and left him for dead in the gutter, boy, what a city, he will tell her, boy. And everything will be all right again. Everything will be just fine and dandy.

How long have you been doing this, Ben?

Too long.

How long is too long? he wonders. Well, that all depends on the meaning of the word "is," doesn't it? What was *was*, so who cares when the first one was, or what she looked like, or whether she was any good or not, or what led him into that place in the first place? Why is he here now, for that matter, listening to Sinatra singing while a very black whore showers in the other room? She must've been absolutely terrific, that first girl, otherwise why is he *still* here, wherever here is? The truth is he does not know where he is. Has perhaps not known his exact whereabouts since that first thrilling time. If, in fact, it was the first. Or even thrilling. Who remembers? Who can possibly remember?

* * *

She looks clean-scrubbed and fresh-faced and she is wearing a fluffy white robe belted at the waist. Barefooted, she looks to be about five-seven or -eight. She is a very tall Masai woman who has just come from the well and is tending her cattle with a long stick in her hand, although her toe nails are painted green, he notices.

"You didn't make yourself a drink?" she says, surprised.

"I was just sitting here enjoying the music," he says.

"Did I take too long?"

"No, no."

"What shall I fix you?"

"What have you got?"

"Anything you might like," she says.

"Little gin on the rocks would be fine," he says.

"Gin on the rocks," she says. "Coming up."

He listens to the music. Closes his eyes and listens.

"My father used to play trumpet," he says.

"No kidding?"

He opens his eyes. She is kneeling in front of the cabinet now, the flap of the robe falling open over one knee, reaching in for the bottle of gin.

"Had his own big band," Ben says.

"What made you think of that?"

"I don't know. Sinatra?"

There is a flash of upper thigh as she rises, a fleeting glimpse of crisp black pubic hair. The white robe falls again like a curtain, but she knows he caught the display, and cuts a knowing look in his direction as she carries the bottle of gin into the kitchen. He watches as she opens the refrigerator door, takes out an ice cube tray, cracks it, drops cubes into two short glasses.

"You want an olive in this or anything?" she asks.

"Might be nice," he says.

"One, two?"

"Three, why not?" he says.

She comes back into the living room, hands him one of the glasses, and sits on the sofa beside him, pulling her legs up under her, making herself completely at home. The robe parts again. He glances at her shiny brown knees and thighs.

"Nice, huh?" she says.

"Yes."

Her knees? Her thighs? The music oozing from hidden speakers somewhere? The gin with the three olives floating in it? Or just being here in this room together at close to three in the morning? He sometimes feels that morning never comes. He sometimes feels he is trapped in a perpetual nighttime of long-legged, big-breasted, red-lipped girls incessantly beckoning, offering dark and secret candy. He would love to sit here beside this girl—this woman, she's forty, don't forget—and not be so completely cognizant of her legs, sit here sipping his drink without yearning for another stolen peek at her pussy, sit here just drinking peacefully with her and talking quietly to her without being constantly aware of her sexuality.

"Tell me about this guy you killed," he says.

"Nah," she says. "That was a long time ago."

"How old were you?"

"I don't want to talk about it."

"Why not?"

"Cause I'm not proud of it. I went to jail for it. It was just something had to be done."

"Why?"

"Why? Cause his older brother turned me out when I was just sixteen. Cause after his brother died . . ."

"Turned you out? What do you mean?"

"Put me on the street. To peddle my sweet little ass. Was the older brother who branded me with this," she says, and shows him her left wrist with the small blue scorpion on it, stinger tail arcing over its back. "Both of them belonged to this gang called The Scorpions, this was to show he owned me." She flicks her hand as if trying to shake the scorpion off her wrist, and then drops the hand into her lap. "His name was Roger, I cursed him day and night, he finally died of an overdose, I cheered when the son of a bitch turned blue. The one I stabbed was his younger brother. He stepped right in, took full possession of me, put the *red* tattoo on my shoulder, you *mine* now, Sweet Buns, dig?"

She sips at her drink, nods, remembering.

"Beat me day and night, the son of a bitch," she says. "Winston was his name. He was maybe this high," she says, and extends the left hand with the scorpion on the wrist to indicate a person perhaps five-feet four-inches tall. "Used a rubber hose on me

164

so it wouldn't leave no bruises, didn't wish to mar my gorgeous face or bod. One morning, I come back off the street, he asts me Whut you got for me, cunt? How much you bringin home? I tell him Winston, this is what I got for you, this is whut I'm bringin home, and I pull a sling blade out my purse and rip his fuckin throat wide open."

"Just like that, huh?"

"Well, not juss like that, this wasn't no crime of passion, Ben. I killed him cause the sum'bitch turned me onto scag. I been shootin heroin since I was seventeen, Ben. I'm a dope fiend is whut I am. You want to run out of here now?"

"What happened? After you stabbed him?"

"He turned all red on me, the way his brother turned all blue two years earlier. An' I got sent to jail, end of story, cheers," she says, and clinks her glass against his.

"So now you're back to hooking," he says.

"It would appear so," she says drily, and takes a long swallow of gin. "Which is lucky for both of us, right? You get it? Well, I guess maybe you don't," she says. "The brothers used to call me Lucky. Short for Lokatia. Was them who turned out to be lucky, though, wun't it? One of them OD's, the other gets his throat slit, good riddance to bad rubbish. I hated that name Lucky," she says, almost spitting it out. "You like Lokatia?"

"Yes, I do," he says. "It's a good name."

"African," she says, nodding. "It means Gorgeous Gazelle."

"Is that true?"

"No, I made it up just now," she says, and actually giggles. She shoves herself off the couch, long legs flashing again, and goes to where she left the bottle of Gordon's on top of the cabinet and pours herself a fresh drink, and then carries the bottle to him, and arches one eyebrow in inquiry, and when he holds out his glass to her, splashes more gin in over the ice cubes. "Trade was slow tonight," she says. "I'm usually out till three, four in the morning. But I was already on my way home when I spied you in the gutter."

Here it comes, he thinks. Uh, I hate to ask this, Ben, but if we're going to get this show on the road, that'll be a hundred in advance. I know, it's tawdry, as a colleague of mine once remarked, but I do have to —

"You know what I think it was?" she says.

"I'm sorry?"

"The Kennedy boy getting killed. That's why nobody's out on the street tonight. They home watching TV."

"Maybe so. How old were you?" he asks.

"What do you mean?"

"When the President got killed."

"Oh. Three?" she says. "Four? I must've been four."

"Do you remember any of it?"

"Just John John saluting the coffin."

"That was something."

"Otherwise, I was too young."

166

"I was eight," he says. "That's all I remember about my eighth birthday. The President getting killed."

"Your eighth birthday, huh?"

"Yeah. You know, it's funny. All day long, I've had the feeling something happened that day."

"Something did happen. The President got killed."

"Oh, I know."

"So what do you mean, something happened?"

"Something *else*."

"That's enough to have happened."

"I suppose so," he says, and shrugs.

Shehigh makes herself more comfortable on the couch, adjusting her legs, exposing again the long brown flank of her thigh, but only for an instant. Feigning discovery of her indiscretion—or perhaps really discovering that he can see Catalina on a clear day—she pulls a little-girl face and immediately tosses the flap of the robe over her leg again.

"You remember lots of things from when you was young?" she asks.

"Some."

"When's the first time you got laid?" she asks him.

It occurs to him that their only lingua franca is sex. This is not surprising. Sex is Lokatia's occupation and sex is his preoccupation, so why shouldn't they understand each other? The dialogue here is free and easy; there is no need for either a translator or an interpreter. He can just imagine sitting in the living room of the house he himself designed in Topanga Canyon, enjoying a nightcap with Grace and discussing this very same subject matter, oh sure. But here he is in a living room decorated like a Turkish whore house, with beaded curtains and mirrored throw pillows and a frayed Persian rug, and Sinatra singing while a big black and gray tabby and a white cockatoo sit listening like a baggy-pantsed comic and his straight man, and a very black, virtually naked hooker snuggles into his shoulder and encourages him to talk about—gee, guess what, kiddies?—the first time he got laid.

"I don't remember," he says.

"Everybody remembers the first time."

"When was yours?" he asks.

"When I was eleven," she says.

He looks at her.

"True," she says, and crosses her heart with the index finger of her right hand. "It was very romantic. He was a Spanish kid from a Hun-Twennieth and Park. We were in the same Special Reading class at school. Him cause English was a second language, me cause I was dyslectic. We did it on a blanket we spread near the pigeon coops. It was a starry night in July, we could hear the pigeons cooing all the while, it was so romantic, really. It was summertime in Harlem. Everything was summertime."

"What was his name?"

"Hector. Why?"

"I don't know."

"Hector Lopez."

"Have you seen him since?"

168

"Hector? I think he's in jail."

"I mean . . . after that night."

"Oh, sure. We went together all through junior high. Then I got involved with the fuckin Scorpions and summertime ended. Everything ended."

"Eleven was very young," he says.

"Not on my block. How old were you?"

"Nineteen."

"Get out!"

"I mean it."

"Nineteen, I can't believe it!"

"I was a late bloomer."

"A late bloomer? You were a Christmas cactus!" she says, and bursts out laughing. "You get it?"

"Well, I kept trying," he says, "I just never had any luck. I was attracted to older girls, I think that's what it was. I mean there were girls I went out with, girls I took to the movies and all, it wasn't as if I didn't want to. I just never got lucky, is all."

"Well, you got Lucky tonight," she says. "If you want her."

"What's your last name?" he asks.

"What's yours?"

Without hesitation, he says, "Thorpe."

"Mine's Bruce."

"Lokatia Bruce," he says.

"That's me."

"Nice to meet you," he says, and they clink glasses again. The cockatoo lets out a shriek at the sound. "Oh, shut up, Whitey." he says, and the bird shrieks again, and Lokatia laughs.

"Bruce is Scottish, you know," she says.

"Funny, you don't look Scottish," he says.

"It must've been a slave owner's name. You want me to be your slave sometime?"

"I don't know. Would you *like* to be my slave sometime?"

"Lots of white guys like black girls to be they slaves. Yes, massa, please let me suck your dick, massa, all that shit."

"Would you enjoy that?"

"Better than bein a real slave, that's for sure. If you want to try it sometime, we could. Whatever," she says, and shrugs.

The cat suddenly jumps up on the sofa, startling him.

"I really don't like animals, you know," he says.

"Francis seems to like you."

"What does Francis know?"

"He senses things."

All at once, the cat moves onto his lap. He yanks his glass to the side, away from the animal, spilling gin on his pants.

"You don't think you could put him in the bathroom or something, do you?" he says.

"Come here, Francis," she says, and lifts the cat off his lap as if she's picking up a wet towel. "Didn't you ever have a pet?" she asks him.

"Sure, I did."

"But not a cat."

"Not a bird, either."

"Then what, a goldfish?"

170

The cat is on her lap now, pussy to pussy. She is stroking the cat. The cat makes contented purring sounds, his eyes squeezed shut. Lokatia's left hand, the one with the blue scorpion near the wrist, strokes the cat between his ears.

"A dog," Ben says. "My father gave her to me for Easter. Brought her home in a little basket with jelly beans all around her."

"You still got that dog?"

"No. I was only seven."

"What happened to her?"

"I don't remember," he says, and looks at his watch.

"You keep lookin at your watch, you'll make me feel undesirable."

"You're desirable all right."

"Cause I'm an older woman, right?"

"To me, you're a younger woman."

"Right, you'll soon be forty-four."

"November twenty-third."

"The day Kennedy got killed."

"The day Kennedy got killed, right," he says, and looks at his watch again.

"So stop lookin at your watch, I'm so desirable."

"Sorry," he says.

But he has already registered the time. It is twenty-three minutes past three, and his plane leaves at eight A.M.

She swings herself off the couch, irritating the cat, who was beginning to feel altogether too comfortable and secure, and who makes an angry little sound as he leaps to the floor. In the corner of the room, the cockatoo echoes the cat's disdain with a penetrating shriek that surely awakens everyone in the building. She kneels to the cabinet again, exposing a fair amount of thigh yet another time, glances back at him over her shoulder, catches him staring at her, smiles as primly as a nun, and modestly lowers her eyes as she drops the CD into place.

"More gin?" she asks.

"I'm fine," he says.

She sits beside him again. The cat keeps its distance, still disgruntled. The cockatoo says not a word. Lokatia tucks her legs under her again. She sips at the gin.

"So when *was* your first time?" she asks.

"I told you. I don't remember."

"You said you was nineteen."

"That's right."

"So where was it?"

"College. Yale. I'd already met my wife. We were already going together."

"Was it her?"

"Grace!" he says. "Never in a million years."

"Some other college girl?"

"No."

"Then who?"

"I really don't remember."

"Must've been a whore," she says idly, and sips at her drink.

"Maybe," he says.

"Am I right? It was a whore, wasn't it?"

He dimly recalls a back street somewhere on the outskirts of New Haven, remembers driving by a strip-mall store advertising girls modeling lingerie, an orange neon sign in the window declaring OPEN, which the talented woman inside turned out to be in every respect. He remembers telling himself that he was going in there to buy Grace some sexy underwear, though she didn't wear sexy underwear at the time, still doesn't wear sexy underwear, he doesn't remember why he went in there on that cold and dismal November night. He recalls the woman modeling a skimpy bra and open-crotch panties, recalls her saying, "I do a lot of young kids like you." Which he supposed made it all right. She was a bottle blonde, he now remembers, though he can't for the life of him remember her name, if ever he knew it.

"Did she have a dog?" Lokatia asks.

"A dog? Of course not."

"Tell me about your dog."

"Why do you want to know?"

"Cause I like animals. Lots of hookers keep pets, you know. It's cause we lonely."

He looks at her.

Their eyes meet.

"What kind of dog was she?" Lokatia asks.

"A mutt. I think she was part Yorkie, part beagle. Her name was Cookie. My mother named her."

"That's a lousy name for a dog."

"I know. I loved that dog," he says. "She was very cute and very smart."

173

"What happened to her?"

"I don't remember. I was only seven."

"She didn't get hit by a car or anything, did she?"

"No, no."

"Cause lots of animals get hit by cars, you know."

"Yeah, but this was Mamaroneck!

"Right. You were only seven, huh?"

"Well, almost eight. November twenty-third, I told you. Some birthday, huh?" he says. "President gets himself killed. We went to a movie that day, I remember. My mother and I. We used to go to movies a lot. I stayed home from school that day, because it was my birthday. It was supposed to be a treat. We were supposed to go to Serendipity afterward. That's an ice cream parlor. But something happened."

"What happened?"

"I don't remember."

"The President got killed is what happened."

"Sure."

"Let me freshen that," she says, and takes his glass and carries it into the kitchen with her. She opens the fridge again, takes out the ice cube tray, drops ice into each of their glasses. "I sometimes think if I drink enough, I won't hunger for the shit. But it don't work that way," she says. "Gettin to be about that time, in fact. Don't worry, I won't start shakin or nothin, I got the dragon under control." She puts the tray back into the freezer compartment, and comes back into the living room, to where the bottle of Gordon's is sitting on the cabinet. She pours

174

liberally into each glass and then comes back to the sofa. Sinatra is singing with Barbra Streisand now. They sound as if they truly might have been lovers once long ago, telling each other all about the crushes they have on each other.

"They recorded this in separate studios, you know," Lokatia says, and hands him his glass.

"Thanks," he says.

"Miles apart from each other."

"I know. Amazing."

"Cheers, Ben," she says.

"Cheers," he says.

They drink. She takes his hand in hers. She pats his hand the way she did in the taxicab, when he was hurting all over.

"What happened to your dog?" she asks.

"The ASPCA came to take her."

"Why?"

"Because she wouldn't pay attention. She used to crap all over the house."

He falls silent, remembering.

"They were supposed to come while I was at school," he says, "but they got there late. They were putting her in a cage when I walked in the house. I begged my mother not to let them take her. She kept telling the guy he should have got there earlier."

"So what happened?"

"He took the dog. And I stopped talking to my mother."

"Forever?"

"No, no."

"Do you talk to her now?"

"She had a stroke two years ago," Ben says. "She's in a nursing home now. We never talk now."

"You were only seven, huh?"

"Well, almost eight. That was a long time ago," he says, and looks at his watch again.

"You notice how every time we start talkin serious here, you look at your watch?"

"I didn't realize that."

"But it's true."

"And I didn't know we were talking so seriously." Something is nudging his memory.

I'd better get out of here, he thinks.

"You know," he says, "maybe I ought to go. I know you must be tired . . ."

"Don't go yet," she says.

"I have a plane to catch."

"Plenty of time yet."

"I'll be late."

Something terrible will happen, he thinks.

He remembers his mother changing her seat. A woman wearing a hat sat down in front of her, so she moved one seat in.

"It must've looked like I was sitting alone," he says.

"What do you mean?"

"Empty seat on either side of me. That day. My birthday."

He falls silent. Across the room, the cockatoo picks up a nut, cracks it in his beak. The room is very still. He can hear the cockatoo working the nut between his jaws.

"What happened that day?" Lokatia asks.

"I don't remember."

"Did somebody sit down next to you?"

"I don't remember."

"Somebody make a move when he saw you sittin alone?"

"I don't know."

"Some man sit down next to you?"

"I don't know."

"Some woman?"

"I really don't know."

"Did somebody bother you, Ben?"

"I don't remember."

"Some person touch you?"

He shrugs.

"While you were watching the movie?"

"I don't know."

"Is that what happened, Ben?"

He shakes his head.

"Why didn't you tell yo mama what was happenin, Ben?"

He shakes his head again.

"Ben? Why didn't you juss tell yo mama?"

He turns to look at her.

"I wasn't talking to her," he says. "She gave away my dog."

At three-thirty in the morning, here in this room with her, there is the sound of traffic muted on the muzzle of the night below, the muffled sound of voices from television sets or radios turned low, the occasional sound of a toilet flushing or a baby crying, or someone mumbling in sleep, and now, yes, the sound of a couple moaning in ecstasy somewhere in the building. Lokatia reaches up to touch his face with the hand that has the blue scorpion tattooed near the wrist. She tucks her head into his shoulder, rests her left hand gently on his chest. He feels quite content here with her in his arms, her hand resting familiarly on his chest.

"Ben?" she says.

Her voice is very low.

"I got to go take care of myself now."

"Okay."

"You don't have to leave," she says.

"Well, I think I'd better . . ."

"I'm sorry," she says. "But you know how it is, huh? I got my candy, you got yours."

She sighs heavily, pats his hand, and wearily shoves herself off the sofa. The cockatoo shrieks as she walks swiftly to the beaded curtains hanging in the kitchen doorway, and tosses them aside. The curtains click behind her as she goes into the kitchen, stir slightly in her wake, hang motionless and still again. He sits staring at the curtains as if expecting her to return at any moment. He can hear her rattling around in the kitchen drawers, can hear her swearing softly. He looks at his watch. It is thirty-seven minutes past three. His plane leaves at eight o'clock. He has to get to the airport. He has to fly home. But where is that? How did he ever manage to get so fucking lost?

178

What the hell had she meant?

I got my candy, you got yours.

In the ladies' room, they are all talking about the death of the President. His mother and all the other women have just learned about what happened in Dallas. He can see the ankles of women under the doors of occupied stalls, legs apart, can see high-heeled shoes, legs apart, can see long-legged women in short skirts putting on bright red lipstick at mirrors over stark white sinks, combing their hair, combing long blond hair, combing long black hair. He jiggles from one foot to the other in the center of the room. He is eight years old, embarrassed that his mother still takes him into the ladies' room with her, frightened by what has just happened to him, excited by the shocking news and the high shrill voices of the women everywhere around him. Some of the women are crying now. A stall door opens and a girl wearing a mini skirt and high heels comes strutting out still pulling up dark green pantyhose, stepping around Benjy, "Ooops!" she says, smiling at him. Did it really happen? Or was it a dream? He hurries into the stall and unzips his fly. Urine trickles and spits from his penis, and then at last gushes forth in a strong steady stream. He closes his eyes and throws his head back.

Washing his hands at the sink, he can hear the women commiserating about the President. "Isn't it awful what happened?" his mother says. Warm water runs over his hands. He looks up at his own reflection in the mirror over the sink, and sees on his

179

face the secret knowledge of what he shared in the dark with a stranger, and is suddenly overwhelmed with shame and sorrow and guilt. Instead of going to Serendipity for ice cream, his mother takes him home to Mamaroneck.

He does not know how many minutes he sits there alone in Lokatia's living room, the cockatoo silent, the rain beginning to taper outside. At last, he rises from the sofa, and blows his nose on a tissue he takes from a box on the end table, startling the cockatoo, who shrieks in response. His wallet—with the travelers checks Lokatia never asked for—is sitting on the end table beside the box of tissues. He tucks it into the right hand pocket of the jeans. Francis the cat is sitting just outside the kitchen, staring at the beaded curtains, waiting for his mistress to emerge. Ben parts the curtains, and steps inside. Lokatia is standing at the counter. A blackened tablespoon is on the countertop. A syringe is in her right hand.

"I have to go now," he says.

"Okay, Ben," she says.

"I'm sorry," he says.

"For what?" she says.

"Are you sure you have to do this?" he asks.

"Just say no, huh?" she says, and grins like the little girl she once must have been. "You get it?" she asks.

He nods bleakly. He goes to her. Takes her in his arms. Kisses her on the forehead. Holds her away from him. Looks into her eyes.

180

"I'll see you," he says, though he knows their paths will never cross again after tonight. Unless he meets her again in some other city sometime, as he very well might, a white girl next time, wearing a red wig next time, or a Chinese girl wearing very dark lipstick, or a Latino girl smoking a long thin cigar, another Cindy or Fatima or Heidi or Kim or Tiffany or Peggy Sue, another someone, another anyone, another woman or girl in yet another city or town someplace, anyplace, ever and always somewhere.

I got my candy, you got yours.

He guesses he knows what she meant.

He guesses at last he knows.

He looks at his watch.

It is forty-six minutes past three.

Time is moving so very swiftly.

"Goodbye, Lokatia," he says.

"Goodbye, Ben," she says.

He goes to the beaded curtains, and parts them, and walks to the front door and out of the apartment and down the steps to the street.

The rain has stopped.

A heavy fog is rolling in.

He steps down off the curb and looks up the street for a taxi. On the next corner, a young black girl is crossing the street against the light. She is wearing a tight mini skirt and very high-heeled shoes. Her blouse is cut low over her breasts. She is smoking a cigarette. As she comes toward the curb, the light changes, bathing her in its red glow. She glances in his direction, hesitates when she spots him, smiles, waves tentatively to him. In the distance, in the mist, Ben sees the dome light of a vacant taxi.

He raises his hand.

By eight, the morning fog
must disappear . . .

Ed McBain

CHAPTER
SEVEN

The three detectives leave the crime scene at about nine A.M. and go for breakfast in a diner on Seventieth and Third. They sit together in a window booth, drinking hot coffee and eating bacon and eggs. Emma and the guy from Homicide work in the same building on Broadway, all the way uptown on the West Side, but they've never met each other before now. The guy from Vice works out of a building here on the Upper East Side, another planet. He is telling them the strangled girl was a known hooker.

"Worked at a massage parlor on Seventy-fourth and Third. Used the name Heidi on the job. Her real name is Cathy Frese. Twenty-six years old, new in the city."

The guy from Vice is maybe in his early to mid-forties, a good-looking man in a rough-hewn sort of way, dark hair going gray at the temples, brown eyes, what her father would call "a black Irishman." Irish manner about him, too, if there is such a thing. Emma supposes she herself has an Irish manner. The guy from Homicide is Italian. He is in his early fifties, Emma guesses, and dressed in what her father would call a "natty" way, wearing a tan tropical suit she swears is silk, a snap-brimmed straw hat of a deeper hue, beige button-down shirt, summery tie with alternating yellow and blue pastel stripes. His name is Anthony Manzetti, and he is telling them the One-Nine Precinct called around six-fifteen this morning to report a girl strangled in an alleyway on Seventieth and First. The guy from Vice has been called in because one of the blues recognized the dead girl as a neighborhood hooker. Emma was called in because it appears the girl was raped.

"What's Special Victims working just now?" Manzetti asks.

Special Victims was already called that when Emma joined the squad eight years ago. Until 1988, it was called the Sex Crimes Squad. She guesses Special Victims sounds more politically correct. Manzetti's squad used to be called Homicide North. Now it's Manhattan North Homicide Task Force, which makes it sound like an invading army. Manzetti is looking for an M.O. that will wrap the case in five seconds flat, fat chance.

"Nothing like this," Emma says.

"How about your phantom rape artist?" the guy from Vice asks.

This is sort of an inside joke. Special Victims has been chasing a black guy in a woolen watch cap for the past three years now, with still no arrest. His poster is in store windows all over the Upper East Side, but he just keeps doing his thing.

"Not his style," Emma says.

She's not quite sure she likes the guy from Vice, maybe because they kind of work different sides of the same street. Vice used to be called the Public Morals Division but for the past four years it's been called the Vice Enforcement Division, which makes it sound like they're rooting for the bad guys. Are they here to *enforce* vice? her father would ask. Make it stronger somehow? Help vice flourish and grow in this fair city?

"You know," she says, "I'm sorry, but I didn't catch your name before."

"Morgan," he says. "James Morgan."

"Emma Boyle," she says, and extends her hand.

"Nice to meet you," he says. "You know the James Bond joke?"

"No," Emma says.

Manzetti shakes his head.

Morgan grins in anticipation.

"James Bond walks into this bar," he says, "and takes a stool next to this gorgeous blonde. He looks her in the eye, extends his hand, and says, 'Bond. *James* Bond.' The blonde looks back at him and says, 'Off. *Fuck* off.'"

Manzetti laughs. Morgan laughs with him. Two Good Old Boys hooting it up over the bacon and eggs. Emma merely smiles and nods. To her, the joke seems inappropriate when they're here to discuss a girl who was strangled and raped. Well, the job, she thinks. Twelve years on the force, they still have to test you with fuck, piss, shit, cunt.

"So how do you want us to proceed?" Morgan asks.

"As if he's a moving target," Manzetti says, "three-point triangle on his tail. Emma, you come at it like a run-of-the-mill rape . . ."

Run-of-the-mill rape, she thinks.

"Check your Lousy File, see if you've got anything matches the M.O . . ."

"I'm sure we don't," she says.

I just *told* you we don't, she thinks.

"Well, just to make sure. See who's on the street doing mischief, find out where he was this morning around dawn."

Emma nods.

She is already thinking this will lead to zero. She is thinking her team doesn't investigate many rapes resulting in murders. She is thinking she can count such cases on the fingers of one hand. She is thinking Anyway, a rape-homicide is always investigated as a homicide, not a rape, so what's Manzetti trying to pull here? Is his plate too full just now? Is he trying to dump this one on the local talent?

"Jim, I want you to come at it like some whore got killed cause of her line of work. Maybe her father or her brother or her boyfriend didn't like what she was doing. Or maybe it was a disgruntled john, or a jealous girl in the same stable, or a pimp deciding she held out on him, whatever. Or just some guy don't like hookers, whatever."

"Along those lines . . .," Morgan says, and lets the sentence dangle.

188

Master of suspense, Emma thinks.

"Yeah, what?" Manzetti says.

"We had a disturbance up the XS two, three . . ."

"The what?"

"The XS Salon. Where the vic worked."

"What kind of disturbance?"

"Two, three weeks ago. Some drunk got out of hand, started pushing two of the girls around."

"What's that got to do with . . .?"

"Cathy Frese was one of the girls."

Manzetti looks across the table at Emma. Emma nods maybe.

"You think he might have gone back?" Manzetti asks. "Is that it?"

"It's possible," Morgan says. "Getting laid is an obsession with these people. They ain't normal, you know. All they do is think about sex day and night, it's the only thing on their minds."

"Check him out," Manzetti says.

"So what do I call you?" Emma asks. "James? Jimmy? Jim?"

"Well, I'll tell you," he says, and turns toward her and grins. Big Irish grin. They're walking crosstown toward the XS Salon, dodging light morning traffic as they cross Second Avenue. John F. Kennedy, Jr. was found dead in the ocean yesterday, but the city doesn't seem to be overly distressed today. A twenty-six-year-old girl was found strangled and raped in an alleyway at six this morning, but the city is just going about its usual business three and a half hours later. "My mother still calls me James," he says, "and my father still calls me Jimmy. Everybody else calls me Jim. You can take your choice."

"Which do you prefer?"

"I guess Jimmy," he says, and shrugs. "How about you? Is Emma what you like?"

"It's what most people call me."

"Not Em?"

"I hate Em."

"Emma Boyle," he says, trying the name.

"All over again."

"What do you mean?"

"Boyle's my maiden name. I'm in the middle of a divorce."

"Sorry."

"No big deal," she says.

But it is.

They walk in silence for several moments.

"Is he in the job, too?" Morgan asks.

"No. He's a lawyer."

"Is that how you met?"

"Yes. In court. He was defending a guy we sent away for twenty years."

"Good start."

"I thought so."

"What happened?"

"The job happened," she says.

The day has turned sticky and hot.

Emma is wearing a wheat-colored linen suit over a lavender cotton blouse open at the throat. Her dark brown hair is clipped short, falling in bangs on her

190

forehead. She would prefer going barelegged on a day like today, but the job dictates pantyhose and low-heeled pumps that match the suit. All in all, she could be any woman walking to her office on Madison or Lex—except for the snub-nosed Detective Special in her tote bag. Morgan is wearing a white short-sleeved shirt under a blue Dacron suit. A shoulder holster under the jacket shows the butt of a nine-millimeter semi-automatic pistol. They walk side by side, moving through miasmic heat.

"This XS Salon we're going to," Morgan says, giving the word "Salon a deliberate French spin, "is a whore house, never mind what it says in their magazine ads. But if we tried to bust every one of these little places, we wouldn't be able to focus on the big boys anymore. Where the mob's concerned, prostitution and dope go hand in hand. We look to get 'em on RICO, send 'em away for a long long time. We're not only into prostitution, you know. We're after the policy racket, bookmaking, loan sharking, ticket scalping, the whole nine yards."

On Third Avenue, he leads her to the front of a four-story, red-brick tenement squatting between a Korean grocery and a bar called The Shamrock. Newspapers outside the grocery store carry the headline Bodies From Kennedy Crash Are Found. A subhead under a photo of Senator Kennedy and four of JFK, Jr.'s cousins reads PLAN IS FOR CREMATION WITH ASHES TO BE SCATTERED AT SEA. As they approach the door to the building, Morgan says, "It's B for Beautiful."

She doesn't know what he means until he reaches out to press the only bell button with a nameplate on it, the letter B in outline, filled in with a red marker. A girl's voice comes from a speaker set in the doorjamb above the bell buttons.

"Yes?"

"Police," Morgan says. "Want to buzz us in, please?"

"One moment, sir," the girl says.

They wait.

And wait.

"Putting on their panties," Morgan says, and smiles knowingly.

They wait.

"Come in, sir," the girl says at last, "we're on the first floor."

A buzzer sounds. Morgan twists the doorknob, opens the door, and allows Emma to precede him into a small foyer. They immediately recognize as blood the dried stains on the black-and-white tiles underfoot. This is not a crime scene, but they step around the stains gingerly, and then climb a steep flight of steps to the first-floor landing. Walking familiarly to a door with the brass letter B hanging on it, Morgan knocks on it sharply. The door opens at once. A very fat black man wearing a sweat shirt over Bermuda shorts, white socks, and sneakers stands in the doorway, a red light glowing behind him.

"Police," Morgan says, and shows his detective shield.

192

"What seems to be the trouble, Officers?" the black man asks.

"No trouble," Morgan says. "We're looking for a man who might've been here last night."

"Okay to come in?" Emma asks, and reaches into her tote for her shield on its leather fob. "Detective/Second Grade Emma Boyle," she says, "Special Victims Squad." She drops the shield back into her bag. "And your name, sir?"

"Jefferson."

"Is that your first name or your last?"

"My whole name's Jefferson Moore."

"Okay if we come in, Mr Moore?"

"What for?"

"Talk to some of your girls."

"There's hardly nobody here just now," Moore says. "We don't open till ten."

"Whoever's here," Emma says.

"Well, come in, I guess," he says.

They step past him into a small entryway and then beyond that into an empty room where a threadbare, velvet-covered couch rests against the wall. Moore closes and locks the entrance door behind them.

"They's juss me and one of the girls here juss now," he says. "We don't get too many people needin massages in the mornin hours."

"Massages, huh?" Morgan says.

"Yes, suh, this is a massage parlor, is what it is."

"Uh-huh," Morgan says. "Besides Cathy Frese, who else was working last night?"

"I don't know no Cathy Freeze."

"Try Heidi."

"Don't know her neither. Don't know none of the girls work nights. You got to ask the night manager about that."

"Harry Davis? Is that who was here?"

"That's his name. You know him?"

"He knows me," Morgan says. "Is he here now?"

"Was you the one here on that holdup last week?"

"No. I was up here two, three weeks ago, you had some drunk making a fuss here. Is Davis in or not?"

"No, suh, he's the night manager. He don't get here till six P.M."

"You got his phone number?"

"Yeah, but he don't like to be bothered at home."

"Bother him," Morgan says.

"You mention the word 'homicide,' they'll give up their own mothers," Morgan says.

He is talking about the list of names Davis gave him on the phone. They are driving across the Queensboro Bridge in a Vice Division sedan, the air conditioner rattling, the car stiflingly hot even though they've rolled down all the windows. Emma throws her suit jacket onto the back seat, over Morgan's. Her cotton blouse clings to her. She can feel beads of perspiration rolling down her chest and into her bra, between her breasts.

"I'm still trying to place this first one," Morgan says, "Consuelo Gomez." He takes his right hand from the wheel, taps his temple with the index finger, and says, "I've got a computer right up here, but

194

there are too many names in it. I think she uses the name Blanca on the job. She used to go to Queens College. I think she got pregnant or something, had to quit school, been hooking all over town the past five or six years. You got any kids, Emma?"

"One. A daughter."

"So what's gonna happen?"

"What do you mean?"

"The divorce and all."

"I'm fighting for custody right this minute."

"How come? The mother usually . . ."

"My husband says I'm too busy to raise her. Too busy being a cop, he says."

"So who's been raising her till now?"

"Exactly my point."

"What's the judge have to say?"

"He's still deciding."

"Who has the kid meanwhile?"

"His mother. Temporary custody."

"Your husband's mother?"

"Bitch of the world."

"Like *my* mother-in-law," Morgan says, and grins. "Must be an accident up ahead," he says, and hits the horn. It is a signal for drivers all up and down the line of traffic to begin honking. Morgan shakes his head in annoyance. Emma takes a Kleenex from her tote, dabs at her upper lip. She feels sweaty and tired and unattractive. Everywhere around her, there is the din of automobile horns. "How'd she seem last time you talked to her?" she asks.

"Who's that?"

"Cathy. The night that drunk pushed her around."

"He did a real number on her. Split her lip, there was blood all over the front of this baby doll nightie she wears." Morgan turns from the wheel, looks at her. "She wanted to kill him," he says.

The girl standing in the open doorway is some five-feet six-inches tall, a full-figured girl with curly black hair and dark brown eyes, wearing a pair of blue jeans and a red tube-top blouse. No makeup, no lipstick. She seems to be in her early twenties, fresh-faced and clean-scrubbed, but according to Morgan she's been hooking all over town for almost six years.

"How you doing, Consuelo?" Morgan asks, and grins. "Or should I call you Blanca?"

Anger flashes in her dark eyes.

"How'd you get this address?" she says.

"Harry gave it to me."

"I'll kill him."

"You hear this, Emma?" he says, and grins again. "Nothing better happen to him, huh? We just heard a death threat."

"He had no right telling you where I live."

"I could've got it from the files."

"No, you couldn't. I've never been busted."

"Anyway, we're here," Morgan says. "Offer us some lemonade."

"Lemonade, sure," she says.

"This is Detective Boyle," he says. "Few questions we'd like to ask you. Okay to come in?"

196

She glances at Emma appraisingly, gives Morgan a dirty look, and then steps aside to let them enter. The apartment is cool and tidy and somehow barren. A small kitchen is to the left as they enter. In the living room, sunlight streams through windows overlooking low rooftops. Emma and Morgan sit on a cheap modern sofa with their backs to the windows. Consuelo sits in a straight-backed chair facing them. An air conditioner hums. A clock ticks.

"So what is this?" she asks.

"Somebody killed Cathy Frese," Morgan says.

"What?"

"Little Heidi."

"Jesus! Where? Up the place?"

"On the street," Morgan says.

"Outside the salon?"

"Few blocks away."

"I'll tell you the truth, that's what scares hell out of me."

"What's that?"

"Some john waiting for me outside. The weirdoes we get up there?" she says, and shakes her head.

"You didn't see anybody waiting outside for Cathy, did you?" Morgan asks. "This morning?"

"I left after she did."

"Any other time?"

"No. It's just the whole idea scares me."

"She didn't *leave* with anyone this morning, did she?" Emma asks.

"Harry would've busted her head."

"Why? Was *he* doing her, too?" Morgan asks.

"Go ask him."

"We will," Emma says. "Do you remember an incident with some guy who was drunk? Two, three weeks ago? Do you remember him?"

"Yeah, what about him?"

"Did he come back last night?"

"If he did, I didn't see him."

"Who was the other girl he roughed up, would you remember?"

"I think it was T.J. You know her?" she asks Morgan. "She wears these little *Wizard of Oz* shoes? Red sequins on them? You ever see her up there?"

"Alice," he says, and taps his temple.

"Yeah, Alice, that's what she calls herself up there. She did a lot of three-ways with Cathy."

"How about you?"

"Only once or twice. In fact, Cathy and me almost did one together last night."

"Almost?"

"Yeah. Guy wanted a room with a little blue light in it. I asked her did we have a room with a little blue light, some of these guys we get, I have to tell you. What it was, I went upstairs to take this john down because his time was up, and then I helped him find his raincoat in the closet, there's like this little closet as you come in. He found his coat . . .

"This one's mine," he said, and took the coat off its wire hanger.

"You still here?" Heidi said, and grinned at him, the gold tooth in her mouth flashing.

198

"I'm waiting to talk to the manager," he said.

"I'll go get him," Blanca said. "We got a room with a little blue light, Heidi?"

"You want a little blue light?" Heidi asked him.

"How about both of you and a little blue light?" he said. "I've got plenty of time coming."

"He thinks he has time coming," Blanca said, and started out of the room.

"No kidding?" Heidi said, and grinned as if she'd just heard something very comical. "You really think so, Michael?"

"Was that his name?" Emma asks. "Michael?"

"That's what she called him."

"Why'd he want to see the manager?"

"He thought he had time coming."

"What's that mean?"

"He thought he didn't get his full hour or something, who the fuck knows? Harry threw him out on his ass."

"What do you mean?"

"Threw him down the stairs, beat the shit out of him."

"What time was this?" Emma asks at once.

"Two, three in the morning, who knows? He wanted to do me and Cathy in the time he had coming."

"And you say Cathy knew him?"

"Called him by name."

"Michael."

"Michael."

"What was his last name?"

"If that was even his *first* name," Consuelo says. "None of these guys give you their right names, am I right, Jimmy?"

"None of them," Morgan says. "What'd he look like?"

"Average-looking guy."

"Meaning?"

"Who knows what these guys look like?"

"Remember what he was wearing?" Emma asks.

"Sure. A gray cashmere jacket, dark gray flannel trousers, a blue button-down shirt and a dark blue tie."

"But you don't remember what he looked like."

"I notice what people are wearing."

"You say you went upstairs to get him . . ."

"Yeah. Cause his time was up."

"Who was he with?" Morgan asks.

"He was alone."

"I mean who'd be *been* with?"

"Oh. Josie and one of the other girls, I don't know who."

"Josie?" Emma says.

"Zampada. Up there, she goes by Fatima. She lives in Brooklyn. Right over the bridge."

"Looks like an Arab spy, right?" Morgan says, and taps his temple.

"You think so?" Consuelo says, and shrugs. "But you know, I don't think Cathy knew him *that* way, you know what I mean, this guy Michael, whatever his name was. I mean, they were just like trains that pass in the night, you know? Hello, goodbye, nice to see you, let's fuck, and Harry throws him down the stairs. I don't want to tell you how to run your business, but I'd be lookin for the guy who smacked her and T.J. around that time."

"Where does this T.J. live?" Emma asks.

"She's on Harry's list," Morgan says, and reaches into his jacket pocket for his notebook.

"She thinks she looks like Judy Garland," Conseulo says. "If you go see her, humor her."

CHAPTER
EIGHT

Except for her brown eyes, Terri Jean Ryan doesn't look at all like Judy Garland. She isn't even wearing the signature red-sequined slippers she wears when she's Alice at the XS. When Morgan asks about them, she says simply, "That's for the job," and goes back to folding the laundry she's just carried up from the laundromat around the corner. Her television set is tuned to CNN. The newscaster is telling them that while most Americans are pleased that no expense was spared in locating the Kennedy plane, many are still wondering why the government exhausted such unusual efforts on the case. Occasionally, she glances up from the laundry to the TV screen. Her apartment is in the Ninth Precinct. Morgan tells both T.J. and Emma that he used to work out of the Ninth, when he first started as a patrolman.

"Used to be a lot of drugs in this precinct, it's much better now, gentrification. Back then, we had young people squatting in abandoned apartments here in Alphabet City, these 'Too-Late Hippies,' I used to call them, feathers in their hair, no bras. They used to get beat up all the time by junkies who came crashing in. This was some wild precinct for a new cop, I gotta tell you."

T.J. is folding towels now. She listens to Morgan as if he is talking about another city here, this long-ago precinct when he was a rookie cop. Now there are decent restaurants all up and down the avenues, little theater groups, even art galleries. Emma tries to imagine a much younger Morgan strutting the streets in his brand new blues. She herself used to work out of the Three-Two up in Harlem, on West a Hun' Thirty-fifth and Seventh—which by the way was no picnic either. The male cops there used to jimmy open her locker and piss in her shoes, made her feel right at home, you know. She caught one with his penis in his hand one time, about to let go. She rammed her baton into his back, and he pissed all over his own pants. That was the last time she found soggy shoes in her locker.

"So what's this about Cathy?" T.J. asks.

They figure Consuelo called ahead, told her to expect a visit from the Law. They're not surprised. T.J.'s apartment is on the third floor of a building on East Sixth Street, just off Avenue A. At ten to eleven that morning, they can hear the sounds of summer traffic below. The windows are wide open, but there isn't the faintest hint of a breeze. On CNN, a black guy and a blonde woman who looks cross-eyed are exchanging views on whether or not JFK, Jr. should have taken the plane up when weather conditions were so bad.

"Somebody raped and strangled her," Emma says.

T.J. takes the comment casually, not a flicker of emotion crossing her face as she continues folding the laundry. She glances at the TV screen again. They are showing for the umpteenth time the photograph of John John saluting his father's coffin.

"I once had a guy said he worked for the State Department in Washington," she comments idly.

"Tell us about this drunk a few weeks back," Emma says.

"What drunk?"

"Guy who got rough with you and Cathy."

"As if I remember," T.J. says.

"This would've been two, three weeks ago," Emma prompts.

"You know how many drunks we've had up there since?" T.J. asks, and looks up at her. There is in that look her entire autobiography. There is nothing sexy or inviting about this person wearing blue jeans and a tight cotton sweater. She is simply a barefoot, freckle-faced, overweight woman of about thirty, with reddish-brown hair, sweating profusely as she folds her laundry on a stiflingly hot Thursday morning in an apartment without air-conditioning. One would never guess she sells blowjobs uptown. Her hands are her only delicate feature. She spreads the laundry, flattens it under long slender coaxing fingers, folds, flattens, folds again. She is wearing a wedding band on her right hand. Emma wonders if she's a widow. Or is she divorced? Does she have children who now live with her ex-husband's mother?

"You did a three-way with him and Cathy, remember?" Emma says.

Again the look from T.J. The look says Do you know how many three-ways I've done with Cathy over the past three weeks? Do you know how many three-ways I've done in my lifetime? I'm thirty years old, the look says, and I've been a hooker since I was seventeen, do you know how many fucking three-ways I've done? Please. This is what Emma reads in the look. She almost wants to get out of here. The hell with it, she thinks. We'll get the information somewhere else. But where?

"Try to remember," she says. "Detective Morgan and his partner were there that night, does that help you?"

"You were flirting with my partner," Morgan says, and winks at her.

"Oh sure, flirt with a fuckin Vice cop," T.J. says. She picks up a stack of folded towels, carries them to a closet, opens the door, puts them on a shelf inside, and comes back to the table where the rest of the laundry is piled.

"He found you very attractive," Morgan says, and winks again.

"Yeah, thousands of men find me very attractive," T.J. says drily. "That's why I have a million dollars socked away. Cause all the men who come up the XS find me very attractive."

"This guy picked you out of the crowd, didn't he?" Morgan says.

"Proves my point," T.J. says, continuing the vaudeville routine. "He was drunk."

Emma has heard this kind of banter before between cops and cheap thieves, Hey, Willie, when did they let you out? Hello, Officer Muldoon, you're puttin on a little weight. Good old buddies. Two sides of the same coin, heads or tails. She has heard cops say that without crooks they'd be out of a job. She has heard cops say they feel more at ease with law breakers than with honest citizens who come in with a complaint. Civilians, we call them, she thinks. And wonders when she herself stopped being a civilian and became a cop.

"Do you remember him?" she asks.

"Had a little mustache, didn't he?" T.J. asks Morgan.

"Don't ask me," Morgan says, "I never saw him. We got there after he split."

"Par for the course," T.J. says, grinning. "Never a cop around when you need one. I think he had a little mustache," she tells Emma.

"Was he white or black?" Emma asks.

"I don't do black men," T.J. says.

"How come?" Morgan asks.

"Big whangers."

"That's hearsay, Your Honor."

"Oh yeah? Try sticking one up your ass sometime."

"Watch it," Morgan says, "there's a lady present," and winks at T.J. yet another time.

"I got hurt one time doing a black guy," she says. "That was it for me, man. Never again."

"What else besides the mustache?" Emma asks.

"He was about Jimmy's size," she says, and looks Morgan over. "Five-ten maybe, a buck ninety or so."

"You're short an inch and five pounds," Morgan says.

"Close though."

"How old?" Emma asks.

"Late thirties, early forties."

"What color hair?"

"Brown."

"Eyes?"

"Who notices eyes, this business?"

"And you say he had a mustache."

"I'm pretty sure. A little mustache."

"Tell me what happened?"

"Cathy already told Jimmy what happened."

"I'd like to hear it, too," Emma says.

Morgan looks at her. Shrugs. Nods to T.J. that it's okay to repeat the story. Two old buddies here. Opposite sides of the same coin. Without hookers, there'd be no Vice cops.

"He must've come in sometime after midnight," T.J. says. "He'd been drinking a lot, he picked Cathy cause she was little Heidi, you know, and me cause I look like Judy. I guess he likes virgins. Judy Garland," she explains. "People say I look like Judy Garland."

"I can see the resemblance," Morgan says. He does not wink this time. He's not exactly sulking, but his body language is telling Emma You want to handle this, go right ahead, girlfriend. One day I'll piss in your shoes.

"We went up to this big room we have on the third floor," T.J. says, "the girls call it The Honeymoon Suite, we use it for three-ways a lot. There's a big king-sized bed with this beautiful painting over it, it's like a naked gypsy girl."

Now, as her delicate slender hands fold and flatten and fold the blouses and jeans and panties and slips, she remembers that the drunk called himself Stanley—

"These guys never use their real names," she says.

—and told them he was an actor, he'd been in a lot of movies, he said. Well, he didn't look like any movie star she or Cathy had ever seen, but they went along with it, anyway, what the hell. This was after the party was over and all—

"Complete satisfaction," she says drily, and rolls her eyes in a mock swoon.

—and they were just sitting around bullshitting and waiting for his hour to be up, he had about five minutes left on the clock, he was already dressed and ready to leave. She remembers Cathy asking him what movies he was in, and he told her he was in *The Sixth Sense*, was his most recent one, the scene in the restaurant where Bruce Willis is with his wife, did they see that movie? Stanley was one of the people eating at a table in the restaurant. But he was also in *Saving Private Ryan*, the scene at the beginning where everybody on the beach is getting killed, he was one of the soldiers on the beach.

"So Cathy, the big mouth, says, 'What you mean is you're an *extra*, ain't that it?' and the guy, being drunk and all, gets on his high horse and says, 'No, I'm an *actor!* Those scenes required a great deal of preparation,' and Cathy busts out laughing. So he slaps her. So I tell him, 'Hey, Mr Hanks, keep your fuckin hands to yourself, okay?' So he slaps me, too. Well, we both jump off the bed, and run for the hall, with him chasing right behind us. He grabs Cathy by the hair, she has this long blond hair, and he starts calling her a cunt and a whore and whatever else he can think of, bitch, slut, and *really* hitting her, like *hard*, I mean, never mind the slaps. Cathy starts screaming bloody murder, we *both* start screaming, in fact, and Stanley panics and runs out of there. I mean, he's *out* of there, down the stairs and out in the street, I mean *out!* We called the cops, anyway. A day late and a dollar short, right?"

"Just the way Cathy told it to me," Morgan says, and smiles pleasantly at Emma.

"What else can you tell us about him?" she asks.

"Like what?"

"Tattoos, scars, birth marks, any other identifying . . .?"

"He was just your everyday john," T.J. says wearily. "No better, no worse, no different from any of the others. They're all the same, each and every one of them."

She is carrying folded underwear into the bedroom when they let themselves out of the apartment. On the television screen, the anchors are describing the makeshift shrine on the sidewalk outside Kennedy's TriBeCa apartment . . .

"Mounds of flowers," the blonde is saying, "and candles . . ."

"Flags and balloons," the black man says.

". . . and photos of a small boy in short pants saluting his dead father's coffin," the blonde says.

In the street outside, as they walk to the car, Morgan says, "Couple of things."

"Yeah?" Emma says.

"First, I been dealing with hookers a long time now . . ."

"And I've been dealing with . . ."

"I just don't need . . ."

". . . rapists a long time. So if you're about to tell me . . ."

"I'm telling you I don't need advice on how to deal with hookers."

"Who the hell gave you any advice?"

"You wanted to hear the story from her, isn't that what you said? Why? You think it was gonna be any different from the story *I* heard?"

"I just wanted to get her version. As opposed to Cathy's."

"Just don't ever again diss me in front of a two-bit whore, okay?"

"Fine."

"And don't look so pissed off. If we're gonna work together, we gotta be honest with each other."

"Okay."

"Okay?"

"I said okay."

210

"Good."

"What's the second thing?" Emma asks.

"What?"

"You said a couple of things."

"The second thing is we ought to arrange some signals we can use. If we're gonna be working together any amount of time. Like if I touch my nose, for example, it'll mean you're Good Cop, I'm Bad Cop. Or if I call you Em instead of Emma . . ."

"I told you I don't like being called Em."

"That's just what I'm saying. If I call you Em in front of somebody we're questioning, that'll mean Don't go there. Same as if you call me James. Don't go there, leave it be, shift the topic to something else."

"Okay, but I don't think we'll be working together that long. That we have to arrange signals."

"How come? You know something I don't know?"

"We have a name. Stanley."

"I had the same name three weeks ago. It doesn't mean a thing. In fact, we have *two* names, if you want to get technical. Michael *and* Stanley. Both phony. These guys never use their real names."

"Stanley was drunk," Emma says.

"*Even* when they're drunk," Morgan insists.

"I'm saying if Stanley *is* his real name . . ."

"It's not, believe me."

". . . and *if* he's an actor."

"That was all bullshit."

"Maybe not. He gave them the names of both movies he was in."

"He was trying to impress them. You heard T.J. One guy told her he worked for the State Department."

"He got upset cause they called him an extra."

"All part of the act."

"But if he really *was* in those movies, he got paid for his work. And if he got paid, there's a record someplace."

Morgan thinks this over for a minute.

"Maybe," he says, and nods.

"Let's make some phone calls," Emma says.

The lieutenant in command of the One-Nine Squad on East Sixty-seventh Street knows Emma from other rape cases she's worked in the precinct, especially the one Morgan earlier called "The Phantom Rape Artist," the black guy in the watch cap who has every cop on the Upper East Side running around in circles. He gives her and Morgan desks and telephones upstairs and tells them to yell if they need anything. The first call they make is to Manzetti, who tells Morgan at once that they already have two witnesses to what happened this morning. Surprised, Morgan turns to Emma and says, "You'd better pick up, he's got two witnesses."

Emma lifts the receiver on the extension phone. "Hi, Tony," she says. "You kidding?"

"No, we're gettin lucky here all of a sudden," Manzetti says. "There's this guy's a bartender in an after-hours joint on Second Avenue, he gets off work at three-thirty, four o'clock in the morning. He walks up to Third, and is heading uptown where he lives a few blocks away when this cab speeds by and splashes him with water from a puddle, all that rain we had last night, you remember? The cab pulls in just ahead, drops off a passenger, and pulls away. But he gets the license plate number, which is the same number as the medallion. It's also on both side doors and in a light on the roof, there's no question he got the right number, it's only three digits and a single letter."

Emma is wondering where all this is going.

"Well," Manzetti says, "the bartender's really pissed off, you know? When he wakes up today — which is around ten o'clock or so — he walks over to the One-Nine, which is the precinct where he got splashed . . ."

O-*kay*, Emma thinks.

". . . so he can make a complaint because this was a new suit he was wearing and all. The sergeant he talks to takes down the cab's license plate number and then asks where the incident occurred . . ."

"I'm ahead of you," Emma says.

"Seventy-fourth and Third," Manzetti says.

"The XS Salon," Morgan says, nodding.

"You got it. That's where the cabbie dropped off his passenger. Guy was still standing outside the place with a *blonde* — you hearing this? — when the bartender leaves. Well, the sergeant is for a change alert, they just had a freakin homicide this morning and the vic happened to work on Seventy-fourth and Third. So he takes the guy upstairs to the detective who caught the squeal, who gets a descrip . . ."

"What'd he look like?" Morgan asks.

"Five-ten or so, medium build, dark hair."

"Could be our Stanley."

"Who's our Stanley?"

"Guy who caused the trouble up the XS I was telling you about. Emma thinks he might have given them his real name—cause he was drunk and all. We're just about to call the Screen Actors Guild, see if they got anything on him."

"He's a movie actor?"

"An extra."

"Well, let me know," Manzetti says dubiously.

"Who's your second witness?" Emma asks.

"A black cleaning lady going home from doing offices. She saw what looks like the same guy beating on a blonde, her words, on the corner of Seventieth and Second, this is now around four-fifteen, four-thirty, she didn't look at her watch, she just got the hell out of there fast. So if we get anybody we can parade for these two people, we're maybe getting someplace."

"Anybody call STED?" Morgan asks.

STED is the acronym for Surface Transit Enforcement Division. If Emma had that medallion number in *her* possession, first place *she'd* call would be the Taxi Enforcement Unit at STED. In New York City, every cab driver is required by law to fill out a so-called trip sheet, on which he writes down the location and time of every pickup and drop-off he makes. Individual cab owners, fleet owners, and lease managers all keep these trip sheets on file until

214

they're eventually turned over to the Taxi and Limousine Commission. Morgan was getting back to basics. A cab had dropped off a possible suspect who was waiting outside the XS at close to the time Cathy Frese left work this morning. The trip sheet would tell them where the passenger was picked up. So *had* anyone called STED?

"Working it now," Manzetti says. "There's a hundred and four cabs in this particular fleet, they park in a garage here on the West Side. The night dispatcher'll go through the trip sheets soon as he gets in."

"Be nice to know," Morgan says.

"You realize, of course . . ."

"I realize."

"That a little homicide isn't the first thing on these guys' minds."

"How about the ME?" Emma asks. "Is a little homicide the first thing on his mind?"

"Listen, at least he told us she's dead. Maybe he thinks that's enough."

"Can one of your people give him another call?"

"Sure," Manzetti says, but the weariness in his voice indicates his people have already made enough calls to the Medical Examiner's Office.

"We're here at the One-Nine," Emma says. "If you get anything, let us know."

"You, too," Manzetti says, and hangs up.

There are four listings in the Manhattan Directory for the Screen Actors Guild at 1515 Broadway. They would go there in person, but in any homicide investigation, time is of the essence and if they can get what they want on the phone, they'd much prefer it. Cathy Frese's body was found by a woman walking her dog at six this morning. If indeed someone had seen a man assaulting her at four-fifteen A.M., chances are she was killed not too long afterward. They will know more positively once they get the autopsy report, although an accurate post mortem interval is often difficult to establish, especially during the summer months when the body is slow to cool. It is now eleven-fifteen A.M. If indeed Cathy was killed sometime between four-thirty and five o'clock, the killer already has a lead time of six to seven hours. In police work, such a lead is often conclusive: the killer can be lost to them forever.

Morgan dials the general listing for the Guild while Emma dials the listing for the Guild's Membership Department. At the very moment she is being connected to a man named Nelson Shears, Morgan is being told by a receptionist on another line that he can get the information he needs from a Mr Nelson Shears in the Membership Department. He hangs up and listens to Emma.

"This is Detective Boyle," she says, "Special Victims Squad." She listens. "N.Y.P.D.," she says. "We're trying to locate an actor who may have been an extra on both *The Sixth Sense* and *Saving Private Ryan*. Well, that's just it," she says, "we don't have his name. Not his full name, anyway." She listens, and then says, "I would imagine quite a few. Though possibly not on *The Sixth Sense*. That wasn't as massive a movie, was it? We have a first name for him, if that's any help. Well, wouldn't he have to join the Guild to work as an extra? That's what I thought. So isn't there a record someplace of who got paid for working on those films? These people pay social security, don't they? Even if they're only extras? Gee, I'm terribly sorry if I sound snippy, Mr Shears, is that the word you just used, snippy? I sure hope there wasn't anything sexist intended in the choice of that word, snippy. This is a homicide we're investigating, you see, and I would sincerely appreciate your cooperation here. Yes, I'll wait, sure I will. Thank you."

She looks at Morgan, rolls her eyes. Morgan nods sympathetically. She waits. Taps her fingers on the desktop. Continues to wait.

"Hello?" she says. "Yes, who am I speaking to now, please? Miss Hennings, how do you do, this is Detective Boyle, I'm investigating a homicide, and I'm trying to get the name of a man who may have done extra work on two . . . yes, *may* have done. That's what I said. And *may* also have committed murder, as I mentioned. We have a first name for him and we have the two movies he says he worked on . . ." She listens. "*The Sixth Sense*. And *Saving Private Ryan*." She listens again. "I would imagine so, yes. Well, whichever would be easier for you, we're really trying to get to this man as soon as we can." She listens again. "Stanley," she says. "I'm sorry, that's all we have. He's in his late thirties,

217

early forties, if that's any help. Five-ten or -eleven, weighs around a hun'eighty, a hun'ninety. Dark hair. Uh-huh. Uh-huh. Well, *could* you do that, please? Let me give you a number where I can be reached." She reels off the number on her cell phone and then listens again. "Uh-huh. DreamWorks, did you say? Would you have a number for them? And the other company? Hollywood Pictures? And . . . Spyglass, did you say? Could I have that number, too, please? Thank you, Miss Hennings, I'll be waiting for your call."

She hangs up, looks across the desk to Morgan.

"She says there were a zillion extras on *Ryan* . . ."

"I'll bet."

". . . but she thinks she may have better luck with *Sixth Sense*. She's going to check with Pension Plan and Health, see if they've got anything for a Stanley who worked on both movies. She didn't sound too hopeful."

"Miracles happen," Morgan says, but he doesn't sound too hopeful, either. "She's got your number," he says. "There's nothing we can do till she calls back. Why don't we go see Josie Zampada?"

"Who's Josie Zampada?"

"Fatima," he says, and taps his temple. "Remember what Consuelo said? She lives in Brooklyn, right over the bridge." He opens his notebook, runs his finger down the list of names Harry Davis supplied. "Nope," he says, and looks up, surprised. "Probably laying her," he says, and shrugs.

"Let's see if there's anything on her up the squad."
He pulls a desk phone to him, dials. "Lou," he says,
"it's Jimmy. Hit the computer for me, will you?
I need an address for a hooker named Josie Zampada,
trade name Fatima, works up the XS. Have we got
anything?" He waits. He looks up at the ceiling.

"Who's that you're calling?" Emma asks.

"My partner."

Emma is hoping Miss Hennings at the Screen
Actors Guild will call back this very moment with a
last name and an address for their movie star friend
Stanley. This will save them a trip to Brooklyn and a
wild goose chase looking for Michael, who also has
no last name. She is wondering whether she should
call both DreamWorks and Hollywood Pictures, get
them working on Stanley as well. She really believes
he's a better suspect than some guy who wanted a
room with a little blue light.

"That's her," Morgan says into the phone. "Let
me have it."

When they get to Josie Zampada at ten minutes to
twelve that morning, she is sprawled in a striped beach
chair, taking the sun in the park across the street from
her garden apartment. As they approach, she lowers
the foil reflector she's holding under her chin,
recognizes Morgan at once, frowns, sits up, and holds
up her hand to shield her eyes from the sun. She has
long black hair and pale blue eyes and she's wearing a
skimpy blue bikini that scarcely conceals her full
breasts and narrow hips. Morgan's earlier description

of her seems completely fitting; she does look like some sort of exotic foreign agent.

"What's this?" she asks, annoyed.

There are mothers sitting on benches everywhere around them, rocking baby carriages. Emma has the feeling Josie is controlling her anger, her voice low, the pale blue eyes darting.

"Cathy Frese was killed this morning," Morgan says.

"This is where I *live*," she says tightly. "I share the apartment with a girl studying tele-communications at NYU, she thinks I'm a salesperson at Bloomies. Who sent you here? Harry?"

"You're in our computer," Morgan says. "Cathy Frese was killed this morning," he says again.

"Tell us about a guy named Michael," Emma says.

"Who the hell is Michael?"

"A john you and Cathy . . ."

"Come on, cool it, willya?" Josie says.

"Where *would* you like to talk?" Emma asks.

"I wouldn't," Josie says.

She bends over, reaches into a striped bag at her feet. Emma can see the nipple of one breast. So can Morgan. He stares openly, just as if he's never before seen a half-naked woman in any of the whore houses he's busted. Josie pulls out a package of Virginia Slims, sits up, shakes a cigarette loose, lights it. In the distance, a church bell tolls the hour. It is twelve noon. The bonging of the bells serves as a signal.

220

Mothers everywhere in the park rise from the benches, begin wheeling baby carriages home. Josie puffs on her cigarette, watching the exodus. Two women linger near the jungle gym, but they are too distant to hear any conversation from this end of the park.

"Michael," Morgan reminds her.

"Who remembers names?" Josie says. "You think any of these guys is different to me from any of the others?"

"*This* guy got beat up by Harry last night."

"Oh, him."

"Comes the dawn," Morgan says.

"Remember him now?" Emma asks.

"Yeah. Michael. From L.A."

"Did he give you a last name?"

"Even the *first* name wasn't his. He got it from a kid he knew when he was six."

"What'd he look like?"

"Dark hair, brown eyes, nothing special. None of these guys are anything special."

"How tall?"

"Five-ten, eleven, something like that."

"Fat, skinny, what?"

"Average. A buck-sixty, a buck-seventy, in there."

"What'd you talk about?"

"He told me he was an architect. These guys all say they're something they ain't. You don't know how many johns come up the salon and tell me they're diplomats at the U.N. They're all full of shit."

"What else did you talk about?"

"Fucking young girls," Josie says. "He likes to fuck young girls."

"He must've really dug Cathy then, huh?" Morgan says.

"Should've, but he didn't. He had his choice, he didn't pick her."

"How come?"

"Who knows? When he first came in, I thought he was gonna choose *me*, in fact. Gave me the once-over, you know the way they do . . ."

"But he *did* choose you," Emma says, puzzled.

"Not right then. He asked for me later. But not when he first came in. He looked me straight in the eye, and then he turned away to where Cathy was standing in the doorway to the back . . ."

. . .the long leggy look of a thirteen-year-old about her, cupcake breasts under a short, sheer, white, baby doll nightgown . . . the image of a precocious teeny-hopper. She was wearing high-heeled, white satin slippers with puffy white pom-poms. No panties. Long blond hair on her head. Blond hair shaved close below. Single gold tooth in the corner of her mouth. Lounging in a doorway that led to the further reaches of the apartment, an amber light glowing somewhere behind her. She threw him a sultry look when she was introduced as Heidi.

"But you say he didn't choose her."

"Nope. He asked who Cindy was . . ."

"And you are?"

"Cindy. See anything you like?"

"Yes. You."

222

". . .and settled on her. They went upstairs alone together."

"Which one is Cindy?" Morgan asks. "Refresh my memory."

"Tall busty blonde with frizzy hair."

"Right. What's her real name?"

"*That's* her real name! Crazy, am I right? To use it up there?"

"How'd *you* happen to get in the act?" Emma asks.

"What do you mean?"

"The three-way."

"Oh. He told Cindy he wanted both of us. He sent her downstairs for me."

"Changed his mind about you, huh?"

"I guess so."

"How come?"

"I have this strange mysterious power over men," she says, and winks at Morgan. He winks back.

"What else did he say about himself?" Emma asks.

"Not much."

"Did he say he was married? Single? Div . . ."

"I don't know about the married part, but he's got a twenty-one-year-old daughter."

"Where? Here in the city?"

"He didn't say."

"Did he mention where he was staying?"

"No."

"Was it with his daughter?"

"I have no idea."

"Or a hotel? Did he mention a hotel?"

"Not to me."

"To Cindy maybe?"

"They were alone for a while, who knows what lovers' secrets they whispered in each other's ears," Josie says, and narrows her eyes like Fatima the spy, and then grins slyly, as if she has just made a secret joke only Saddam Hussein would understand.

"Guess we'll have to ask her," Morgan says.

"Guess so," Josie says, and flips the reflector back under her chin again.

"Is she on our list?" Emma asks.

Morgan checks it. "No," he says. "You know where she lives, Josie?"

"Nope."

"Got her phone number?"

"Nope."

"What's her last name, would you know that?"

"Gee, I can't remember."

"Know how we can get in touch with her?"

"Sure," Josie says. Her eyes are closed, sunlight bounces off the foil reflector, highlighting her cheekbones. "Wait outside the salon at six tonight."

As they walk to where he parked the car, Morgan dials his office and asks his partner to hit the computer for an XS girl named Cindy, no last name. He listens for a moment, and then says, "Never mind after lunch, do it *now*, Lou, you have my number," and breaks the connection. "Wanted to wait till after lunch," he tells Emma. "You know what it is, he thinks this is just a

224

dead hooker here, we don't have to break our balls on it, that's his thinking, there's no rush. Meanwhile, our guy has a seven-hour lead." He unlocks the door to the car. Emma takes off her jacket, tosses it onto the back seat. The moment he starts the car, she slides the window down on her side.

"I need an hour," she tells him.

Morgan turns to look at her, puzzled.

"I have to go see my husband. I'm sorry."

"Nothing we can do, anyway," Morgan says. "Not till somebody gets back to us."

"I wish we could get to this other girl sooner."

"Maybe Lou'll find something on the computer."

"By six tonight he'll have a *twelve*-hour lead."

"Look at the bright side," Morgan says. "If our guy's still in the city, he doesn't know we've got anything yet. The minute we find out where he is . . ."

"Our guy? Who's our guy, Jimmy? So far, we've only got a couple of names."

"That puts us ahead of the game," Morgan says. "Where should I drop you?"

"Forty-eighth and Madison."

"Thing you have to remember is these guys all lead double lives," Morgan says. "I know these guys, believe me. Michael, Stanley, *whoever* he is, he's probably got a wife and two kids, he's an insurance salesman lives in Larchmont. Most of them were abused one way or another when they were kids, they got bad memories go back half a century, all of them sex-related. It's the same with the girls. In her other

225

life, Cathy Frese was a virgin in a white baby doll nightie, no panties, a shaved pussy. Heidi, hm? They all got some kind of gimmick, these girls. They all try to look like anything but a whore."

Emma is thinking that Cathy Frese wasn't wearing a baby doll nightgown when she saw her sprawled in that misty alleyway early this morning. Cathy Frese hadn't looked like a virgin and she hadn't looked like a whore, either. She had merely looked like any young woman who'd been brutally raped and murdered. Emma suddenly wonders if Morgan has any daughters of his own.

"You mentioned a mother-in-law," she says. "Are you still married?"

"Divorced for six years now."

"Any children?"

"A thirteen-year-old daughter. Drop-dead gorgeous and smart as hell. Well, she goes to St. Mary's on the Mount, you know the school? Nuns, uniforms, the whole bit. They're very strict, but boy, is she learning! I get her every other weekend and on alternate holidays. I just had her for Easter, I'm getting her again this weekend. I hope this fuckin case doesn't run over."

"What's her name?"

"Fiona. My wife chose it. They look exactly alike. Long blond hair, blue eyes. She's a good-lookin woman, my ex. A bitch, but good-lookin."

"You still get along with her?"

"She hates me."

"Why?"

"Who knows? My daughter adores me, she hates me. Maybe she resents I'm such a good father." He nods, pleased with himself. "Who's your money on?" he asks. "Michael or Stanley?"

"So far they're both just names," Emma says. "How about you?"

"Michael, I think. Guy starts complaining about being short-changed, hits on Heidi and Blanca right after he comes down from a three-way upstairs, causes some kind of disturbance that gets him kicked out of the place, what does that sound like to you?"

"What does it sound like to you?"

"It sounds like a guy pissed off enough to maybe wait outside and go after Heidi when she comes down."

"Why Heidi?" Emma says.

"He can't take it out on the guy who beat him up, so he goes after a girl looks like a teenager, he doesn't even know *why*."

They drive across the bridge in silence. Emma is thinking Michael may already be back in Los Angeles telling his wife what a good boy he was here in the Big Apple. She is thinking Stanley may already be on his way to Florida to be an extra in a beach movie. The crosstown traffic creeps across the city streets. Outside the car, people are moving as if through a thick viscous haze. When Morgan at last pulls the car to the curb on Madison, it is almost one-thirty.

"Try your partner again," Emma suggests.

Morgan dials the number. He lets it ring and ring.

"Guess he decided to wait till after lunch, after all," he says. "I'll run back there, hit the computer myself."

"If you get a chance, call that lady at the Guild, too."

"Sure. What's her name again?"

"Hennings. Let me know if you get anything."

"Otherwise I'll see you outside the XS at ten to six. You've got all my numbers, stay in touch."

Emma reaches over the back seat for her jacket. Morgan watches her. She slides out of the car, puts the jacket on, hoists her tote from the floor of the car.

"See you," she says, and closes the door. She watches as Morgan pulls the car from the curb and moves it into the stream of uptown traffic. The sidewalk is crowded with lunch-hour pedestrians. She remembers something Morgan said as they were coming across the bridge.

Most of them were abused one way or another when they were kids, they got bad memories go back half a century, all of them sex-related.

The pedestrians move past her and around her. Any one of them could be a Stanley or a Michael, rushing by on the sidewalk here, haunted by memories he can't fathom, trying to figure out what led him to a point in his life where he ended up killing a young girl on the street.

The thought is chilling.

She hurries into the building.

228

CHAPTER
NINE

It's peculiar how Andrew's office now seems such a strange and forbidding place to her. It used to be as intimate to her as her own office on Broadway. A sanctuary. A place to which a person could retreat from the city. Sometimes you needed to hide in this city. But now it is a cold and somewhat sterile fortress on the twenty-seventh floor of the building, its windows facing east, relentlessly cool on this day when the temperature outside is ninety-seven degrees.

Andrew himself looks natty . . .

Thank you, Dad, she thinks.

. . . in a blue tropical suit that was hand-tailored at Chipp's, where she went with him to pick out the fabric. He is wearing a paler blue button-down shirt, and a blue silk tie patterned with minuscule ruby-red dots. She knows the tie. She bought it for him on a sudden whim one day.

"It's nice to see you," he says. "How have you been, Em?"

"Fine," she says.

She hates being called Em. And she has *not* been fine. She has been missing her daughter terribly. She has been considering defying the court order that gave Andrew's mother temporary custody of their little girl. She has been thinking of taking the train to Westport, Connecticut, and kidnapping Jackie. She has been thinking of shooting Andrew's mother if she has to. Anything to get her daughter back.

"Andrew," she says, "I think it's absurd that I can't see Jackie."

"Honey, I'm not the judge," he says, and lifts his shoulders and opens his palms to her in the classic What Can I Do? body language. She resents him calling her honey when she's no longer his honey, wonders in fact if she ever *was* his honey now that she knows he was seeing another woman for the last two years of their marriage.

"The court order is predicated on neglect," she says. "I know, and you know—don't deny it, Andrew—that I have never neglected Jackie from the minute she was born. I was a little disoriented when you left, I admit that, but I was in the middle of hiring someone to stay with her full time when your mother pulled her end run . . ."

"I had nothing to do with my mother's motion to the court."

"You could have said something."

"I could have, yes. But I happen to agree with her."

He looks content and puffy and paunchy sitting in his hand-tailored suit behind his designer desk in his corner office on the twenty-seventh floor, enjoying the fact that his mother prevailed, enjoying the insane notion that she, Emma Boyle Cullen, could possibly

230

in a hundred million years be an unfit mother. *I happen to agree with her*. You smug little bastard, she thinks, but she clenches her fists in her lap, behind the tote so that he can't see her hands, he knows all her tricks and tics, and she very calmly says, "Andrew, why don't you ask her to let me see Jackie this weekend?"

"Sure," he says.

"You will?"

"Sure. I know what her answer will be, but sure. I'll ask her."

"I would appreciate that."

"No problem."

She is tempted to ask how Jackie is, ask how her own daughter is, when he looks at his watch and says, "Em, I'm really sorry. I've got someone coming in at three, and I haven't even looked at the file."

"I know you're busy," she says, and rises swiftly, and goes to the door without even shaking hands.

She rings the B for Beautiful bell button and when a girl's voice says, "Yes, Miss?" she announces herself as Detective Boyle, Special Victims Squad, and tells the girl to buzz her in, please. She waits for at least three minutes, and is about to press the bell button again, when an answering buzz sounds. She throws open the outside door. The blood stains have been washed off the black-and-white tiles in the entrance foyer. She climbs the steps to the first floor, and knocks on the door with the hanging brass letter on it. The time on her watch is 2:57 P.M.

The black man who answers the door is not the same one they talked to earlier today. By contrast, he is some six-feet two-inches tall, wearing tight blue jeans and a tank top undershirt, with prison-gym muscles bulging everywhere and jailhouse tattoos on the biceps of both arms. He grins amiably, introduces himself as Harry Davis, tells her he hopes the names he gave Detective Morgan proved helpful, and cordially invites her in.

They pass through the foyer with its red light, and through the small room with the couch beyond, and then make an abrupt left turn into a corridor at the end of which is an open door leading to a small office. A small television monitor above Davis's desk shows the sidewalk outside the building's entrance door. Another monitor shows the first-floor corridor and the area immediately outside the door marked with the letter B. He offers her a seat.

"I came in early today," he says. "To tidy up my office. Now I'm glad I did."

She figures he came in early because Cathy Frese was murdered and the police have been snooping around. He smiles, his eyes frankly appraising her. She has made his day, the smile says, the eyes say, this hot and tired thirty-four-year-old woman who has a two-year-old daughter living in Westport, Connecticut, with her grandmother instead of at home in Chelsea. You are young and beautiful and desirable, his shining smile says, his twinkling brown eyes say, and you smell of all the perfumes of Araby instead of the sweat and grime of the nasty city outside. She suddenly wonders how many young girls Harry Davis has conned into believing that fucking strangers for money is a life of romantic adventure. Here you go, girls, short hours and high pay, a no-risk occupation replete with exciting men and snappy dialogue! A thrill a minute! Mr Charm here. Shove it up your ass, she thinks.

"This guy you threw down the stairs," she says.

"He was threatening me," Davis says at once.

"I'm not looking for a shitty assault bust," she says. "One of your girls got killed this morning."

"So I understand. He *was* nonetheless threatening me. And the girls who work here aren't *my* girls, by the way. I'm merely the night manager. I normally come on at five, make sure everything's in order for the night shift, which starts at six. This is a massage parlor, Detective. You'll find nothing out of order here. Ask Detective Morgan. He knows this is a respectable establishment."

"So you beat him up."

"No. Just hustled him out."

"Threw him down the stairs."

"Showed him the way out. Look, the man was *looking* for trouble."

"Why do you say that?"

"Why? Gee, maybe because *first* he told Blanca he had time coming, and *next* he asked Heidi to come back to his hotel with him, which he *had* to know was against . . ."

"Asked her what?"

"*What time do you quit here?*"

"Around three-thirty, four o'clock," Heidi said. "Why?"

"I was thinking after we get this time business straightened out . . ."

"The time business, right."

"After you and me and Blanca find that room with the little blue light . . ."

"Oh, sure, the blue light."

"You might want to come back to the hotel with me."

"Gee, a hotel," she said, and rolled her eyes in mock wonder.

"It's not far from here, Fifty-sixth and Sixth," he said. "What do you think?"

"I think it's not allowed, is what I think. But let's talk about it later, okay?" she said, and raised her eyebrows to indicate someone was standing behind him.

"How do you know this?" Emma asks.

"It was me standing behind him," Davis says.

"What time did Cathy leave here, would you know?"

"Around four o'clock."

"Anyone leave with her?" Emma asks. "Any of your customers?"

"That's not allowed."

"Anyone waiting for her downstairs?"

"I didn't go downstairs."

"Any of the other girls go downstairs around that time?"

He hesitates.

234

"Who?" Emma says at once.

"Cindy might have left around then."

"Cindy who? What's her last name?"

"I don't want to get her in any trouble."

"Is that why she wasn't on your list?"

"Cindy Mayes. I don't have her phone number and I don't know where she lives. *That's* why I didn't put her on my list."

"Then it wasn't just an oversight."

"I just told you what it was."

"Will she be here tonight?"

"Six o'clock," he says, and nods.

"Tell her I'll be here, too," Emma says.

"Be happy to," Davis says, but he is no longer smiling.

She calls the number she has for the Vice Enforcement Office and asks to talk to Jimmy Morgan, please. The guy on the other end tells her Detective Morgan is away from his desk just now, and asks what this is in reference to.

"This is Emma Boyle," she says, "Special Victims Squad. Jimmy and I are working this homicide together . . ."

"Oh yeah, hi, this is Lou Greenberg, his partner. Can I tell him anything if he calls in?"

"I was supposed to meet him outside the XS Salon at . . ."

"Know it well," Greenberg says.

". . . at ten to six," Emma says, "but something came up. Cut him off at the pass, will you?"

"Will do. Anything good?"

"Maybe. Right now, I'm heading for the Palmer Continental, on Fifty-sixth and Sixth. Ask him to call me, he has my mobile number. Incidentally, I've got a last name for Cindy."

"Who's Cindy?" Greenberg asks.

The desk clerk at the Palmer Continental tells Emma he does not have any first-name Michaels from Los Angeles registered at the moment, nor were there any registered this past week, he's terribly sorry. Emma asks him to check for any first-initial M's from Los Angeles, which she can tell is a nuisance for the clerk, but hey, *she's* terribly sorry, this is a fucking homicide, you know? There are no M's, either. She tries describing him, which she knows is a hopeless task, but she plunges onward regardless, five-feet-ten, -eleven inches tall, around a hundred-and-seventy pounds, dark hair, brown eyes, remember anyone like that? No one at the front desk recalls anyone fitting that description. Or, more accurately, they remember at least a dozen men fitting that description, which is tantamount to no positive identification at all.

According to Harry Davis, what started the altercation between him and this Michael character was the fact that the man had been drinking too much. Since the Palmer is the only hotel on Fifty-sixth and Sixth, and since Michael said he was staying here, a possibility is that he began drinking here before starting his prowl last night.

She heads into the bar.

236

The bartender is a man in his early forties, she guesses, with black hair combed sideways to conceal encroaching baldness. He is wearing a little black bar jacket and a white shirt with a black bow tie. He looks surprised when she places her shield on the bartop and announces herself as a detective from the Special Victims Squad.

"We're looking for a man who may have been in here last night, possibly a hotel guest," she says. "All we have is the name Michael and a description that may or may not be accurate. Five-ten or -eleven, weighing around a hun'seventy, dark hair, brown eyes. See anyone like that in here last night?"

"You're kidding, right?" the bartender says. "Every guy *in* here last night looked like that."

It is almost a quarter to five now, the hotel bar is rapidly filling with people drifting in after work. Most of the men are wearing business suits. The bartender's right, they all look like they're five-ten or -eleven, with medium builds and dark hair and eyes. The bar is full of Michael clones. Maybe the whole world is full of Michael clones. Maybe they'll never find him. Maybe he'll live happily ever after in L.A. and environs without the N.Y.P.D. ever zeroing in on him. It's a depressing thought.

"Can I get a Coke?" she asks.

"Sure."

He goes to the end of the bar, takes a glass from behind him, pulls down a handle on a dispenser with three other handles. A dark fluid she supposes is Coke flows into the glass. He carries it back to her, sets it down in front of her on a little cocktail napkin. She guesses the Coke's going to cost her sixty-five dollars, this place.

"The guy we're looking for would've been wearing a gray cashmere jacket," she says. "Dark gray flannel trousers, a blue button-down shirt with a dark blue tie. See anybody like that?"

"How old would he be?"

"Early forties," she says, and picks up the glass, and takes a long swallow.

"Alone or what?"

"He may have been cruising."

"What time would this have been?"

"Don't know. He might've been going out for the night."

"Like around now?"

"Could've been. Could've been later."

"Like seven, eight o'clock?"

"Maybe."

"Cause there was a guy came in around seven-thirty last night might be him. Forty, forty-five years old, dressed in blue and gray, like you said. He was hitting on a girl sitting at the bar here."

"A hooker?" Emma says.

"No," he answers at once, offended. "What makes you think *that*?"

"Well, sitting alone at the bar," Emma says, and shrugs.

"Don't you ever sit alone at bars?"

I sit alone at bars, yes, she thinks. I do that a lot these days.

238

"She comes in here two, three times a week," the bartender says, "sits alone here for an hour or so. I thought she was a hooker, too, at first, same as you did. But she's just lonely, you know?" He shakes his head. He looks suddenly balder all at once. His brown eyes look suddenly more mournful. "Beautiful redhead," he says, "you wouldn't think she'd have to cruise. You'd think she was married already, with kids of her own. Are you married?"

"I'm getting a divorce," Emma says. "You didn't hear this guy's name, did you? While they were talking."

"I wasn't listening."

"How'd they get on?"

"Fine. Had a few drinks, left here together."

"Who paid for the drinks?"

"He did."

"How?"

"Charged them to his room."

"What was the room number? Do you remember?"

"You know how many people charge drinks to their room?"

"Did you happen to hear the *girl's* name?"

"I didn't have to, she comes in here all the time."

She looks at him.

"Karen Tager," he says.

From the Manhattan directory in the lobby, Emma copies the phone number for a Tager, K., no address, and then flips open the lid on her cell phone. It is now five-fifteen P.M. She dials the number, and lets it ring ten times, finally assumes the woman hasn't come home from work yet, *if* she works, or else has already gone out for the evening. She clears the call and then immediately dials Homicide's number.

"Manzetti," his voice says.

She tells him where she is, tells him everything she's learned so far, tells him about the girl this Michael character picked up in the hotel bar . . .

"How'd you get the hotel?"

"Night manager at the XS."

"This is moving too fast."

"Let's hope. I'll let you know if I reach her."

"How does all this sit with you?" Manzetti asks.

"What do you mean?"

"Guy who frequents whore houses suddenly turning into a homicidal rapist."

"I know what you mean. Most of our . . . ."

"You're breaking up," Manzetti says. "I'm losing you, Emma."

"Stay with me," she says, and moves to another part of the lobby. Everywhere around her, men and women are moving in and out of the hotel bar. There is lively chatter. There is hugging and laughter. Men and women embrace, kiss each other in greeting. Sudden tears rush to her eyes. She brushes them away with the back of her hand. "How's that?" she asks into the phone.

"Much better."

"What I was about to say, most of our rape arrests are guys who've done burglaries, you know, some of

240

them, auto theft, even your two-bit Mom-and-Pop stickups, like that. But they aren't career *rapists*, they're career *criminals*. I'm not even sure there *is* such a thing as a career sex criminal."

"So how do you figure him?"

"Well . . . we once busted a guy who'd raped five women at knife point, physically molested four others. Before then, he'd spent eight grand on prostitutes in a two-year period. If our guy *is* a sex addict . . ."

"You think he is?"

"I don't know enough about him yet. But *if* he is . . ."

"I'm losing you again."

"I said *if* he is—hello? Tony? Can you hear me? Tony? *Shit!*" she says, and angrily stabs the END key. She looks at her watch, and then walks swiftly and purposefully out of the hotel and into the sultry heat of early evening. She signals to a cab, gets in, and gives the driver the address of the XS Salon on Third Avenue, interrupting his phone conversation in Urdu with someone she feels certain is plotting to blow up Grand Central Station. She searches in her tote bag for Manzetti's number at Homicide, dials it as the driver keeps babbling. When Manzetti comes on the line, he immediately says, "We were cut off."

"I know. Could you please get off the phone?" she asks the driver, and when he says, "I have rights, too, madam," she snaps, "I'm a police officer! Get off the goddamn *phone!*"

She waits for silence. It is sullen, but it comes.

"What I was saying, it doesn't have to follow that just because the guy's a sex addict, he does a rape."

"How about he's just one of your burglars or car thieves or *whatever* who raped her cause he was pissed off at her?"

"Could be."

"Could be one or the other, is that what you're saying?"

"One or the other, yes," Emma says.

Or both, she thinks.

"Only thing is he was staying there at the Palmer. That doesn't fit, does it?"

"Why not? There are rich sex addicts, Tony. Rich rapists, too."

"What time did he check out, do you know?"

"He may still *be* there. We don't even have his real name yet."

"Cause we've got him outside the salon at four this morning. How long would it take from the Palmer that time of night? Ten, fifteen minutes?"

"About that. Tony, I have to go. I don't want to miss Cindy."

"Who's Cindy?" he asks.

Cindy Mayes—if she is Cindy Mayes—is wearing a long white cotton T-shirt dress that falls amply to her ankles, where white Reeboks complete the impression of someone who's just come up from a long walk on the beach, as well she may have. She is wearing no makeup. Not a trace of liner, lipstick, or blush. Her complexion has a freshly burnished look, her frizzed blond hair is alive with natural highlights, her blue eyes sparkle with vitality. She is really a quite beautiful young girl, stepping boldly into the doorway of the salon, pressing the B for Beautiful bell button, and looking up familiarly at the surveillance camera. She is recognized at once. A buzzer sounds just as Emma says, "Miss Mayes?"

Cindy turns, her hand on the doorknob.

"Police officer," Emma says, and flashes the tin. "Mind if we have a few words?"

"Shit," Cindy says, and whirls away from the door. She looks up at the camera, says, "Later," to it, waves toodle-oo, and falls in beside Emma as she starts walking away from the building.

The sidewalks at three minutes before six on this steamy Thursday evening are thronged with office workers heading for subways and busses. Emma, wearing the same soggy linen suit she's been wearing since six this morning, feels part of the sweaty masses, this amorphous, anonymous crowd of workers heading home after a grinding day—except that *she's* not heading home just yet, *her* grinding day isn't quite over yet. It is not yet dusk, evengloam is not yet upon the city. But there is that expectant hush to the streets, the odd quiet that comes over the city before nightfall, an air of anticipation that signals excitement and sometimes danger.

"This is about Cathy, isn't it?" Cindy says.

"Yes," Emma says.

She can't help feeling somewhat envious. Cindy's workday is just beginning. *She's* been on the beach all day, young Cindy here, and can well afford the athletic stride, the quick pace of their march down Third Avenue. They are approaching Seventy-second Street. Emma is a little out of breath. She spots a coffee bar called *La Traviata*, asks, "Okay here?" and Cindy shrugs Who cares?

The place is empty save for a very fat woman reading a newspaper and using a mobile phone, her belongings spread everywhere around her. Cindy orders a latte mochaccino, whatever that may be. Emma sticks with a double capp, cinnamon and chocolate sprinkled over the foam. They take a table far from the fat lady who seems to have moved in for the summer. She is telling someone on the other end of her phone that the "cells" look just terrific. She is either a corrections officer or an animated film maker or an oncologist. An overhead fan circulates air redolent with the aroma of freshly brewed coffee. An air conditioner high on the wall hums noisy accompaniment.

"Do you have a name?" Cindy asks.

"Emma Boyle."

"Are you a Homicide detective?"

"Special Victims." She shows her shield again. "Detective / Second Grade," she says.

"Is that good?"

Emma looks at her.

"I mean, is it high up or something?"

"It's okay," Emma says. "First would be better."

"How much do you make?"

"Tell me about this morning," Emma says.

"I'll bet I make ten times what you make."

"I'll bet you do," Emma says. "What time did you leave the XS this morning?"

"Around four o'clock. How do you know about me?"

"Did you see Cathy Frese around that time?"

"Listen, I don't want to get in any trouble here."

On the phone, the fat woman is saying "Very high fidelity, you can hear butterflies." Maybe the "cells" she's talking about are cellular phones. Maybe the lady's into electronics. Or maybe she's just full of shit, Emma thinks, another New York phony carrying her office to the coffee bar, talking loud and loose and trying to impress the world at large, little realizing she's beaming her act to a two-bit whore who makes ten times what the lowly Detective/ Second in the rumpled linen suit earns. Emma suddenly realizes how angry she is. And thinks she may be angry only because someone raped and killed Cathy Frese. But knows that isn't it. She's angry because of Andrew Cullen. She's angry because his fucking mother stole Jackie from her. Or maybe she's just angry in general these days.

"What kind of trouble do you think you might be getting into?" she asks.

"Somebody killed Cathy, right?" Cindy says, and her grimace adds the word "Duhhh." She sips at the mochaccino. Foam gives her a momentary white mustache. She licks it clean with a neat little tongue. Emma imagines her doing a three-way with Michael the night before. "You're here because you think I

245

may know something about it. I don't. So let's not look for trouble, okay?"

"Let's look for whatever I *have* to look for, okay?" Emma says. "Your girlfriend was killed, so let's cut the crap. Did you see her this morning when you were leaving the salon?"

"Yes," Cindy snaps.

"Was she alone?"

"Yes."

"Sure about that?"

"Positive."

"Did you talk to her?"

"Yes. We said goodnight."

"And?"

"I walked off to the subway."

"What'd *she* do?"

"She stood there waiting."

"For what? For who?"

"How would I know?"

"Did you see anybody pull up in a taxi?"

"No."

"See a man get out of a taxi and walk over to her?"

"No."

"Did you see somebody named Michael getting out of a taxi at that time?"

"Who's Michael?"

"You did a three-way with him around one, two this morning."

"Who says?"

"Any number of people."

"I don't remember anybody named Michael."

She shakes her head, sips at her coffee. Her face is blank.

"You and Fatima," Emma says. "Dark hair, brown eyes, around five-ten or -eleven," Emma says. "Did you see him outside the XS at around *four* this morning?"

"I don't remember seeing anybody who looked like that."

"How do you know Cathy was waiting for someone?"

"Well, she was *standing* there, I assumed she was *waiting* for someone. Otherwise, why was she *standing* there? Are you sure you're a detective?"

"Yes, I'm positive," Emma says. "She didn't *say* she was waiting for someone, did she?"

"She said goodnight, see you tomorrow, is what she said."

"Did she *ever* mention waiting for someone after work?"

"Never."

She ducks her head, sips coffee and foam from the cardboard container. Emma waits for her to raise her head again. Waits to look into those clear blue eyes again.

"You're sure about that?"

"Yes, I'm positive," Cindy says, and again ducks her head.

Across the room, the fat woman is packing her tent. Emma waits. The woman waddles at last to the front door. A bell tinkles as she opens the door. The contained heat of the day rushes into the room like a plague of rattling locusts. The door closes behind the fat woman. The room is silent except for the whirring of the overhead fan and the hum of the air conditioner high on the wall.

"What are you afraid of?" Emma asks.

"Who's afraid?" Cindy asks.

But she is.

Emma knows she is.

She lets the number ring once, twice, three times . . .

"Hello?"

A woman's voice. Wary. Apprehensive. Even in that single word. Emma wonders why.

"Karen Tager?"

"Yes?"

"This is Detective Boyle, Special Victims Squad? Okay if I come there and talk to you?"

"What?"

"This is Detective . . ."

"Yes, but why do you want to talk to me?"

"A woman was killed, Miss Tager, we're trying to find the man who may have done it."

"Well . . . how would I . . . I mean, what would I know about . . .?"

"May I come there, Miss Tager?"

"Well . . . all right, but . . ."

"Could you let me have the address, please?"

"Well, okay," she says, and gives Emma the address and apartment number. "But I still don't . . ."

"See you in a little while," Emma says, and presses the END key. She dials Vice at once, gets a detective she's never spoken to before, asks for Jimmy Morgan, and is told he's gone for the day. She locates Morgan's home number in the little muddle of cards she collected early this morning, and dials it. It rings twice, and Morgan picks up.

"Jimmy Morgan," he says.

"Hi, it's Emma. You got my message, huh?"

"Yeah. What's happening?"

"I think I've got a lead. Woman this Michael character picked up at the Palmer. I'm on my way to see her now. Can you meet me?"

"Where?" he says at once.

CHAPTER
TEN

The building on Greenwich Avenue is a three-story walkup stuccoed over in brown, with black fire escapes running to the top floor from just above a teal-colored awning that shades a ground-floor French pastry shop. The entrance door to the building is just left of the bakery, painted black to match the fire escapes. Two steps lead up to the door; a brass kick plate protects its lower edge. Immediately to the left of the doorway is a store-front beauty spa with a sign that makes the entrance look like a golden minaret. The street at six-forty-seven P.M. is busy with pedestrians and automobiles. Emma is on the phone again, standing just in front of the black door, when Morgan cruises by in the Vice Squad sedan and toots the horn. He signals to her that he's going to park around the corner, then makes the turn and the car vanishes from sight.

"...but there had to be blood, am I right?" she's telling Manzetti. "What he did to her? So this Michael character couldn't have walked into the Palmer with blood all over his raincoat, right? If it even *was* him. So maybe there's a raincoat down a sewer near the crime scene someplace. Yeah, *could* you put some blues on it? That'd save us a lot of time. Thanks," she says, and is about to hit the END key when Manzetti says, "Hold it, here's Danny with something."

She waits.

"The ME's report," he says. "*Finalmente*."

She continues waiting. Static riddles the line.

She's afraid she will lose him again. She seems to keep losing people, this phone.

"ME's name is Malone," he says, "do you know him?"

"No."

"Good man, I've worked with him before. Anyway, this is it." He clears his throat, and begins reading. "She was strangled manually, neck grasped from the front. They found curved impressions of the thumbnail and grouped abrasions caused by other fingers. They also found contusions and tears of the thyro . . . I don't know how to pronounce this . . . the thyrohyoid membrane?"

"Yeah, go on."

"Also fractures of the hyoid bone, thyroid and cricoid cartilages. Large effusions of blood in the submucous layer of the larynx and pharynx. Impression of the assailant's teeth on the girl's cheek, be nice if we can find a suspect to do a bite imprint. Here's the stuff about her hair . . . tortuous and deformed roots . . . patches ripped from her head while still firmly attached to it. Jesus. Cause of death: violence of a nature sufficient to produce a fatal compacting of the throat organs."

He pauses.

He is reading ahead.

She waits again.

"Here's the rape stuff," he says. "She was all torn up, Emma. Forced entry seriously lacerated the posterior commisure and produced a lesion similar to a birth tear unquote. They found dried semen in the pubic hair and on the thighs and vulva. Spermatozoa in the vaginal smears. Multitude of foreign pubic hairs, too, but the girl was a hooker, so that was to be expected. We've got plenty to compare if we ever catch this guy."

"Here's Morgan now," she says. "We'll get back to you after we talk to the redhead."

"She's a redhead?"

"I thought I told you, sorry."

"I would've liked a blonde better. Establish an M.O."

"I gotta go, Tony."

"Go," he says.

"Who was that?" Morgan asks, nodding to the phone.

"Manzetti," she says, and drops it into her bag. "He just got the ME's report, the guy was a fucking monster."

"Tell me about it," Morgan says, nodding.

"Did you ever reach that lady at the Guild?"

"Yes. Nobody named Stanley worked on both those pictures."

"So scratch Stanley," she says, and nods glumly.

"Easy come, easy go," Morgan says.

A Chinese delivery boy on a bicycle goes zipping past on the sidewalk. Morgan takes an angry slap at his rear wheel. The kid turns to him, is about to say something when Morgan gives him a look. The kid pedals off in a hurry. Morgan turns back to Emma. He shrugs, grins. This city, he is telling her. She shrugs, grins back. This city, she agrees. And turns to scan the bell buttons for a Tager, K.

She knows at once that Karen Tager is a rape victim.

The woman doesn't even have to open her mouth. Emma knows. Perhaps it's the way she instinctively backs away from Morgan as they come into the apartment—and then immediately smiles at him. This is a woman who's been violated. Emma has met this woman before.

She greets them in pajamas over which she wears a green robe that matches her eyes. She tells them she's sorry, but she was getting ready for bed when they called. She gets up at three-thirty every morning because she has to be at work at five. She's a phlebotomist, she tells them, and waits expectantly, knowing they will ask what that is. She explains that she draws blood.

"Thank you for letting us come here," Emma says.

"How'd you get my name?" Karen asks.

"The bartender at the Palmer gave it to us."

"Freddie? Really? Why? You said on the phone that a woman had been killed. I don't see what my being at the Palmer . . ."

"Did you meet a man named Michael last night?" Morgan asks.

"Michael?"

"Yes. At the Palmer bar."

"Well . . . yes, I did," she says, and her green eyes suddenly open very wide. "Oh my *God*," she says. "Did he *kill* somebody?"

"We don't know yet, Miss Tager. Did you leave the hotel bar with him?"

"Yes, but I don't know anything about . . ."

"Where'd you go?"

"An Italian restaurant around the corner. Who did he kill?"

"What time did you finish eating?"

"Nine-thirty, ten o'clock. Who'd he kill?"

"Where'd you go then?"

She hesitates.

"Miss Tager? Where'd you go then?"

"Back to the hotel."

"To the bar again?"

She hesitates again.

"Miss Tager?"

"No. We went to his room."

Morgan merely glances at Emma. They are both experienced detectives. And although they have never worked together before, there is a shorthand they both understand. He is asking her to pick up the questioning. He is telling her a woman will get better results from this point on.

"How long did you stay in his room?" Emma asks.

"I was only there for a few minutes."

"Do you remember what time you left?"

"I guess it was around ten-fifteen."

"Where'd you go, Miss Tager?"

"Home."

"Was he alone when you left him?"

"Yes. Well, yes. What'd you think? We were just the two of us, he was alone when I left, yes."

"Why'd you leave?"

"He tried to rape me," Karen says.

Here it comes, Emma thinks.

"Tried?"

"Yes. I ran right out of there."

"Good."

"You don't believe me, do you?"

"Of course I do."

"Well, your partner doesn't."

"I believe you," Morgan says.

"Then why are you smirking that way?"

"Sorry, I didn't know I was."

Emma glances at him. He is definitely not smirking. In fact, there is a very serious look on his face and in his eyes. She does not know what is wrong with Karen Tager or why she has suddenly decided to lie. Nor does she understand what woman's intuition or cop's insight is telling her this girl sitting in the easy chair across the room there is lying, but she would stake her life on it. Whatever this Michael character did or didn't do later on last night, he did not try to rape Karen Tager after dinner.

"So you ran out of there around ten-fifteen or so."

"I think it was about then. He's married, you know. He told me he was expecting a call from his wife. In fact, he has a twenty-one-year-old daughter. She lives in Princeton. His father plays trumpet. *Used* to play trumpet. He had his own band."

"Was that the last time you saw him? When you left his room?"

"I called him later. But that was the last time I actually saw him, yes."

"Why'd you call him?"

"To tell him what I thought of him."

"What time was that?"

"That I called him?"

"Yes."

"Around eleven or so. I was already in bed."

"He was still there at eleven?"

"Yes.

"What room was it, Miss Tager?"

"What?"

"What room did you call?" Morgan says impatiently. "What was his room number?"

"Oh. 721."

"You're sure about that?"

"Positive. Michael Thorpe. Room 721."

Bingo, Emma thinks.

The hotel manager tells them that the person who occupied room 721 from early yesterday morning to early *this* morning was not a *Michael* Thorpe but a Mr *Benjamin* Thorpe from Los Angeles, California. He

256

gives them Thorpe's address and telephone number in Topanga Canyon, and tells them he would allow them to inspect room 721, but a new guest has already checked into it. If there's anything else he can do to . . .

"What time did he check out this morning?" Morgan asks.

"Six-thirty-one."

"Give us a list of all the phone calls he made from the time he checked in to the time he checked out," Emma says.

The computer printout of Benjamin Thorpe's hotel bill shows ten outgoing calls on July 21 and three on July 22. It is now six minutes to eight. Emma calls Manzetti's office, and somebody on the squad tells her he's in the field. She gives him the number of her cell phone, even though Manzetti already has it, and asks that he call back as soon as he checks in.

"He's out," she tells Morgan, and gets on the pipe to her own office. She tells a detective there named Susan Hawkes that she'll be faxing her a list of numbers for which she'll need corresponding names and addresses. "If the phone company gives you trouble with addresses . . ."

"The *phone* company!" Susan says, and Emma visualizes her rolling her eyes.

". . . just settle for localities, we've already got the numbers. I also need a list of all planes leaving New York for Los Angeles anytime from, say, seven this morning to whenever tonight."

"Newark, too?" Susan asks.

"Newark, too. How's the rape business?"

"Quiet."

"Let me know if you pick up a white male, medium height, medium build, dark hair, dark eyes, okay?"

"Sounds like my husband," Susan says.

"Sounds like everybody's husband."

"How soon do you need this stuff?"

"Now," Emma says.

"Okay, m'dear, shoot me the fax."

Standing at the fax machine in a little alcove off the cashier's office, feeding the several pages of Thorpe's hotel bill into it, Emma says, "Did I tell you I went to see Cindy?"

Morgan is sitting in a leather-and-chrome chair near the machine. "Cindy, Cindy," he says, and taps his temple. "Tall busty blonde, frizzed . . ."

"That's the one. She left the salon same time as Cathy this morning. Says she didn't see anyone, but I think she's hiding something. She knows what Thorpe looks like, she's the one who did the three-way with him."

"I guess that's *one* way to remember a person," Morgan says and grins. He is silent for a moment. The fax machine whirs and beeps. He glances at it. "Couple of things," he says, and looks up at Emma.

Uh-oh, she thinks.

"If we're gonna be partners on this thing . . ."

"We are partners, Jimmy."

"Yeah, that's what I thought, I thought we were investigating this thing together. But it's turning out

258

to be you're some kind of lone wolf, Emma. You go back to the XS alone, you talk to the bartender here at the Palmer alone . . ."

"I was trying to save . . ."

"I know, time is of the essence. But now I learn you *also* went to see this girl Cindy alone . . ."

"I know, I'm sorry."

"I mean, I *do* have experience, I'm an experienced Vice cop, and the dead girl *was* a hooker, Emma, you *do* remember that, don't you?"

"You're right, I'm sorry."

"All I'm saying is we're either in this together or we're not, Emma. I want to catch this son of a bitch as much as you do, believe me."

"I believe you, Jimmy."

"Okay then."

"Okay."

"Are we finished with the domestic dispute?" she asks, and smiles.

"We're finished," he says.

Emma's phone rings. She snaps open the lid.

"Boyle," she says.

"Emma, it's me," Manzetti says. "Where are you?"

"The Palmer," she says.

Morgan mimes *Who is it?*

She mouths the name *Manzetti.*

"Can you meet me on Sixty-eighth and York?" he says. "Somebody broke into the dead girl's apartment."

* * *

Even though Manzetti's people were here earlier today, apartment 22 did not become a bona fide crime scene until someone broke the lock on the door and illegally entered the premises. Homicide's morning visit was merely routine, a matter of course; a murder victim had lived here, the possibility existed that among her belongings they might find some clue to her death.

Now, as the three detectives trudge up the steps to the second floor, two uniformed cops are busy hanging yellow plastic CRIME SCENE tape in the hallway. The original lock dangles from brass screws on the splintered doorjamb, but a Medeco lock, and a hasp that will later be fastened to door and jamb, are sitting in a box on the floor just to the right of the door. A plastic-encased Crime Scene notice has already been tacked to the front door. At twenty past eight on this oppressive Thursday evening, the uniformed cops look very earnest and serious, perspiring in their blues as they work.

"Super noticed the broken lock on her way up to the roof," Manzetti says. "Evening, boys."

"Sir," the cop with the roll of tape in his hands says, glancing at the shield pinned to Manzetti's jacket pocket. The other cop almost salutes.

"When was this?" Emma asks.

"She goes up the roof to feed her pigeons every afternoon around three-thirty, four o'clock," Manzetti says. "Saw the busted lock, called Nine-One-One, told them it's the apartment of somebody got killed this morning. Funny thing is, she had the lock changed just a few days ago."

"Who?" Morgan asks. "The super?"

"No. The Frese girl. So now somebody breaks in. That's some kind of coincidence, don't you think?"

Emma wonders if it's some kind of coincidence.

Manzetti is pulling on white cotton gloves. He grasps the doorknob, twists it, eases the door open. A rush of contained heat spills into the corridor.

This is where the vic lived, Emma thinks.

Mind the vic, she thinks.

Leo Gephardt was in his fifties when Emma earned the gold shield and got assigned to the detective squad he commanded at the Three-Two. He'd never had a woman working for him before, didn't know what to do with her at first. Finally decided the experience might be educational for both of them. Used to turn over the squad's shittiest squeals to her. She figured this was favoritism; he was, after all, her mentor.

Mind the vic, he used to say.

Limped around the squadroom like a broken sparrow. Got shot in the leg when he was still a patrolman trying to talk a hostage-taker out of dropping a six-year-old kid out the window. Some cops felt a rookie cop had no business negotiating with a hostage-taker in the first place. Some cops even felt Leo *deserved* to get shot. Leo told them, "Hey, if you can't take a joke, go fuck yourself."

He used to call Emma "The Girl from Downstairs," referring to the days she'd spent walking a precinct beat. The Three-Two Squad investigated every kind of trouble, they called it euphemistically, from street gangs to dope dealers to holdups, lots of those, to burglaries, even more of those, to your parking-lot shootouts at the local Mickey D's, to your more exotic and extraordinary occurrences like the ninety-year-old lady they found naked and smoldering in her own bathtub after she'd poisoned herself and her six cats.

Mind the vic, Leo used to say.

Meaning pay attention to the vic, learn all there is to know about the vic—and you'll get the perp. Mind the vic, find the vic, find the perp.

She follows Manzetti into the apartment.

At first, it looks like rage.

It takes Emma several moments to realize it was merely haste.

Whoever destroyed the front-door lock and came charging in here was in one hell of a hurry. Wanted to get in and out fast, find whatever he was looking for, leave the premises. The apartment is a bleak studio with a bathroom the size of an upright coffin, a kitchen not much larger, and a single window opening on a brick airshaft. There are dirty plastic containers in the sink, the remnants of a dinner from some neighborhood takee-outee joint. Several empty Diet Iced Tea bottles are on the kitchen counter top. A glance into the fridge reveals a slab of butter that looks rancid, several wilted celery stalks, a container of something growing mold, a carton of milk with an off-sale date that expired a week ago, and several hard rolls wrapped in plastic. Whatever the intruder

262

was looking for, he didn't hope to find it in the kitchen. None of the cabinet doors are ajar, none of the small drawers under the counter are open.

The bedroom portion of the apartment is another story.

There is a sofa-bed in the room, and it is open. Onto this bed, the intruder has thrown what appears to be every piece of clothing in the apartment. Jackets and slacks still on closet hangers have been hurled onto the bed together with an overcoat and a windbreaker, a parka, a shawl. Dresses and skirts have been thrown helter-skelter across each other, on top of each other. There is also a dresser in the room, a white wooden piece that looks as if it may have come from Ikea. Its drawers have been pulled free of the body and overturned onto the bed, white cotton panties from Bloomie's flung onto lace-edged silk panties from La Perla, starched and folded white cotton blouses tossed haphazardly onto long-sleeved nylon shirts with French cuffs, tube tops and tunics, sweaters, T-shirts and tanks. Blue, knee-high socks are strewn on the pillows, pantyhose in rainbow colors trail onto the floor, red garter belts and open-crotch panties mingle with full white cotton slips and black nylon halfslips slit to the thigh. Strappy sandals with stiletto heels, Beanie-Baby beaded mules, mid-heel slides, flat black patent Mary Janes, blue suede toe-ring thongs, all are thrown everywhere, anywhere, on the bed, on the floor.

The clutter in the room is a medley of fashions and styles, a bedlam of sophistication and naiveté, the seeming confusion of someone new to the big city and searching for a way to define herself, urgently seeking a way to *become* someone here, become *anyone* here. Cathy Frese's tiny space seems to have housed a female in flux, a young girl on the way to becoming a grown woman. But she was twenty-six years old.

On a covered radiator in the minuscule bathroom, they find a shoe-box. In that box, there are photographs of friends, or perhaps relatives, in some green wooded place. In that box, there are letters from relatives, or perhaps friends, in a town named Driggs, in the state of Idaho. In that box, there is an address book containing the names and addresses of people who live very far from this city and the life Cathy Frese led here. A Forever bracelet made of string is buried somewhere at the bottom of the box.

"What the hell was he looking for?" Morgan asks.

Emma looks at the jumble of clothing on the open sofa-bed.

What was *Cathy* looking for? she wonders.

And again thinks *Mind the vic*.

It is a little before nine when they return to the hotel. The information Emma requested is waiting at the front desk.

17/21–7:01 PM Ritter-Thorpe Associates
   Los Angeles, California

7/21–7:07 PM American Airlines
   Raleigh, North Carolina
7/21–7:10 PM Benjamin Thorpe
   Los Angeles, California
7/21–7:20 PM Charles Harris
   Princeton, New Jersey
7/21–7:40 PM Heather Epstein
   New York, New York
7/21–7:55 PM Arthur Davies
   New York, New York
7/21–10:30 PM Benjamin Thorpe
   Los Angeles, California
7/21–11:30 PM Heather Epstein
   New York, New York
7/21–11:40 PM B&R Enterprises
   Baltimore, Maryland
7/21–11:57 PM XS Salon
   New York, New York
7/22–4:45 AM Heather Epstein
   New York, New York
7/22–4:48 AM Lois Ford
   New York, New York
7/22–5:33 AM Benjamin Thorpe
   Los Angeles, California

Emma's partner has also faxed them three pages listing departures for Los Angeles from Newark, La Guardia, and Kennedy, forty-one flights in all, divided among Continental, United, and American. The earliest flight left at 6:10 this morning, an American Airlines flight scheduled to arrive in L.A.

at 11:13 A.M. The last flight tonight is scheduled to leave from JFK at 9:10 P.M.—ten minutes from now.

Over coffee in the hotel lounge—

"We ought to start paying rent here," Morgan suggests.

—they discuss their next move.

"There were eight flights leaving between eight and nine A.M.," Emma says. "He could've caught any one of them."

"*If* he left," Morgan says.

"Well, look at this list of calls," Emma says. "He phoned home at five-thirty-three A.M., an hour before he checked out. Probably to say what flight he'd be on."

"Or he may still be in the city," Morgan says. "Let's try some of these numbers."

The first call they make is to the number listed for a Charles Harris in Princeton, New Jersey. A little girl answers the phone.

"This is the Harris residence," she says.

"May I talk to your father, please?" Emma asks.

"Who's calling, please?" the kid says.

"Detective Emma Boyle."

"Who?"

"Detective Emma Boyle," she says again. "Could you please get him for me?"

"He's not here. I'll get Mommy."

Emma covers the mouthpiece. "A kid," she explains to Morgan.

"Still up at this hour?" Morgan says sourly.

Emma waits. At last, a woman's voice comes on the line. She sounds very frightened.

"Hello?" she says. "Did my daughter say you're a *detective*?"

"Yes, ma'am," Emma says. "Who am I speaking to, please?

"This is Margaret Harris. Is something wrong? Oh God, I *know* what it is. Something's happened to my father!"

"Your father?"

"He's in the city. Has there been an accident?"

"What's your father's name, Mrs. Harris?"

"Benjamin Thorpe. Has something happened to him?"

Emma hesitates for a moment.

Morgan looks at her, puzzled.

"I'm sorry, ma'am," she says, "I must have the wrong number." And breaks the connection at once.

"What?" Morgan says.

"His daughter."

Morgan says nothing. His look says he does not like the way she handled this. She almost expects another one of his little lectures. Couple of things, Emma. Instead, he merely sighs heavily and says, "Let's try the next one."

At twelve minutes past nine that night, two minutes after the last plane to Los Angeles takes off, two blues from the One-Nine Precinct arrest a man molesting a twelve-year-old girl on her way home from the movie theater on Seventy-second and Third.

Because news of the rape-murder has spread throughout the precinct, the arresting officers immediately alert the detectives upstairs, who in turn call Homicide crosstown. Manzetti and his partner, Danny Harmon, arrive at the precinct at a quarter to ten. Just about then, Morgan and Emma are entering the traffic on the East River Drive, on their way to East Seventeenth Street.

"Let's talk about your NYSID, okay?" Manzetti says.

He is holding in his right hand the New York State arrest record of the man who sits on the other side of the table in the One-Nine's interrogation room. The man's name is Edward Nelson. His police record shows his height as five-feet-eleven, his weight as one-eighty-five. But his last arrest was eight years ago, and he appears to be a little heavier now. His eyes are brown, his hair brown. He has no identifying scars or tattoos. He could indeed be the person described by the two witnesses this morning.

Danny Harmon is sitting beside Nelson; he has been working homicides since he was twenty-six years old when he made a spectacular arrest on the Park Slope Strangler case in Brooklyn. He is now forty-seven, a burly Irishman with smoldering brown eyes and a ruddy complexion, very black hair. Manzetti is standing, facing them both. Occasionally, he paces. He is beginning to smell blood here. He is beginning to think that maybe they just got lucky. Sometimes, though not too often, you get lucky in this business.

268

"You've been a busy little boy," Manzetti says.

The man says nothing. He is an experienced felon, but he has not yet asked for an attorney. Manzetti figures he's waiting to see how this preliminary interrogation goes. The minute it gets rough, Nelson will start spouting his rights and asking for a telephone. They all know their rights better than any lawyer does.

"Your first arrest was twenty years ago for Attempted Rape, a Class-C felony," Manzetti says, reading from the yellow sheet. "You did seven and a half at Ossining for that one. Soon as you got out, you were arrested again for Promoting Prostitution, judge took pity on you, I see, you only got probation. Ten years ago, you were busted for Public Lewdness, conditional discharge, you're a very lucky fellow, Eddie. Well, maybe *not* so lucky. Year after that, they got you on Carnal Abuse of a Child, another *sett'e mezz* at Sing Sing, nice work, Eddie. You just got out and you go after a twelve-year-old, very nice."

Nelson says nothing.

"Where were you this morning at around four o'clock?" Manzetti asks.

"Sleeping," Nelson says.

"Where's that? Where do you sleep, Eddie?"

"In Brooklyn. I live in Brooklyn."

"But you cruise Manhattan, huh?"

No answer.

"Know anybody named Cathy Frese?" Manzetti asks.

"No. Who's that?"

"Heidi? Know a girl named Heidi?"

"No."

"Ever visit a massage parlor on Seventy-fourth and Third?"

"I don't go to massage parlors."

"I'll bet you don't. How many girls of your own did you run, Eddie?"

"I don't know what you mean."

"When you were pimping. Back at the beginning of your illustrious career. How many girls?"

"I took the fall, I done the time," Nelson says. "You got no right questioning me about ancient history."

"Ancient history, huh? How about this morning? Is that ancient history, too?"

"I don't know what the fuck you're talking about, this morning."

"Were you anywhere near Seventy-fourth and Third at four this morning? Little after four this morning?"

"No."

"Somebody thinks he may have seen you getting out of a cab around that time. Approaching a blonde waiting there."

"He's mistaken."

"Maybe so. We'll get him in here later, run a little line-up, how about that, Eddie?"

"You gonna run a line-up, I want a lawyer."

"We got another witness thinks she saw you a little later, on the corner of Seventieth and Second, getting funny with the same blonde. We'll invite her to the line-up, too. Did you get funny with a blonde this morning, Eddie?"

"I was sleeping this morning."

"How about tonight? Were you sleeping tonight, too?"

"I was in the movies tonight."

"Oh? Are you a movie star, Eddie?"

"I *went* to the movies."

"How about *after* the movie, Eddie? Were you sleeping, or did you try to feel up a twelve-year-old girl waiting for a bus?"

"I never take busses."

"Did you approach a twelve . . .?"

"I only take the subway."

". . . year-old girl named Naomi Kramer . . ."

"I take the Number Five train from Fifty-ninth Street to Brooklyn."

"So what were you doing on Seventy-second Street, Eddie?"

"I told you. I went to see a movie."

"The arresting officers caught you with your hand practically in the cookie jar, how about that, Eddie?"

"I want to talk to a lawyer."

"Fine."

"Now."

"Fine. You got your own lawyer, or you want us to get one for you?"

"I got one," Nelson says.

Big surprise, Manzetti thinks.

* * *

Heather Epstein is five-feet-seven or -eight inches tall, a wide-shouldered, big-breasted girl with long blond hair and blue eyes. She is wearing at ten o'clock that night a green mini skirt, lime-colored panty-hose, a matching blouse with tiny brown buttons, and platform shoes that add another two inches to her height. Emma guesses she is in her early twenties. Her one-bedroom apartment is furnished with the casual abandon of a college dorm, a computer on a desk in the corner, unpainted bookcases against the walls, a stereo setup, mismatching furniture. There are framed photographs of herself and what appears to be her extended family on every flat surface but the floor. She looks like she would be right at home in Florida or Arizona—but her accent immediately betrays her as a native New Yorker. She asks them if they'd care for a cup of coffee or anything—

"I wouldn't mind," Morgan says at once.

"None for me, thanks," Emma says.

—apologizes for it being only instant, and goes into a small kitchen just off the entrance door, leaving the two detectives alone to wander the living room. Morgan picks up a framed photo on one of the bookcases.

"Older sister," he says aloud.

"Or mother," Emma says.

"Dead ringers."

"Pretty girl."

Morgan nods. Heather is coming out of the kitchen with a coffee cup, a container of skim milk, and a small bowl containing packets of brown sugar, Equal, and Sweet "n Low.

"Thanks very much," Morgan says. He still has the framed photo in his hand. "Your sister or your mother?" he asks.

"What?" Heather says. "Oh. My sister, actually."

"Strong resemblance," he says and puts the picture back on the bookcase. He sits beside Heather on the sofa, reaches for a packet of brown sugar, tears it open, and pours it into the coffee cup. "Nothing for you?" he asks Heather, and smiles. This is turning into a social visit, Emma thinks. Dead girl in an alley this morning, killer maybe roaming loose in L.A., Morgan's having a demi-tasse at the Waldorf.

"I'm all coffee-ed out, thanks," Heather says, and smiles. It occurs to Emma that she might be flirting with him. It further occurs to her that he might be flirting, too. Well, he's single, she thinks. Yeah, but twice her age. Hey, I'm not her mother, she thinks.

"Miss Epstein," she says, "we have a list of phone calls a man named Benjamin Thorpe made . . ."

Heather is already nodding.

". . . from his hotel room last night . . ."

She keeps nodding.

". . . and it shows three calls made to you, one at seven-forty P.M. last night, another at eleven-thirty, and a third one early this morning. Do you remember any of those calls?"

"Yes, I do," she says and nods and smiles somewhat hesitantly, and then — surprisingly —

blushes like a little girl. In her lifetime, Emma has questioned enough people to know when a person is concealing something. Morgan detects something here as well. He nods pleasantly, and smiles, and then says, "What'd you talk about, Heather?"

"Oh, this and that," she says, and blushes more furiously. "You told me on the phone . . ."

"How do you happen to know him?" Emma asks.

"He was, um, giving a lecture at school," Heather says. "Cooper Union. I'm a student there. I'm studying architecture there."

"When was this?"

"Last April. Did he do something?"

"What makes you think that?"

"Well, on the phone you said you were looking for him . . ."

"Few questions we'd like to ask him, yes."

"So did he do something?"

"How well did you know him, Heather?" Morgan asks.

"Not too well at all."

"How'd he happen to call you?"

"I guess he wanted to talk."

"What about?"

"Gee, I don't know. We only talked for a few minutes."

"Can you tell us what you talked about?"

"Well, actually, he wanted to go out with me," she says, and pulls a face. "The first time, anyway. I told him I was busy. Actually, I was on my way to a party."

274

"What sort of relationship did you have with him?" Morgan asks, and sips at his coffee, watching her.

"We were friends, I guess you'd say."

"What kind of friends?"

"He called me every now and then, that's all."

"From Los Angeles, do you mean?"

"Yes."

"How often?"

"Well, every now and then."

"Once a month?"

"Well, more than that, actually."

"Twice a month?"

"I guess. Though he hasn't called me for a while. I mean, before last night. I can't remember the last time he called. He thinks he can just call, you know, and I'll jump."

"Ever go out with him?"

"Once."

"Did you know he was married?"

"Well, yes. But we only went out together once. Actually, we didn't even go out. He came here, that's all."

"When was this?"

"Last April. I told you."

"And he's been calling you since, is that it?"

"Every once in a while."

"Why does he call?"

"Well, to *talk*," she says, and giggles. "Why do you think?"

"What do you talk about?"

"Well."

"Yes?"

"Am I in any sort of trouble here?"

"No, Heather."

"Because . . . if I am . . . I think I'd like to call my father, you know? He's a lawyer."

"Does your father know Benjamin Thorpe?"

"Of *course* not! But if Ben *did* something and you're trying to get me involved, then maybe I ought to . . ."

"Miss Epstein," Emma says, "a young girl was killed early this morning . . ."

"Oh my God!" Heather says.

"And we think Benjamin Thorpe . . ."

"It wasn't Lo, was it?"

"Who's Lo?"

"My friend who was here last night. He didn't follow her home or anything, did he?"

"What makes you think he'd do something like that?"

"Well, he sounded sort of . . . well, desperate. I mean, he doesn't usually sound so . . . I don't know . . . *desperate.*"

"Why'd he call you a second time last night, Heather?"

This from Morgan. He has put his cup down on the coffee table and is leaning toward her now. She sits beside him on the couch, her legs tucked under her, her shoes off. She has begun chewing the lipstick off her mouth. She doesn't answer him for a moment. She looks at him as if wondering whether

276

she can trust him or not. He nods subtle encouragement. He's either an excellent cop or he's coming on to her. Or maybe both. Either way, he seems to be getting results.

"Heather?" he says. "Tell us why he called you again around eleven-thirty last night."

"Well," Heather says, and begins chewing her lip. "I guess he wanted to come over."

"Here?"

"Yes."

"Did he come here?"

"No, I wouldn't let him. Lo thought it was a riot. Him wanting to come here."

"Why was that, Heather?"

"That Lo thought it was funny? Well, he's a man in his forties, you know. So here he is suggesting . . ."

"I meant why'd he want to come here?"

"Why? Well . . . you know."

"Tell us."

"You know," she says, and again blushes. "He . . . wanted to be with us, I guess."

"Be with you?"

"Well . . . have sex with us. Me and Lo."

"Did he say that?"

"He did, yes."

"But you said no."

"I said no. He really sounded desperate. I was a little scared, to tell the truth."

"Desperate how?"

"Well, the way he kept insisting."

"On what?"

"Coming over. And wanting to, well, I told you, have sex with me and Lo."

"Did you ever have sex with him?" Morgan asks.

Point blank, Emma thinks.

"Well, just that once," Heather says.

"Which once?"

"The time he gave the lecture. And came here afterward. But that was just the two of us."

"What about these phone calls from L.A.?" Morgan asks.

They're phone fucks, Emma thinks. She looks at Morgan. He is thinking the same thing. They are in the same business, after all, more or less. *Her* guys are merely *his* guys who've lost complete control. That's the only difference. Heather said Thorpe sounded "sort of desperate" last night, but how desperate is "sort of desperate?" Emma wonders. She feels pretty certain she knows what kind of man they're dealing with here, but engaging in phone sex—or even visiting a massage parlor—is something quite different from raping and strangling a young girl, tearing out her hair, savagely biting her. Quite different. But it's possible. Listen, it could be possible. Guy on the town suddenly loses it, that's possible. Nothing's ever what it seems, she thinks.

"All we did was talk," Heather says.

"What about?" Morgan asks.

"Things."

"What things?

"Just things."

278

"Sex?"

"Sometimes."

"Heather . . . did you have phone sex with him?"

His voice is soft, his eyes are intent on her face. He looks like he's hypnotizing her. Emma remains silent. Let him run with it, she thinks.

"Well, yes," Heather says. "Sometimes."

Her voice is a whisper. She and Morgan could be alone together here. She could be sitting in the darkness of a confessional. He could be on the other side of the screen, listening in the dark.

"Did he want to have phone sex last night?" Morgan asks.

"Yes."

"With you alone? Or with both of you?"

"Me alone."

"And did you, Heather?"

"No. Actually, he didn't ask me. He said he wanted to take me out. But I knew he wanted to. He only calls when he wants to . . . you know . . . do it on the phone. He thinks all he has to do is call me any time of the day or night."

"Do you have phone sex with him every time he calls?"

"Yes."

Her voice so low Emma can hardly . . .

"Heather?"

"Yes. Every time."

"But not last night."

"No."

Morgan nods.

"When he spoke to you that second time," Emma says, "did he mention where he might be going?"

"No, he just wanted to come here, that's all."

"Why'd he call a third time?"

"I don't know."

"Well, he called at a quarter to five this morning . . ."

"I know."

"Well, what'd he want?"

"I don't know. I hung up."

Emma sighs heavily. "Thanks a lot, Miss Epstein," she says. "We appreciate your time."

Heather swings her legs off the couch and slips into her shoes. "I hope you get him," she says. "If he did it."

"If he did it, we'll get him," Emma says.

"Thank you, Heather," Morgan says, and shakes her hand. "We appreciate your help. Just be careful in the future, okay?" he says. "You and your friend both. Lo? Is that her name?"

"Well, Lois, actually," Heather says, and opens the front door for them. "Lois Ford."

In the hallway outside, Morgan says, "He's beginning to fit the profile all the way down the line, isn't he? Calls Heather here in the middle of the night, and three minutes later he's on the phone with her girlfriend. For all we know, he's out there looking for another vic right this fuckin minute. These guys are obsessed, you know, They try to stop themselves, but they can't, they're obsessed. They think about sex every minute of the day, they can't stop thinking about it. Right now, right this minute, he's thinking about sex, I'll bet a million dollars on it. Running girls through his mind, memories of every girl he ever knew or hoped to know, turning them over in his mind. I know these creeps, believe me, I've been with Vice for almost a hundred years now. We better catch this guy soon, before he—"

Emma's cell phone rings. She flips open the lid, and hits the SEND key. It's Manzetti.

"We got a guy here who looks ripe," he says. "We're picking up the two witnesses from this morning, going to run a little line-up in twenty minutes or so. You and Jimmy up for it?"

CHAPTER
ELEVEN

Every time Emma walks into this big white building with its red trim and blue windows, she feels as if she's stepping into an American flag. Squatting solidly on the corner of 133rd and Broadway, the structure is home to Homicide, Special Victims, the Department of Housing Preservation and Development, the Child Welfare Organizing Project, the Harlem Bay Network Mental Health Association, and a dozen other profit and non-profit organizations that share offices in the virtual shadow of the elevated train tracks running past outside. Emma's office is on the sixth floor; Manzetti's is on the fourth.

As they take the elevator up, she calls the XS Salon and asks to speak to Cindy Mayes. It is now almost eleven o'clock, five hours since she had her last conversation with the girl. When she comes on the line, her voice is clear and crisp, a trifle edgy. She sounds intelligent and young and beautiful. Even on the phone, she sounds beautiful.

"This is Cindy," she says.

"This is Detective Boyle," Emma says. "I . . ."

"Yes, what is it?" Cindy asks.

The elevator doors open. Morgan steps out into the fourth-floor corridor, and Emma follows him. Signaling for him to go on ahead to Manzetti's office, she walks to the windows, phone to her ear, and looks out at Broadway. In the dark, an elevated train rumbles by on the tracks outside.

"Cathy's apartment was broken into this afternoon . . ."

"I don't know anything about that."

"Her super says she just had the lock changed on her door. Would you know . . .?"

"I'm sorry, we're very busy up here just now."

"Would you know why Cathy had her lock changed?"

"No, I'm sorry, I don't."

"Did she ever *mention* changing . . .?"

"Look, I really don't have time for you just now."

"*Make* time," Emma says.

"I can't, really. I have to go. I don't want to get in trouble here. I have to go."

"Cindy . . .," Emma starts, but there is a click on the line.

She looks at the phone.

Shit, she thinks.

There is only one suspect, and Manzetti is reluctant to load the stage with too many police officers. These days, you make one false move, the case gets kicked out later on. He can look into the future and visualize Nelson's lawyer jumping up and asking the judge to exclude a positive ID merely because out of six possible choices, five of them were cops.

The lawyer's name is Rabinowitz. He has defended Nelson before, and apparently done a very good job of it since the punk walked on two occasions. On the other hand, Nelson spent seven-and-a-half in the slammer on each of two other occasions, so maybe a five-oh batting average ain't so terrific, after all. Rabinowitz spends at least fifteen minutes arguing that under the Miranda ruling, his client is not obliged to leave a bite mark in the apple Manzetti offers to him. Manzetti knows the ruling the way he knows his own name. But it takes four calls to the D.A.'s Office downtown to convince Rabinowitz that asking Nelson to bite into the apple is the same as asking him to put his finger to his nose or take off his hat. At last, Manzetti gets a bite impression he can compare against the bite mark on Cathy Frese's cheek.

While they sit in Manzetti's office, trying to decide what they can do here to balance the Eddie Nelson line-up scales a bit, Morgan asks one of the Homicide dicks to fax the L.A.P.D. for a routine check on a Benjamin Thorpe out there in Topanga Canyon. Manzetti suggests they can maybe transport some other felons from the holding pen at the Two-Six, but then *their* attorneys would start squawking about God knows what technicality endangering their rights to a fair trial. It's not as if they have three or four suspects here. All they have is Nelson, who claims he was home asleep while someone was raping and strangling Cathy Frese.

This is now twenty minutes past eleven, and Rabinowitz is beginning to squawk already about holding his client too long without charging him. He was earlier protesting that under the Miranda rules they couldn't run a line-up on Nelson without a court order, which they know, and he *also* knows, is complete and total bullshit. They realize, however, that they better get this thing rolling soon, or Rabinowitz will find a *genuine* technical reason to spring his man out of here.

There aren't too many civil-service people working in the building at this hour, just your usual cop grunts and your cleaning people, so they put Nelson up on the stage with a uniformed cop they pull off patrol in the Two-Six, two Homicide detectives from right here on the fourth floor, and two guys who a minute ago were scrubbing sinks and toilet bowls. One of the cleaning men is black. One of the Homicide dicks is black, too. This means there are two blacks, three whites, and Nelson—who is also white—up on the stage.

Morgan suggests that maybe he ought to join the group of usual suspects, give it a heavier tilt toward the white side since the two witnesses described the guy they saw this morning as white, and it might be nice if they were presented with a reasonable choice. Manzetti thinks this might be a good idea, but then they'd run into the initial problem of loading the stage with too many law-enforcement types. If Morgan stepped out there with the others, that'd be four cops, three of them white, two civilians, and Nelson, who is also a civilian—of sorts. He opts for the original six. Actually, it's a good mix.

The black detective is about six-feet tall and weighs about a buck-ninety. In contrast, the black cleaning man is about five-eight, Emma guesses, a slight slender balding man with a thin mustache over his lip. The white detective is about the size and weight the two witnesses described. So is the uniformed cop, who is now wearing a lightweight trenchcoat over blue jeans and a cotton sweater. Three of the six men are wearing trenchcoats. The other three are wearing suits or sports jackets. Manzetti explains to the two witnesses that if they want the suspects to do anything for them, take off a coat, for example, or walk across the stage, or even say anything in particular, that's perfectly all right within the Miranda guidelines.

The two witnesses are sitting in the front row of chairs in what looks like a small theater, with three rows of chairs arranged before a raised platform behind a thick pane of glass. One of them is the white bartender who saw someone getting out of a cab to join a blonde outside the XS Salon at four this morning. The other is the black cleaning woman who saw a man "beating on a blonde" on the corner of Seventieth and Second about fifteen minutes later. Manzetti, Harmon, Morgan, and Emma are all sitting in the very back row of chairs, the idea being that no one can later say they influenced the witnesses in any way, either by hand signal or voice prompt. Rabinowitz is sitting in the middle row, his legs crossed. He is what Emma's father would call a "dapper little man." Someone in the room behind the glass panel throws a switch and the stage is filled with bright light.

The six men walk out in single file and take positions in front of the big black number markers on the white wall—one, two, three, four, and so on. There are also height markers painted in black on the white wall behind the stage. In smaller numbers, they sprout vertically, five feet, five-feet-one, five-feet-two, and on up to six-six. Nelson enters first, walks stage left, takes a position in front of the number 6 marker, and then turns to face the glass. The black detective is next, number 5, then the white detective, 4, and so on, the black cleaning man, the white officer, and lastly the white cleaning man, all of them taking positions in front of the number markers. The black female witness intently studies each man as he crosses the stage and occupies his numbered position. Emma thinks they all look as if they could easily have slain their own mothers in their beds this morning.

It would be nice if you could have a line-up for the participants in a divorce, she thinks. It would be nice if you could parade the disputing parties before an objective witness, have that person say "Yes, he is the guilty one, she is the guilty one," pick from the pair up there the one who is responsible for the dissolution of the marriage. Although in her case it would be an academic exercise, wouldn't it? We all *know* why this marriage is ending in divorce. It is ending in divorce because Andrew Cullen plays around. That is the long and the short of it, ladies and gentlemen, you need not scrutinize that couple on the stage any longer. Andrew Cullen plays around with other women, and his beloved wife Emma cannot abide such behavior.

But then, of course, and on the other hand, what did Emma contribute to this volatile mix? Was she attentive enough, loving enough, sexy enough, *whatever* enough? Was she plainly and simply *enough?* Andrew blamed it on her job. How many times in the throes of hot embrace had Emma been summoned to the squadroom or the hospital to interrogate yet another woman or girl raped or abused by yet another man? How many times? Try a hundred and sixty-five rapes in the borough of Manhattan so far this year, how does *that* sound for the number of times Emma Boyle Cullen was called out of bed in the middle of the night, try that for size, honey. And how many times had she seen that look of knowledgeable forbearance cross Andrew's face and flash in his eyes when the lady detective was called away to do her duty in the middle of the night, or in the middle of dinner, or in the middle of an afternoon stroll in the park with their two-year-old daughter, how many times had the telephone on the bedside table or in her tote bag summoned her to work? And how often could a man endure *coitus interruptus*—well, surely you exaggerate, madam, surely there are *other* rape-squad detectives who share the duty with you, surely you did not answer each and every one of those calls this year, surely you overstate your case.

Okay, shall we divide the number of rapes by— what? Six? Seven? Even ten? How long could a man tolerate such intrusion into his private life before seeking solace and companionship elsewhere, how long? Not long enough, she supposes. Because now they are separated and now a male judge has decided—as apparently Andrew himself previously decided—that being a rape-squad detective is not an occupation compatible with either a seven-year-old marriage or a two-year old daughter—and yes, by the way, it *is* a rape squad. Never mind what they're calling it these days. It is a *rape* squad. *Rape* is what we deal with here. Women being violated by men. Yes. And believe me, Your Honor, playing around with another woman—a *multitude* of women, in fact—is rape. I submit, Your Honor, that Emma Boyle Cullen was repeatedly raped by Andrew Cullen during the past two years of her marriage, which are all the years she knows about for sure, ever since her daughter was born, in fact, but God knows how many years before then. Raped. Yes, Your Honor. And you have the gall to take my daughter away from me? You have the fucking balls to do that, Your Honor? To join in the fucking rape? To join the fucking *club*?

"You okay?" Morgan whispers.

"Yes, I'm fine," she says.

But she isn't.

"Do either of you recognize the man you saw this morning?" Manzetti asks the witnesses. The male witness turns to see where the voice is coming from, and then looks back at the stage again. The black woman, who earlier studied the supposed offenders as they came onto the stage, one of them possibly the *real* offender, now studies them with even closer scrutiny.

The room is silent.

On the stage, everyone tries to look nonchalant. Even Edward Nelson, who may or may not have killed Cathy Frese but who most certainly was caught with his hand in a young girl's bloomers, tries to look nonchalant. All six gentlemen up there on the stage could be partners in a respectable law firm. Put Andrew Cullen up there with them, he'd look right at home. But Andrew Cullen is a rapist, did you know that, Your Honor? Andrew Cullen has been raping Emma Boyle Cullen for the past two years, Your Honor, and now he's stolen my daughter and taken her to Westport, Connecticut, where there are no rapists and ergo no need for a rape squad or a rape-squad detective, not in lily-white Westport, Connecticut, oh no indeed.

"See anyone?" Manzetti prompts.

The black woman turns to look at him where he sits in the back row with the other detectives. Cranes her neck at all of them. Squints at them in the dark.

"No, sir, I do not," she says.

"How about you, sir?" Manzetti asks.

"Nobody," the bartender says.

A uniformed cop walks onto the stage to lead the six men out. Nelson isn't going anyplace except downtown for booking. Manzetti thanks the two witnesses and asks another cop to show them downstairs. They both look offended, as if they should have been paid for their time.

"Thought she was gonna pick *you* for a minute," Harmon tells Manzetti. "Way she was looking back here."

"They always look to the back row for a clue," Manzetti says. "To them, it's like a television quiz show they wanna win, some kind of freakin game."

Some game, Emma thinks.

"Let's see how we make out with the apple," Manzetti says.

"Who's for a beer?" Harmon asks.

At this hour, the night shift has just been relieved and the tiny bar on 131st and Broadway is packed with uniformed cops and undercovers from the Two-Six, Homicide detectives wearing what they wore to work that afternoon, male and female officers alike gathering to wind down after a day that started at three-forty-five P.M. and did not end until half an hour ago—except for the detectives who were unlucky enough to have caught the Cathy Frese squeal at six this morning.

Emma feels very much at ease in these surroundings. Perhaps it's because she's Irish, or perhaps it's because she's a cop. The bar is very definitely an Irish-looking and Irish-sounding bar, the distinctive accents of Brooklyn and Queens lilting on the air as if these men and women are in County Clare sipping beer on the banks of the Fergus, instead of on Upper Broadway a block from the Hudson. None of these men or women are drinking hard liquor. There are pitchers of beer on the table and sitting on the bartop because these men and women aren't here to get drunk—most of them will be going home to wives or husbands—but merely to talk about the day's work. They are in a dangerous occupation, these men and women, and these nightly confabs are not unlike debriefings after a bombing raid or an incursion into enemy territory. This is CopLand After Dark.

"Was there anything from the Coast?" she asks Harmon.

"Nothing," he says.

"Any record on Thorpe?" Morgan asks.

"Clean as a whistle. Nothing in their files."

"Did they roll by his house?"

"All the lights were on, nobody home."

"What time did they go by?" Manzetti asks.

"Around eight their time. They'll make another run along about eleven. What time is that here?" Harmon asks. He spots a female officer he knows, most likely from the Two-Six, standing at the bar with a couple of Homicide detectives. He waves to her, and she comes on over. She is a delicate Hispanic woman, perhaps five-feet-three-inches tall, in her mid-twenties, still in uniform, strapped with a nine bigger than she is, hanging in a black leather holster on her right hip.

"They're three hours behind us," Morgan answers, and looks her over.

"I hear you just took the test for third," Harmon tells the woman. He, too, is giving her the eye. She's really quite pretty. Black curly hair sprouting from under her peaked uniform hat, full hips swelling above the holster belt, good breasts filling her tailored uniform shirt. Emma wonders if they piss in her shoes back at the precinct.

The girl is lingering by the table, not sure whether or not she should join them, four detectives and all. Uniformed cops know immediately who is or who isn't a detective. It's the same sense that allows enlisted men in the military to know who's an officer, even if they're off the base wearing civvies. Harmon has not yet introduced the girl.

Perhaps he senses Morgan's interest and is protecting his own turf. Or perhaps he's just a male chauvinist pig cop who doesn't think women need to be introduced, especially if they're cops. Sometimes Emma gets sick to death of the whole damn thing.

"Who's your rabbi?" Manzetti asks.

The expression is a holdover from the old days, when somebody had to sponsor you for the blue-and-gold shield, and it didn't hurt to have powerful friends in high places. There were hardly any Jewish cops at that time, so the expression was meant to be ironic—or perhaps anti-Semitic. Back in those days, it was a given that nobody had a shot at rising above the rank of captain unless he was Irish. Nowadays, you could be black and get to be police commissioner. Lucky Irish Emma, who is still a Detective/Second after twelve years on the force.

How long will it take little Chiquita Banana here to get to be captain?

"I'll see you later, huh, Danny?" the girl tells Harmon, but her eyes dance over Morgan, who immediately says, "Have a seat. We'll teach you some detective tricks."

"Detective tricks, huh?" she says, and slides into the booth alongside Manzetti.

"Emma Boyle," Emma says, and extends her hand across the table.

"Tess Ortega," the girl says, and takes Emma's hand.

The other detectives—all except Harmon, who knows her—belatedly introduce themselves. Morgan holds her hand a trifle too long for comfort, so she eases it back with a roll of her eyes, telling him he's coming on too strong here in the company of other cops, so cool it, *amigo*, okay? For now, anyway. Morgan catches the clue, big detective that he is, and backs off. Emma figures if anything's going to happen here between them, it'll be after everybody else at the table goes home. From what she guesses, however, a Homicide cop like Harmon isn't about to relinquish the field to a mere Vice cop from the East Side.

Manzetti's married with three kids. He has no time for, and very little interest in, The Dating Game. While Morgan pours a beer from the pitcher for Tess, and Harmon reaches over to the bar for a bowl of pretzels to offer the girl, Manzetti asks Morgan if he thinks this Thorpe character is really their guy.

294

"On a scale of one to ten?" Morgan says.

"Whatever."

"If he's still here in the city, I'd rate him a solid nine. If he's back in L.A. already, that's another story. Lots of planes left early this morning. He checked out of the Palmer around six-thirty. If he caught any one of those early-morning flights, he'd have been in L.A. by noon or thereabouts."

"So where is he? The cops out there drive by at eight, all the lights are out?"

"Could be out to dinner."

"Unless he's still running on New York time. In which case, he'd be asleep by now."

"*We're* not," Emma says brightly.

"We didn't fly three thousand miles across the continent."

"Listen," Tess says, "am I supposed to be hearing all this?"

"The question is are you supposed to be *listening?*" Morgan says.

"Cause if my being here is gonna jeopardize a case or anything . . ."

"Yes, you're very dangerous to our case," Morgan says.

"You are a very dangerous woman," Harmon says.

"Let's say he's still here," Manzetti says. "In New York."

"Okay."

"Where?"

"This is a rape-murder we're talking about," Morgan explains.

"Really?" Tess says.

"Guy nailed a young hooker on Seventieth Street early this morning," Harmon says. "You familiar with the East Side at all?"

"No," Tess says. "I work over here, and I live in the Bronx."

"There's this massage parlor on Seventy-fourth and Third," Morgan says. "This guy was there last night, caused some trouble. We think he might've gone back after the girl."

"He was after every other girl in the city, why not her?" Harmon says.

"He killed more than one person?" Tess says, her eyes wide.

"No, he made a dozen phone calls is all," Morgan says. "Trying to hook up with somebody."

"Anybody," Harmon says.

"Is that what rapists do?" Tess asks. "Give their victims a phone call first?"

"That's just what bothers me," Emma says.

"Me, too," Manzetti agrees at once.

"What's that?" Morgan asks.

"Rape isn't about sex," Emma says. "It's about power."

"And this guy last night was *all* about sex," Manzetti says, nodding.

"From minute one," Emma says.

"Let me see that list of calls again."

Emma starts digging in her tote. Morgan lifts the pitcher, and pours beer all around. A male cop in uniform wanders over to the jukebox, giving Tess the eye on the way, and drops in some coins. Britney Spears's "Baby One More Time" fills the smoky air. Across the room, some male and female cops in street clothes begin singing along on the "Baby, all I need is time" refrain. Emma finds the printout of phone numbers Thorpe called from his room, and the corresponding list of names and locations Susan Hawkes faxed to her. She unfolds both pages, hands them to Manzetti. He glances only cursorily at the numbers, and then studies the names.

17/21–7:01 PM Ritter-Thorpe Associates
    Los Angeles, California
7/21–7:07 PM American Airlines
    Raleigh, North Carolina
7/21–7:10 PM Benjamin Thorpe
    Los Angeles, California
7/21–7:20 PM Charles Harris
    Princeton, New Jersey
7/21–7:40 PM Heather Epstein
    New York, New York
7/21–7:55 PM Arthur Davies
    New York, New York
7/21–10:30 PM Benjamin Thorpe
    Los Angeles, California
7/21–11:30 PM Heather Epstein
    New York, New York
7/21–11:40 PM B&R Enterprises
    Baltimore, Maryland
7/21–11:57 PM XS Salon
    New York, New York

7/21—4:45 AM Heather Epstein
   New York, New York
7/22—4:48 AM Lois Ford
   New York, New York
7/22—5:33 AM Benjamin Thorpe
   Los Angeles, California

"Okay," Manzetti says, "his office we know, American Airlines we know, his home we know. Who's Charles Harris?"

"His daughter in Princeton," Emma says.

"His daughter's name is *Charles?*" Tess says, and winks at Morgan to let him know she's just kidding. Morgan winks back. Harmon winks, too, to let them know he's in on the joke and is still in the running. Emma is beginning to wish she'd gone straight home to bed, all this winking and blinking.

"Heather Epstein, you already went to see," Manzetti says.

"He has phone sex with her on a regular basis," Morgan explains to Tess.

"But not last night," Emma says.

"No, last night he was out killing a young hooker," Harmon says.

"Who's Arthur Davies?"

"No idea," Emma says.

"Called him around eight."

"Or her. It could be the guy's daughter he was reaching out to."

"Or his wife," Morgan says.

"You married?" Harmon asks Tess.

298

"Not anymore."

"Another call to his own house at ten-thirty, then little Heather again at eleven-thirty . . ."

"Getting desperate around then," Morgan says.

"How do you know?"

"Little Heather told us."

"What's B&R Enterprises in Baltimore?"

"Phone sex line," Morgan says.

"How do you know?"

"Vice sees all, knows all."

"Seriously."

"We have a list."

"Here's the XS Salon," Manzetti says.

"Eleven-fifty-seven."

"The night is young," Harmon says, and winks at Tess.

"Back to the hotel and another call to Heather . . ."

"Who hung up on him," Emma says.

"And then Lois Ford three minutes later."

"Busy, busy fellow," Harmon says.

"Any idea who this Ford girl is?"

"Little Heather's girlfriend," Morgan says. "He wanted to do a three-way with them."

"This is getting entirely too sexy for me," Tess says, trying to look scandalized.

"Here's the final call to the old homestead," Manzetti says.

"Say hello to the wife and kiddies," Morgan says.

"Are *you* married?" Tess asks him.

"Not the last time I looked."

"When was that?"

"When I left the house this morning."

"Where's that?"

"I live downtown. In SoHo."

Tess looks him over. Emma is beginning to wonder which of the two detectives has the edge here. This is like watching animals in the wild, the way they're doing their little mating dance for the pretty little cop in the tailor-made blouse. Morgan feigns disinterest, pours himself another glass of beer.

"Think he could be in Jersey?" Manzetti asks. "With the daughter?"

"He wasn't there when I called. In fact, she was worried something might have happened to him."

"So where the fuck *is* he?" Manzetti says, "Excuse me. If he's here, I mean."

"I know."

"In the city, I mean."

"I know."

"Be two in the morning here by the time the L.A. cops roll by again," Harmon says.

"He could be raping somebody else by then," Morgan says.

"*Killing* somebody else," Harmon says, nodding.

They're trying to impress little Officer Ortega here, Emma realizes, letting her in on the big time world of murder and rape, never mind your traffic violations or domestic disputes. We are big macho detectives here, they are saying. Which one of us would you prefer for the night, Officer? Or how about both?

Manzetti sighs heavily, washing both hands over his face. He gets up, yanks his trouser belt higher on his waist, and then reaches for his glass, and finishes his beer.

"I'm bushed," he says. "Let's pick it up again in the morning, okay?"

"Sure," Emma says.

Pick it up *where?* she wonders.

CHAPTER
TWELVE

She takes a taxi over to the East Side.

The streets are still packed with pedestrians. Hot nights in New York do that. People come out. If every night was a hot night, there'd be no crime in the city of New York. Too many people on the street. On a hot night, even your burglars don't like to carry television sets or microwaves. She wonders if there are any statistics on that. The number of burglaries committed on hot nights. She knows the loonies come out when the moon is full, that's a fact. All kinds of bedbugs come out of the woodwork when there's a full moon.

On Second Avenue, she begins walking downtown.

She doesn't realize she's heading for the scene of the crime until she's approaching the corner where the cleaning woman saw a man assaulting a blonde. She turns the corner. Walks up the street past First Avenue. A couple is sitting on the stoop in front of a building two doors down from where Cathy Frese was murdered. They look at her as she walks past. She stops in front of the alleyway between the sushi joint and the shoe repair shop. She tries to visualize the struggle on the street corner, Benjamin Thorpe, or whoever, dragging Cathy up the street and into the alley, where he strangled her. Tries to imagine his hands around her throat, his hands tightening around her throat until she went limp. Did he rape her before he killed her or afterward?

She keeps looking into the alley for a long while.

The couple on the stoop watch her as she walks past them again. Under the street lamp on the corner, she reaches into her tote for the list of telephone numbers she showed Manzetti earlier. She looks at her watch. It is almost a quarter to one in the morning.

Fuck it, she thinks, a girl was killed.

And dials Lois Ford's number.

The girl lives in a walkup between York Avenue and the East River Drive, just a few doors up from a Department of Sanitation garage. Huge white DSC garbage trucks are parked all up and down the street as Emma turns into it from York. On the Drive, at the end of the street, cars flash by in the early-morning hours, their headlights streaking the black river beyond. There are two private parking garages on the street as well, their entrance maws spilling light onto the sidewalk. But the street beyond, where Lois's red-brick building stands, is dark and forbidding, and there are only two lights burning in its face.

Maybe it's just her line of business, but Emma always feels she's being followed. She knows that only a very small percentage of rapes are committed by guys who jump out of the bushes and hold a knife

303

to your throat, she knows that. Your so-called gentleman rapist—there *are* no gentleman rapists—is the one who climbs in your bedroom window after watching you undress and then tries to persuade you that you're really having a good time with him. "It's too bad we had to meet this way," he'll say. Suggesting that, gee, since you're having multiple orgasms here, we could be on a cruise ship to the Bahamas instead. Maybe one day we could even get married. Maybe I'll come back to see you again next week, would you like that? I know you would cause I can see you're smiling, aren't you?

Women learn to smile.

Stare at any woman for longer than ten seconds, she'll smile at you. This goes back to the Dark Ages, when rape wasn't called rape, it was called courtship. You smiled because you were begging for mercy. Please, sir, I'm a nice girl, I'm smiling. Please don't court me, sir.

Emma hates rapists.

And maybe because she'd put away so many of them, she's fearful of reprisal. Terrified that a gang of them will attack her. The East Side Rapists Association. Get the lady cop who's trying to make things hard for us, no pun intended. She always listens for phantom footsteps behind her. She listens for them now. There was a time in this city when you had to watch your perimeter all the time, day or night. This was maybe five, six years ago. You couldn't get too involved in a conversation you were having, you couldn't get too interested in a store window you were passing. You had to be aware all the time of what was happening in your immediate vicinity. You had to cover your own back. Emma supposes it's a lot better now, but she isn't sure how comfortable she'd feel here in this neighborhood at one o'clock in the morning if she didn't have a thirty-eight in her tote bag.

New York is a city on the make. The males here are predatory, the females receptive. Rapists use the status quo as an excuse. They'll tell you the victim wouldn't have been dressed that way if she wasn't asking for it. They'll tell you they're just like any other guy in this city, cruising the singles bars, reading the signals, reacting to the nightly tits-and-ass show. They'll always tell you the sex was consensual. Always. That's a word they learned when they were twelve, consensual. There's not a victim in the world who didn't give her consent beforehand. The second line out of any rapist's mouth is "It was consensual." The first line is "You've got the wrong man."

There is a dim light burning in the vestibule of Lois's building. Why any young girl would choose to live here where anyone can walk up from the Drive and into a building without a doorman and with fire escapes hanging up and down its face is beyond Emma. She checks the periphery, glancing first toward the Drive where the cars whiz past as if there is no speed limit in this city, and next toward York Avenue, where a pizzeria on the corner is still open. The street is deserted. She climbs the three flat steps to the front entrance door, tries the knob, and is not surprised when it opens to her touch.

The inner door is locked.

She looks for the name Ford in the row of bells set in the jamb to the right of the door, finds one for Ford, L. Going to fool a lot of would-be rapists, that initial for a first name. Going to make them think it's Louis Ford living here, or Lawrence Ford. Great protection for a girl living alone, that first initial. Ford, L., apartment 4C. She presses the white button, grips the knob on the inner door, looks over her shoulder, checking again. She knows how many rapes are committed in dimly lighted vestibules where a woman is fumbling to unlock the inner door. A buzz sounds, startling her. She shoves the door open, closes it behind her, begins climbing a steep flight of steps to the fourth floor. The hallways are dim. She would not live in this building for "all the tea in China," as her father is fond of saying. She is somewhat out of breath when she reaches the fourth-floor landing. She waits for a moment, her hand on the banister, breathing hard, before walking down the hall to 4C. She raps gently on the door; it's one in the morning.

"Who is it?" a voice asks.

The same voice she heard on the phone when she called earlier. Young, Somewhat breathy.

"Detective Boyle," she says.

"Just a minute, please."

She hears tumblers turning. Two locks, small wonder. Hears the bar of a Fox lock being dropped to the floor. Smart girl inside there. The door opens a crack, held by a safety chain, even smarter.

"Let me see your badge, please."

Somebody taught her well.

Emma flashes the tin.

The girl studies it. The chain comes off.

"Come in, please," she says.

This is what would be called a studio apartment if it weren't in a tenement. It is essentially one large room with double-hung windows at only one end of it, a bathroom to the left of the entrance door, a tiny kitchen just past that. There is a sofa-bed against one wall of the room that serves as bedroom, living room, and dining room combined, a television set on a stand opposite it. A small table and two chairs are set against the windows overlooking the street. Emma can see a fire escape beyond the windows. Access here would be like falling off Pier 8. On the street below, she can hear the warning beep-beep-beep of sanitation trucks backing up, maneuvering.

"Sorry to bother you so late at night," she says. The apartment is still, the building is still, she almost feels like whispering. "We're investigating a murder."

"Yes, you told me on the phone. It's Mr Thorpe, isn't it? Isn't that why you're here?"

"Yes," Emma says, surprised.

"Heather called me just after you did. You caught me just as I came in. I was out dancing."

She is still wearing what she wore earlier tonight, a beige cap-sleeve metallic-looking blouse over a brown nylon, cheetah-print skirt, ruffle-flounced at the hem. The skirt is short, the blouse scooped low over abundant breasts. Dark brown, ankle-strapped high-heeled sandals match her brown eyes and the brown hair falling straight and sleek to her shoulders and cut in bangs on her forehead. She is not a pretty girl, but she looks sexy and trendy, with just enough eye shadow, just enough blush, just enough lipstick on her pouty mouth. A rapist will tell you she shouldn't dress this way. He will tell you he's only human. He will tell you she's asking for it. He will tell you it was her fault. The victim's fault. I'm just a normal red-blooded American male, he will tell you. It was her fault. Besides, you've got the wrong man. And also, it was consensual.

"She said you think he may have killed someone."

"Well, we're investigating every possibility," Emma says. "Miss Ford, we have a record of calls . . ."

She is already nodding.

". . . Benjamin Thorpe made from his hotel room . . ."

"Yes," Lois says.

". . . yesterday morning. Our list indicates . . ."

"Yes, he called me."

"At four-forty-eight A.M., is that right?"

"Yes."

"Can you tell me what the call was about?"

"Yes. He wanted to apologize."

Emma looks at her.

"He was crying," Lois says. "He called to apologize for his earlier behavior. He said he was a decent man. He said he didn't want me to get the wrong impression of him. He said he didn't know what Heather told me—he'd called earlier, you see . . ."

"Yes, I know."

"Heather, I mean. While I was there. This was around eleven, eleven-thirty. He was afraid Heather might have given me the wrong impression of him. So he wanted to apologize. He was crying very hard. I've never heard a man cry that hard."

"He didn't ask if he could come here, did he?"

"No, he didn't," Lois says.

She looks somewhat disappointed that he didn't. Now that Emma has mentioned it, she seems to be wondering *why* he didn't.

"Did he say *where* he might be going? When he checked out? Did he say he was going back to California?"

"No, he didn't. I mean, he didn't mention California or anyplace else. He just said he was terribly sorry if he'd offended me in any way, and he wanted to apologize. I told him it was okay. I mean, guys come on that way all the time. You really think he killed someone?"

"He might have," Emma says. She reaches into her tote, takes her wallet from it, pulls a business card from behind her Metrocard. "Here's where you can reach me," she says. "In case he calls back."

"Gee, do you think he might?" Lois asks.

"He may still be in the city, we don't know. I'll give you my home number, too," she says, and writes it on the back of the card. "Call me at any time of the day or night."

"Okay," Lois says, and studies first the printed side of the card, and then the number Emma scrawled on the back of it. "Is this a seven?" she asks. "Eight-one-oh-*seven*?"

"Yes."

"Okay," she says again, and nods, and suddenly looks up. "You don't think I'm in any danger, do you?" she asks.

"I'm sure you're not," Emma says.

But she isn't sure at all.

Harry Davis is not at all happy to see her.

This is one-forty in the morning, their busiest time, he tells her, and he does not need a snoopy female in a grungy suit she's been wearing all day, sniffing around scaring the customers and embarrassing the girls. Emma suggests that the girls might feel a little less embarrassed if she called for a paddy wagon and carted the whole fucking lot of them over to the One-Nine, where she can question them each and separately in the privacy of a detective squadroom, would Harry prefer that?

"Just what is it you're looking for, Miss Boyle?" he asks. The use of the "Miss" form of address is an attempt to diminish her status as a detective. She has had this pulled on her before. It is telling her all over again that she is merely a snoopy female in a grungy suit—God, how those words rankle! Eight hundred dollars at Saks Fifth!

"Mr Davis," she says, "Cindy Mayes tells me she saw Cathy waiting downstairs here when she left at four yesterday morning. We have a witness who saw a man get out of a taxi at that same time, and walk over to where a blonde was standing just outside your front door. I want to know who got out of that cab."

"Was he a black man?"

"No, he was white."

"Then, thank God, he wasn't me," Davis says, and grins.

"Is Cindy still here?"

"She is."

"I'd like to talk to her, please."

"She's busy just now."

"I'll wait."

She waits in Davis's office.

There is a sense of busy-ness outside the closed door to the office, telephones ringing, voices echoing, high heels clicking past. There is a sense of business as well, a crisp energetic commerce of the night, money changing hands, transactions negotiated and executed.

Emma waits.

Like an old Irish woman riding a subway to the Bronx, she sits with her hands resting on top of her tote bag.

Cindy does not come into the office until seven minutes past two. She is wearing a flimsy black wrapper over red bra and panties, a red garter belt, black nylons, black ankle-strapped sandals with stiletto heels. She lights a cigarette, sits opposite Emma, crosses her stockinged legs. She looks superbly whorish and eminently at home, an exceptional slut in a kingdom of ordinary tarts. In her blatant presence, it is Emma who somehow feels dowdy and cheap in her grungy suit—the son of a bitch!

"What is it now?" Cindy asks.

Blows out smoke. Jiggles her foot.

"The Rule of Three," Emma says.

"What the hell's that, the Rule of Three?"

"Leo Gephardt. Always ask the same question three times. If you don't get the answer the first two times, you'll get it the third time around. The Rule of Three."

"Who's Leo Gephardt?"

"Captain I once had. He's dead now."

"Shows how good his rule was."

"Third time around, Cindy. You ready?"

"You know how busy we are out there?"

"Who was she waiting for?"

"Who are we talking about now?"

"Cindy, I'm tired."

"So am I. Did you suck a dozen cocks tonight?"

"No, but you make ten times what I do."

"Is that supposed to be sarcastic?"

"Who was she waiting for?"

"That's the fourth time. And I *still* don't know."

"Why'd she change the lock on her door?"

"I have no idea."

"Who was she afraid of?"

"These are new questions, aren't they?"

"Who are *you* afraid of?"

"Does the Rule of Three start all over again?"

"Cindy, I'm really very *very* tired."

"Then whyn't you go home to sleep? Nice girl like you needs her beauty rest."

"Cindy, in just about thirty seconds, I am going to bust your ass from here to Canarsie."

"I don't think so."

"I think so."

The women look at each other.

"You're impeding the progress of an investigation," Emma says reasonably.

"Not if I really *don't* have the answers you want," Cindy says reasonably.

"A *homicide* investigation, no less."

"But I don't know anything about who killed Cathy."

"It's called Obstructing Governmental Administration," Emma says.

Cindy seems to be thinking it over.

"Section 195.05. A Class-A misdemeanor."

"I've never been arrested in my life."

"You can go to jail for a year."

The room is utterly still. From somewhere in the boundless corridors outside the closed office door, Emma hears someone calling "Time!"

"Who was waiting for her?" she asks softly.

"I don't know."

"Cindy . . ."

"Him, I guess."

"Him? Who's him?"

"The guy who *always* waited for her. Listen, I don't want to get in trouble here."

"*Always* waited for her?"

"I don't know. Maybe not."

"*Always*? Is this a steady boyfriend or something?"

"I don't know what he is. He's just some kind of weirdo, that's all."

"Who? Who is he?"

"I don't know. I only know what she told me."

"What'd she tell you?"

"He fell for the Heidi act."

"What do you mean?"

"Treated her like she was half her age. She's twenty-six years old, she's been around the block a hundred times, he treats her like a teeny-bopper. Meets her after work, walks her home, is afraid something's gonna happen to her, somebody's gonna rape her or something, right? She's twenty-six, for Christ's sake, she's only been hooking forever! Dresses her in little pleated plaid skirts, white cotton panties, the whole fuckin Short Eyes trip. She told me she was sick of it but she didn't know how to get out of it. She was afraid to get out of it. She told me she was thinking of changing the lock on her door. She didn't know *what* to do."

"He had a key to her apartment?"

"Yes."

314

"Told you she was going to change the lock?"

"Yes. She was scared to death of him, but she didn't know how to get out of it."

"When did she tell you all this?"

"Three, four nights ago."

"About the lock . . ."

"Yes."

"About being afraid of him . . ."

"Yes."

"Wanting to end it?"

"Yes."

"But she was waiting for him again this morning."

"I guess. I didn't see him."

"You said she was waiting for him."

"Well, she was waiting for *somebody*. I don't know if it was him."

"Don't change your fucking *story* on me, Cindy!"

"I don't know if it was *him!* I didn't see him!"

"Did you *ever* see him?"

"No."

"Did she ever mention his name?"

"Never."

"And you never met him, is that right?"

"Never."

"Never saw him, is that right?"

"Never," Cindy says again.

The Rule of Three, Emma thinks.

But no cigar this time.

The lights outside the Chelsea brownstone are on a timer. When Emma gets home at two-forty-seven that

Friday morning, all the floods are on, illuminating the twelve broad wide steps that lead to the front door and bathing the street level courtyard in light.

She and Andrew lived in this house together from when he was made a partner in the firm six years ago until shortly before last Christmas when Emma found a wrapped gift labeled to someone named Felicia whom she hadn't known existed until that shocking instant. Emma wonders if she will now lose custody of the house, the way she seems to be losing custody of her own child. Everyone says the woman always gets the house. Maybe not when your husband is a full partner in a law firm that handles divorces for hotshot celebrities and real-estate moguls, neither of which Emma is, or hopes to be. She always felt Andrew was embarrassed by her chosen profession. At dinner parties on the legal circuit, women sporting Vidal Sassoon coiffes and Valentino frocks would ask, "And what do you do, Emma?" I'm a cop, she would say. "Oh, really," they would say, "I've never met a cop before." The Supreme Court judge who handed Jackie over to her mother-in-law had apparently never met a cop before, either.

The house is across the street from a public elementary school, which makes it noisy during the day when the kids are screaming around the playground—but then again, no one was ever here during the day. Except Jackie and her nanny, when she was living here with them. The nanny split the minute Emma filed for divorce. Which might have accounted for the judge's decision to place Jackie in "more constant circumstances," his Solomon-like reasoning being that a string of quote unstable and unreliable baby sitters and temporary nannies did not constitute a stable environment for a child in her formative years unquote. After all, what kind of home life could there be for a two-year-old whose father is a busy legal bomber and whose mother is out chasing rapists day and night?

Emma often wonders if her husband was dallying with the nanny as well, a girl from Sweden who was merely blond and beautiful and buxom and named Ingrid after Ingrid Bergman whom her grandmother once met on a yacht at the seaside resort of Sandhamn, according to a story she reverently repeated over and again while sharing the dinner table with them. Not quite a Nanny from Hell, this girl, except for the covetous glances she beamed in Andrew's direction whenever they tucked little Jackie in for the night. Andrew was bedding everything else in sight, Emma later learned, so why not someone under his own roof? Why not a little tiptoe down the hall while Emma was out "chasing rapists day and night," as the judge actually put it when granting Grandma Sylvia's "order to show cause," as it was called in the trade, to which was attached a petition for permanent and temporary custody of the child, so granted. Why not indeed?

There is a Schlage dead bolt lock on the front door. She unlocks it, lets herself in, and hits the light switch in the entry foyer. An overhead imitation Tiffany globe fills the foyer with color. She used to love

coming home. The house is built on three levels—
well, four if you count the ground floor which is
entered from a door off the courtyard and which leads
to the kitchen and pantry and a little garden in the
back. The entry level is on the floor containing what
Andrew used to call "the public rooms," a rather
large living room fronting the street, and a smaller
dining room and serving area toward the back of the
house. There is actually a working dumb waiter in the
house, coming up from the kitchen to the serving area.
Emma's father thinks the dumb waiter is a very classy
touch.

The third level consists of the master bedroom,
Jackie's bedroom, and an adjacent room for the
nanny, when there was a nanny. The very top floor
of the house has a skylighted room Andrew used as a
home office when he was living here. Emma never
goes up there anymore.

The red light on the bedside answering machine is
blinking. She walks to it, sits on the edge of the bed,
hits the button that switches from the time . . .

2:51 AM . . .

. . . to the number of calls . . .

3.

She hits the PLAY button.

"Emma, where are you?"

Her father's voice.

"This is Dad . . ."

No kidding.

"I've been trying to reach you all day long. This
is unusual even for you, Emma. Are you all right?

318

Give me a call no matter what time, I'm worried half to death."

The little Japanese lady inside the machine announces the time of the call as "Thursday, eleven-thirty P.M."

"Em, this is Andrew, it's a quarter to twelve. I asked my mother about this weekend, and she said she didn't think it would be a good idea. Incidentally, if you're wondering why the judge granted her motion, maybe it's because it's almost midnight and you still aren't home. Think about it."

You prick, she thinks.

"Thursday, eleven-forty-seven," the Japanese lady says.

"Emma, this is Tony. The report from the night dispatcher was waiting here at the office when I checked in before going home. It's a quarter past one, I'll be here another ten minutes if you get home by then or you can call me at home at the number I gave you yesterday morning—Jesus, is the case already that old? Incidentally, you ought to get a new phone company. I tried your cell-phone number three times and kept getting a dead zone. Call me."

The recorded voice tells Emma that Manzettti called at one-seventeen A.M. on Friday morning.

"End of messages," the voice says.

Emma hits the rewind button.

She searches in her notebook for the card Manzetti gave her yesterday morning . . .

Yes, Virginia, the case *is* that old already.

. . . finds his home number where he wrote it on the back of the card, and dials it. The phone rings once, twice, three times . . .

"Manzetti," his voice says.

"Tony, it's me."

"Hey, hi. Just a minute, let me find my notes."

She waits. Beyond the bedroom windows, she can see an early morning fog swirling into the garden. Just like yesterday when they found the dead girl in that alleyway. Tendrils of gray curling and twisting among the leaves of the fruit trees already losing their bloom.

"Emma?"

"Yes."

"ARS is the name of the fleet," he says. "The trip originated at Broadway and West Third, all the way downtown. Pickup was at three-forty-five A.M. yesterday morning, drop off on Seventy-fourth and Third at four-oh-seven."

"Sounds about right, that hour of the morning."

"Doesn't help us, though, until we find somebody to parade. How're you making out?"

"I went to see the Ford girl after I left you . . ."

"Oh?"

"Yeah. She told me the reason Thorpe called her in the middle of the night was to apologize. Does that sound like somebody who'd just *killed* a girl?"

"Why not? Who knows with these guys? What time is it out there, anyway?"

"L.A.?" Emma looks at the LED on her answering machine. "Almost midnight," she says.

"I'm gonna give the L.A.P.D. another call. Ask them to run by his house again."

"I also talked to a girl named Cindy Mayes. She works up at the salon, says Cathy was involved with some guy who digs little girls."

"What do you mean involved?"

"In a bad relationship with him."

"The changed lock," Manzetti says at once.

"Could be, don't you think?"

"Likes little girls, huh?"

"Dressed her up like a school kid."

"That explains the cotton panties and starched white blouses."

"All the other kiddie clothes, too."

"Does she know who this guy is?"

"She isn't saying."

"But does she *know?*"

"Maybe."

"Doesn't much sound like Thorpe anymore, does it?"

"Still be nice to know where he is. Let me know what L.A. has to say. I'll be up a while."

"Yeah, me too," he says. "Talk to you," and hangs up.

The moment Emma gets another dial tone, she dials her father's number. His answering machine picks up after the fourth ring.

"Hello, this is Bryan Boyle, please leave a message of any length at the beep."

She tells him she called at five past three, and hangs up.

Now it's her turn to worry about him.

The upstairs bedroom is so located that none of the adjacent brownstones can look down into it. Neither is there any danger of anyone standing below and peering up into the windows; an eight-foot high wooden fence encloses the garden. Tonight, the fog seems to add an additional layer of security. It is as if a gray curtain has been drawn outside, offering further privacy and seclusion. And yet, standing at the French windows, looking down at the tendrils of haze that drift among the blooming azaleas and laurel, watching the mist as it rises past the purple lilacs bordering the fence, Emma imagines a figure darting across the yard in the shifting fog, a watcher outside, peering up at her, a rapist. She draws the drapes.

Slipping out of her shoes, she takes off her jacket and carries it to the closet where there's a bag for dry cleaning. Women with good legs take off their skirts before their blouses; she learned this in a course on behavioral patterns at John Jay College. So she guesses she must think she has good legs because she drops the linen skirt and then puts it into the same dry cleaning bag. Or maybe her legs are really lousy — no, they're not — but maybe they are, and it's just more convenient this way. As flat-footed as a ballerina, she stamps across the bedroom and into the bath-room, where the hamper for laundry is standing against the wall alongside the scale. She unbuttons her blouse, unclasps her bra, steps out of pantyhose and

322

panties, drops all the clothing into the hamper, closes the lid—

What was that?

She is suddenly alert.

Was that a sound she heard downstairs?

She steps tentatively out of the bathroom.

"Hello?" she says.

Grabs a robe from the hook on the bathroom door, slips into it, belts it at the waist, stands stock still, silently listening. Her tote bag is across the room, on the bed.

"Hello?" she calls again.

Silence.

She listens, listens . . .

The sound of the doorbell is ear-shattering.

She is across the room to the bed in three single bounds, her hand dipping into the tote, closing around the butt of the .38 in its clamshell holster, a spring-assisted draw easing the piece into her hand. She whirls from the bed, pads swiftly across the room, hesitates only a moment, listening again, and then starts down the stairs to the entry level, her gun hand leading her.

"Who's there?" she shouts.

"For Christ's sake, Emma . . ."

What?

". . . open the goddamn door!"

She lowers the gun.

"Dad?" she says.

And feels suddenly like a horse's ass.

* * *

Her father is wearing a rumpled seersucker suit over what she guesses is a yellow cotton T-shirt from Gap and soft white leather loafers from Gucci. No socks. His thinning white hair is combed with no attempt to disguise encroaching baldness. His pate and his face are sunburned a fiery red from the two weeks he just spent on Block Island with the woman he calls his "significant other," a Jewish lady named Myra Rifkin, who teaches Documentary Film Making at NYU, where he himself teaches Contemporary English Literature. Bryan Cameron Boyle has bright blue eyes he personally refers to as "twinkling" but which do not appear particularly twinkly at the moment.

"Where the hell have you been?" he asks.

"Dad," she says, "I'm a cop."

"Oh, is that a fact?" he says. "Ask me in."

"Come in," she says.

"I didn't get you out of bed, did I?" he asks.

"Almost," she says.

"Didn't you get my message?"

"I called you back."

"Must've been on my way."

"I'm not twelve, Dad."

"Oh, is that a fact, too?" he asks.

She should be flattered—she knows he was concerned about her—but somehow she's annoyed. She's been a cop for twelve years now, she can drop a cheap thief in his tracks at fifty paces from a dead draw, but here's her father worrying about her because she's not asleep in her own bed by midnight.

"I worry," he says, as if reading her mind.

"Worry about Myra," she says, and is immediately sorry.

"I do," he answers. "Are you going to offer me a drink?"

"Sure," she says.

They walk through the entrance hall into what Andrew used to call "the parlor," the large living room with its bay windows fronting the street. Emma is wearing the bulky terry cloth robe she bought the summer she and Andrew rented the house on Fire Island. That was before Jackie was born. That was before Andrew began playing around. As she lowers the shades, she thinks again that she sees a figure outside in the shifting fog, and then the image is gone, and the shades are down, and there is nothing to fear anymore. Besides, her revolver is now on the small round table in front of the bay windows. There is a lamp on the table, which she now turns on, and a lace doily under the lamp, and then the snub-nosed .38 sitting on the doily. She knows what her father drinks. She goes to the cabinet opposite the fireplace, takes from it a bottle of Tullamore Dew and pours a hefty shot of the whiskey into a Manhattan glass.

"Nothing for you?" he asks.

"I'll be working early."

"Always the job," he says.

"You sound like Andrew."

"Perish the thought. Cheers."

"Cheers, Dad."

The room is suddenly silent. Outside in the fog, she hears a car passing. She does not know what to say to her father. She watches him standing in front of the fireplace, sipping his whiskey.

"We had a suspect who was an extra on *Saving Private Ryan* and *The Sixth Sense*," she says.

"Did you now?"

Sounding very Irish. She hates when he sounds Irish. He does it mostly for his students, so they'll think he's Barry Fitzgerald. Or for Myra, so she'll think he's a hopeless old romantic, which she often calls him to his face. A hopeless old romantic. As if that's supposed to endear someone to a man.

"Briefly," she says.

"Pardon?"

"The suspect. The extra."

"Oh."

"He was only a suspect for a little while."

"You mean he was a suspect for only a little while, don't you?" he says.

"If you say so, Dad."

"Grammar is grammar," he says. And then, to take the edge off his reproach, he adds, "Just between you and I, anyway."

She pretends not to get it.

He shrugs. He knows she got it because it's a long-standing joke between them. Her patrol captain at the Three-Two used to say "Just between you and I, there's no shittier job than policing," avoiding the correct "you and me" as hopelessly lower-class while stepping into shit an instant later.

Emma wishes she could like or even admire Myra Rifkin, but the fact is her father met the woman only six months after he and Emma's mother separated, and began living together six months after that, which remarkable coincidence—just between you and I—seems a bit far-fetched to Emma, hmm? She fully realizes that it was her mother who wanted the divorce, for reasons known only to herself, and which she has never chosen to share with Emma, but this does not excuse her father's haste, in Emma's eyes at least, in choosing another partner before the funeral meats were cold upon the table, to coin a phrase— not for nothing is Emma the daughter of an academic. Her father is sixty-two years old, and Myra is fifty-eight, but she dresses like thirty, with flirty little velvet hats she picks up in Greenwich Village thrift shops and paisley granny skirts and L.L. Bean boots, Jesus! A Too-Late Hippie, Morgan would call her. A *Far* Too-Late Hippie. I have to call him, Emma thinks. Tell him what I learned from Lois Ford. Tell him our prime suspect called her to apologize, does that sound like a man who'd just used his bare hands to tear hair from his victim's head? Fill him in on what Cindy said, too. Morgan likes to stay abreast. Morgan gets upset if she acts like a lone wolf. Which she supposes she is nowadays.

"A penny," her father says.

"It would bore you," she says.

"Try me."

"I'm tired, Dad."

"Is that a hint for me to be on my way?"

"If you like. You're welcome to stay."

"Here's your hat, what's your hurry," he says, and drains the glass and puts it onto the doily alongside Emma's pistol. He looks down at the gun. Everything he feels about her profession fleetingly crosses his face as he looks at the gun. He barely restrains a sigh. "Well, be careful," he says, and is starting for the door, when he stops, and turns, and says out of the blue, "I'm a person, too, Emma," and then merely nods and goes out of the room, and out of the house, and into the fog.

She dead-bolts the door behind him.

Stands in the entrance foyer under the imitation Tiffany globe for several moments, and then turns out the light and goes upstairs to the bedroom. The LED display on her answering machine reads 3:44 A.M. She pulls back the sheet on the bed, climbs in, and turns out the bedside lamp.

CHAPTER
THIRTEEN

She is dead asleep when the telephone rings.

She looks at the luminous dial of the bedside clock. It is almost four A.M. She picks up the receiver.

"Hello?" she says.

"Lois?"

"Yes?"

"This is Ben," he says.

"Ben?"

"Benjamin Thorpe."

"Oh."

"How are you, Lois?"

"Fine. Wh . . . what do you want? Why are you calling me?"

"Just to see how you are."

"It's three o'clock in the morning."

"I know."

"Are you in Los Angeles?"

"No. I'm still here in New York."

"She said you might have gone back to Los Angeles."

"Who? Heather?"

"No, the detective. The one who was here."

"A detective came to see you?"

"Said you *might* have gone back to Los Angeles. Detective Boyle!

"No, I'm here."

She hesitates. Takes a breath. Go ahead, ask him, she thinks.

"Did you kill somebody, Ben?"

"No. What? Did I *what*?"

"Tell me the truth, Ben."

"Who said I killed somebody?"

"She did. Well, might have. She said you *might* have killed somebody."

"No. Of course not. No. That's ridiculous."

"I didn't think so. The way you were crying on the phone last night. You sound a lot better now."

"I am a lot better."

"So where are you?"

"I told you. I'm still in New York."

"They're looking for you, you know."

"Do they really think I killed somebody?"

"A young girl."

"No."

"A prostitute. They think you went to a prostitute last night. After you called Heather."

"Why would I do that?"

"Gee, I don't know," she says broadly. "Why do men go to prostitutes?"

"I don't know any prostitutes. I've never been to a prostitute in my life."

"Oh, I'll bet."

"Never."

330

"Is that why you call Heather all the time? Cause you don't know any prostitutes to call?"

"She's a friend."

"She told me you call her all the time."

"Just sometimes."

"Did you really want to come see us last night?"

"Yes."

"She told me you wanted to come see us."

"I did."

"Both of us, she said."

"That's right."

"It broke my heart, you know. The way you were crying. You didn't have to feel so bad, you know. *I* wasn't the one who turned you down, you didn't have to call *me* to apologize. I mean, it was nice of you and all, but I wasn't offended, really. That's a common fallacy, you know. That a girl gets insulted because a man expresses desire for her. If you want my opinion, only *ugly* girls get insulted. A good-looking girl is flattered by an expression of interest, truly."

"Are you a good-looking girl, Lois?"

"Well, I don't know about that."

"Well, you must know if you're good-looking."

"I don't want to sound conceited."

"What do you look like?"

"I think I'm an attractive woman."

"Are you?"

"I think so."

"Describe yourself."

"That's hard to do. Objectively, I mean."

"Do it subjectively then."

"I don't think I can do that."

"Sure you can. How tall are you, for example?"

"Five-six."

"How much do you weigh?"

"A hundred-and-twenty, but I'd *really* like to lose a few pounds."

"A hundred-and-twenty is a good weight. For five-six, that's a good weight."

"A hundred-and-fifteen would be better, believe me."

"Maybe, but a hundred-and-twenty isn't fat, Lois."

"I'd like to lose five or six pounds."

"Do you think of yourself as fat?"

"Well, not exactly *fat*. But . . ."

"Are you full-figured, is that it?"

"No. No, I wouldn't say full-figured. No. But I could stand to lose a few pounds."

"For example, what are your dimensions, Lois?"

"I really don't know. Only models know their dimensions. I don't know any real girls who know their dimensions."

"Well, for example, what size bra do you wear, for example?"

"I'm a thirty-four B."

"And your panties, for example?"

"Five. I wear a size five panty."

"That's not fat, Lois, I'm sorry."

"I didn't say I was *fat*, per se. I'd just like to lose five or six pounds."

"What color hair do you have, Lois?"

"Brown. I have long brown hair, bangs on my forehead."

"Brown hair and bangs, huh?"

"I hear that one all the time," she says. "What color is *your* hair?" she asks.

"Brown. Well, brownish-black. Dark hair. I have dark hair."

"What do you look like? Tell me what you look like, Ben."

"I'm just your average red-blooded American male."

"I'll bet. Calling young girls in the middle of the night."

"How old are you, anyway, Lois?"

"Twenty. I was twenty in April. How old are you?"

"Too old for twenty, that's for sure."

"Come on, tell me. I've dated older men."

"Have you?"

"Sure. Married men, too. It's impossible to live in this city without getting to know an older married man sooner or later."

"Well, I'm in my forties, let's leave it at that."

"Late forties or early forties?"

"Late."

"Brown hair and bangs," she says, and giggles. "I hear that one all the time."

On the table beside the bed, the electric clock is humming. She has set it for seven A.M. because her computer class starts at nine and she has to go all the way to Brooklyn. The clock now reads four-ten, and

333

she is wide awake. She can hear the DSC trucks maneuvering on the street below. She can hear the rush of traffic on the East River Drive. She can hear Benjamin Thorpe breathing on the other end of the line.

"I'm really sorry Heather wouldn't let us meet last night," he says. "I'm enjoying talking to you."

"Well, Heather's very protective of her turf, you know."

"I didn't realize that about her."

"Oh, sure. Her possessions, too. She once loaned me a pair of earrings—we were going out that night, and I forgot to put on earrings? You'd have thought they were the sacred crown jewels, the way she kept reminding me to return them."

"Are you wearing earrings now, Lois?"

"No. Earrings? I'm in *bed*."

"I didn't know that."

"Nobody wears earrings to bed."

"I didn't realize you were in bed."

"It's four in the morning. Four-fifteen already, in fact."

"I'm sorry if I woke you."

"Stop being so sorry all the time, Ben. You don't have to apologize for everything you do, you know. It's four in the morning, so what?"

"Four-fifteen."

"Right. So what?"

She can hear his breathing.

"What color are your eyes?" she asks.

"Brown."

"Are you tall?"

"I consider myself tall."

"How tall is considering yourself tall?"

"Five-eleven."

"That's a good height, five-eleven."

"I'm comfortable with it."

She hesitates a moment, and then says, "I told her it might have been fun."

"I'm sorry? Told . . .?"

"Heather. You coming over. I told her it might have been fun."

"I think it might have."

"I think she didn't want to share you, is what it was."

"Like the earrings."

"Well, not exactly like the earrings, no."

"Come to think of it," he says, "I guess I don't know any women who wear earrings to bed."

"Unless they forget to take them off," she says. "That happens sometimes."

"Yes, but usually . . ."

"Usually a woman will *not* wear earrings to bed, that's definitely correct."

"What do you usually wear to bed, Lois?"

"Well, that depends."

"On what?"

"On the time of year, I guess. During the winter, I usually wear a flannel nightgown. In the summertime . . ."

"How about tonight, for example? What are you wearing tonight?"

"Now?"

"Right now, for example. What do you have on right this minute, Lois?"

She hesitates.

"Lois?" he says. "What are you wearing?"

"A short nightgown and matching panties," she says.

"What color?"

"Blue. I like blue."

"A kind of baby doll nightgown?"

"Not that short."

"How short?"

"Above the knee. But not as short as a baby doll."

"Does it have lace on it?"

"No, it's just this sheer nylon. Blue."

"Are the panties sheer, too?"

"Well, yes."

"Very sheer?"

"Yes."

"Can you see yourself through the panties?"

"I guess I could. If the light was on."

Her heart is suddenly beating very rapidly.

"Ben?" she says. "You didn't really kill someone, did you?"

"I have never killed anyone, ever, in my entire lifetime," he says. "I promise you. Even during the war, I did not kill anyone."

"How do I know you're not lying to me?"

"I'm telling you the truth, Lois. I spent the entire war in Saigon. I never killed anyone. Not then, not now."

336

"Did you go to bed with prostitutes? In Saigon?"

"Yes. In Saigon."

"You told me before that you'd never been to bed with a prostitute."

"I was lying."

"So how do I know you're not lying now? Because this was a prostitute who got killed, you know."

"Yes, but it wasn't me who killed her."

"Are you telling me the truth now?"

"I swear on my grandmother's eyes."

"Because I have to be able to trust you, you know."

"You can trust me."

"Tell me a secret," she says. She is whispering now. She realizes all at once that she is whispering. "If you want me to trust you."

"I have no secrets."

"Then how can I trust you?"

"Trust me, Lois."

"Tell me what you're wearing," she whispers.

"Just a white T-shirt and slacks."

"What color slacks?"

"Blue."

"Like my nightgown and panties."

"Yes."

"Are you wearing shoes and socks?"

"No. I'm lying in bed."

"Are the lights on?"

"Just a lamp by the bed. Are the lights on there?" he asks.

"No, I'm lying here in the dark."

"Are you covered with a blanket or anything?"

"On a night like this?"

"Or a sheet?"

"No, I'm just lying here."

"Do you have air-conditioning?"

"No."

"Are the windows open?"

"One of them."

"I can hear sirens."

"This city."

They both fall silent, listening to the sirens.

"Ambulance," he says.

"Or police."

"They have a different sound."

"Maybe it's the police coming to get you," she says.

"How? They don't know where I am."

"They'll find you."

"So what? I didn't do anything."

"I hope not."

"I promise. Is it very warm there?"

"Sort of."

"Lois?"

"Yes, Ben?"

"Why don't you take off the nightgown? If you're warm, I mean."

"I'm not too warm."

"Night like tonight," he says.

"I'm really not . . ."

"Hot night like tonight."

338

"Well."

"Take it off, Lois."

"Well."

"Go ahead."

"All right."

She puts down the phone, pulls the nightgown over her head, tosses it to the foot of the bed. She lies back against the pillows again, puts the phone to her ear.

"Okay," she says, "it's off."

"What do you look like?"

"I can't see myself. It's dark."

"Turn on a light."

"Okay."

She reaches for the bedside lamp, finds the switch, turns it on. A warm glow suffuses the bed.

"Okay," she says.

"How do you look?"

"Fine."

"Tell me."

"Tell you what?"

"How you look. Describe yourself."

"I'm this raving beauty," she says, and giggles.

"Describe your breasts, for example."

She takes a deep breath.

"You know," she says, "Heather told me what you do with her."

"Did she?"

"Um-huh. What you do on the phone."

"She shouldn't have told you that."

"But she did."

"That was very naughty of her."

"But she told me."

"Telling you our secrets that way."

They are both whispering again.

"Did it excite you?" he asks.

"Sort of."

"Her telling you what she does with me on the phone?"

"Sort of."

"Have you ever done that with anyone on the phone?"

"No."

"Why don't you take off your panties, Lois?"

"Is that what you ask Heather to do?"

"Yes."

"Does Heather take off her panties for you?"

"All the time."

"Will you call me from Los Angeles when you get back there? Make me take my panties off, too?"

"Take them off now, Lois."

"Will you call me from Los Angeles? The way you call Heather?"

"All the time."

"Order me to take my panties off?"

"Yes. Take them off, Lois. Now."

She catches her breath.

"I have to put down the phone," she says.

"I'll wait."

"Stay there," she says.

"I'm waiting, Lois."

She puts down the receiver, hooks the waistband of her panties in both thumbs, slides them down over her narrow hips, raises her buttocks, pulls the panties down over her thighs and her knees, kicks them off her ankles and her feet. She lies back again, picks up the phone.

"They're off," she whispers.

The watch Emma wears is a thirty-nine-dollar Timex with a shiny black case and a black plastic strap and a dial that lights up blue when she pushes in the winding stem. She hits the stem now, the moment the telephone rings. It is exactly four minutes to five. In the dark, she picks up the receiver.

"Boyle," she says.

"It's me," Manzetti says. "Are you asleep?"

"Well, yes, I was."

"Sorry. I just heard from the L.A.P.D. They rode by Thorpe's house again, there's still nobody home. It's already two in the morning out there, where the hell is he?"

"Maybe he's still here," Emma says.

"Maybe that's why I can't sleep," Manzetti says.

The telephone rings again a few moments later. Her watch reads five-oh-one A.M.

"Hello?" she says.

Someone is sobbing on the other end of the line.

"Hello?" she says again.

"Detective Boyle?" a girl's voice says.

"Yes, who's this?"

"Lois."

"What's wrong, Lois?" she asks at once.

"I'm so ashamed," Lois says.

"What is it? Tell me."

"I'm so ashamed."

"Tell me what happened," Emma says.

This is what you say to rape victims. Tell me what happened. They want to tell you what happened, but at the same time they are ashamed of what happened, feel that they themselves are somehow responsible for what happened. Was my skirt too short, my heels too high, my blouse too low cut? Was I showing too much leg, breast, ass? Was my lipstick too bright? Did I look like a slut? Technically, Lois Ford is not a rape victim. But as she tells Emma what Benjamin Thorpe made her do on the telephone . . .

"Was he calling from Los Angeles?" Emma asks.

"No, New York. He's here in New York."

. . . as she reports in detail the conversation she had with him, a conversation that had started at approximately four A.M. and ended almost forty-five minutes later . . .

Emma looks at her watch.

It is now five-oh-eight.

"Yes, tell me," she says.

As Lois recites what happened, it becomes clear that she was every bit a rape victim as a woman dragged into the bushes and threatened with a knife. She'd been helpless in the hands of a gentleman rapist on the other end of the line, a friendly persuader, an experienced seducer who had done this

342

many times before and who would do it again and again so long as there were women out there to be had for the plucking. Technically or not, Lois Ford had for damn sure been raped.

"How do you know he wasn't calling from L.A.?" Emma asks.

"He said he was in New York."

"Said he was Benjamin Thorpe?"

"Yes."

"Said he was calling from New York?"

"Yes."

"Did he say from where in New York?"

"No."

"Did you ask him?"

"No."

"Is your phone number listed in the directory?"

"Yes. But not my first name. Just an L."

"Do you have caller ID?"

"No."

"What time did he call, Lois?"

"Around four."

"And what time did the call end?"

"Just before I called you."

"Five, ten minutes ago?"

"Yes."

"You're sure it wasn't longer ago than that?"

"I'm sure."

"It wasn't longer ago than a half-hour, was it?"

"No."

"You're positive?'

"Positive."

"All right, then, listen to me carefully. This is what I want you to do."

She calls Morgan and asks him to meet her for breakfast at a diner on Canal Street, convenient to both the Chelsea brownstone and his apartment in SoHo. The streets are still heavy with fog when he arrives at six-thirty in the morning.

"You'd think it was fuckin London," he says.

He is wearing jeans and a lemon-colored cotton sweater. Loafers without socks. Emma has thrown on a green cotton skirt and matching T. She is barelegged and wearing darker green slides with a low heel. They look as if they're both dressed for a day in the Hamptons, but officially, they're not on the job yet. They are just two off-duty cops meeting for breakfast.

"I was up half the night . . .," he says.

"Me, too."

". . . tryin'a dope this thing out. It's a bitch, ain't it?"

"It is," Emma agrees.

"So what's all this you have to tell me?" he asks.

He is eating blueberry pancakes. He slices them with his fork, lifts little triangles dripping syrup to his mouth. He hasn't yet shaved this morning; there is a faint beard stubble on his chin and his jowls.

"Thorpe called Lois Ford," she says.

"You're kidding me!"

"He's in New York, Jimmy. He told her he's in New York."

"Where? Jesus, does she know *where*?"

344

"No. He called for phone sex . . ."

Jimmy is nodding.

"Led her down the garden . . ."

"Naturally, these guys," he says, still nodding.

"I asked her to hit Star 69. I figured if Thorpe got horny, maybe he also got reckless. What you do, you hit the star key on your phone and then the six and the nine . . ."

"I know."

". . . and you get the number of the last person who called. You have to do it within a half-hour after the person hangs up. But it won't work if the caller has a block on his line."

"I know. Zippo," Morgan says, and nods again.

"Zippo," Emma says. "Thorpe called from a blocked phone. But there's something else, Jimmy. This is what's driving me nuts."

He is lifting a wedge of pancake to his mouth. He waits, the fork poised.

"Cathy had a boyfriend."

"What!"

"Some guy who thought she was *really* Heidi."

"What do you mean?"

"Dressed her like a little girl."

"Who told you this?"

"Cindy. "

"You made contact again, huh?"

"Don't get sore. I would've called you, but . . ."

"No, that's okay."

"It was late, Jimmy. I went up there two in the morning."

345

"Up where?"

"The XS."

"Busy at that time, I'll bet."

"Very. She told me this guy waited outside for Cathy after work each night."

"Did she say who?"

"Never met him."

"Did she get a look at him?"

"No. But it can't be Thorpe. He only got here Wednesday."

"Be too much to hope for, anyway."

"Never met him. Never saw him. So she says."

"You think she's lying?"

"I think she's frightened. He's the reason Cathy changed the lock on her door."

"Then he's the one who broke in this afternoon! Shit, Emma, let's go up the XS right this minute!"

"She's long gone, Jimmy."

"See if anybody *else* up there knows this guy. Jesus, all at once this is coming together!"

"You think?"

"Well, don't you? This is a real lead, Emma, this really gives us something to work with! We find this guy, we wrap it!" He gulps down coffee, wipes his mouth and his chin with a napkin. "Here's what I think," he says.

"Let me hear."

"I think we should go back to the XS, see if Cathy's boyfriend actually exists."

"Okay."

346

"See if anybody up there actually ever *saw* the guy."

"Okay."

"What do you say?"

"I say good."

"You wanna go back up there?"

"Yes."

"Ask some questions?"

"Yes."

"Try to zero in on this creep?"

"Yes."

"*Nail* the son of a bitch?"

"Yes," she says, and nods. "Yes, I do."

They sit there grinning at each other. For the first time since yesterday morning, she feels they're really working together.

"But not now," she says. "Nobody'll be there right now."

He looks at his watch.

"They don't come in till ten," she says.

"Okay, I'll meet you there at ten." He picks up the check, looks at it. "You want to split this or what?" he asks.

"Of course," she says, and reaches into her bag for her wallet.

"Three bucks enough for the tip?" he asks, and shows her the bill. There is suddenly a look of such boyish uncertainty on his face that she wants to hug him.

"Three bucks is fine," she says.

*   *   *

On Emma's cheap Timex, it is ten minutes to eight when she gets to Cathy Frese's building on Lexington Avenue. The fog is still thick, the city seems insulated in gray. Tenants are coming out of the building, into the fog, heading off to work. As Emma climbs to the second floor, tenants coming down the stairs glance curiously at the yellow tapes and the policeman standing outside the door to apartment 22.

She shows the officer her shield and her ID card, tells him she's investigating the murder of the girl who lived here, and asks him to unlock the Medeco for her, please. The officer has just relieved the Graveyard Shift, and this is his first day at the crime scene, so he's not sure whether it's okay to let her in or not. Emma advises him to check with his patrol sergeant, and waits while he steps away from her to phone in. A short stout woman comes lumbering up the steps. She is wearing a gray skirt, a red T-shirt, and black clogs.

"Ah, good," she says when she sees Emma.

The accent is Polish or Hungarian, Yugoslavian perhaps, Middle European certainly. Her face is broad and lined. Out of breath after her climb, she places her hands on ample hips and says, "Forgive, please. You want cleaning?"

"Sorry?" Emma says.

"I super," the woman says. "What to do with dry cleaning?"

Emma still doesn't understand.

"Miss Cathy dry cleaning. You want take? I bring?"

348

"Oh. Yes. Sure. Bring it up."

The woman nods and turns away, unhappily surveying the steps down. She is heading below again when the patrolman returns.

"I'm sorry, Detective," he says. "I had to check."

"That's okay," Emma says.

He inserts the key in the Medeco, twists it, snaps the lock open, removes it from the hasp.

"You be all right in there alone?" he asks.

"I'll be all right," Emma assures him, and goes into the apartment. She does not know quite why she came back here, or exactly what she's looking for. The apartment is still. The fog lurks outside the single window in the room, swirls in eddies in the brick shaftway that offers no light on this gloomy morning. She snaps on an overhead bulb covered with a Japanese lantern. There is scarce improvement.

Mind the vic, she thinks. Find the vic.

Find the vic in the clutter of clothing still here on the open sofa-bed, exactly where it was last night when they came here for the first time. Find the vic in the little-girl socks and blouses and panties and shoes and, yes, even the string Forever bracelet. Emma owned a Forever bracelet when she was twelve, wore it day and night, never took it off till it rotted on her wrist.

Or find the vic in the sexy undergarments Cathy Frese might have wished to wear to her place of business, the way Emma sometimes wishes to wear to work something other than the strictly practical outfits the job demands, garter belt and seamed black stockings under a long black skirt, perhaps — surprise, Captain! Wear what the other girls at the XS wore, Cindy in her blatant threads looking like a hooker auditioning for the role of hooker, Julia Roberts pretending she fucks for money, Richard Gere pretending she's a street walker and not a movie star, must be difficult to tell the difference, huh?

Never mind the little white baby doll nightie draped on the body of a twenty-six-year-old woman trying to look thirteen, the shaved pubic area, the tiny breasts and wide innocent eyes, pick me, sir, won't you please pick me? Too bad about the gold tooth in the corner of her mouth. The gold tooth gave away the game. The gold tooth flashed I-Am-a-Whore to the night. The gold tooth signaled wisdom and worldliness, I have been here, I have done this, I am not a naïf in Candyland.

Find the vic, Emma thinks, and tries to remember what it was like to wear a Forever bracelet.

What it had meant to her, if anything.

She cannot for the life of her recall that twelve-year-old girl.

"Missis?"

She turns toward the door.

The super is standing there, holding in her right hand a bluish-green garment on a wire hanger covered with plastic wrap.

"Where to put?" she asks.

"I'll take it," Emma says.

"Comes back yesterday," the super says, and shrugs and hands it to Emma.

350

Emma moves around the sofa-bed . . .
Carries the garment to the closet . . .
Hangs it on the rod . . .
Glances idly through the plastic . . .
Sees a flash of . . .
Gold?
Gold embroidery, is it?
Gold and red embroidery?
And leans in closer to the hanging garment.
"Oh dear God," she says.

CHAPTER
FOURTEEN

When he answers the door to his loft, Morgan is wearing the same jeans and yellow cotton sweater he wore to breakfast not three hours ago. He seems mildly surprised to find Manzetti and Emma on his doorstep, but he grins amiably and says, "Hey, I was just about to come meet you."

Emma is carrying a blue, drawstring canvas bag with the words NYPD and EVIDENCE stenciled on it in white. There is a CHAIN OF CUSTODY tag hanging on the bag, with spaces for signatures acknowledging transfer from one person or entity to another, but so far the only one who's signed for possession is Emma herself. Morgan most certainly recognizes this type of bag, and the tag attached to it, but he makes no comment, asks instead if anyone would like coffee.

"Not me," Manzetti says.

"Thanks, no," Emma says.

She is glancing around the place. The loft is in one of those unrenovated buildings that still exist down here in SoHo, a huge space that is sparsely furnished and spotlessly clean. It is already a quarter past nine but the morning fog still hasn't cleared. It presses now against the kitchen windows, where a small round breakfast table and three chairs rest in an angled nook. Morgan catches Emma's eye, beams at her, says, "Nice, huh? My daughter's coming tomorrow, I spruced it up." Framed photographs of a young girl at various ages line the walls of the entire space, including some recent ones that show a plain-looking girl of twelve or thirteen, with long stringy blond hair and pale vacant eyes. "That's Fiona," he says proudly. "Beautiful, huh?" and beams again at Emma.

Emma yanks open the top of the canvas bag, reaches into it, and takes from it a pleated plaid skirt and a blue blazer.

Sewn to the breast pocket of the blazer is a patch embroidered in red and gold.

The patch reads ST MARY'S ON THE MOUNT.

"It's your daughter's," she says. "Her name tag is in it."

Morgan says nothing.

"Cathy Frese sent it out for dry-cleaning. It came back yesterday."

"Uh-huh," he says.

"Let's talk, okay, Jimmy?" Manzetti says.

"Sure," he says. "Sit down. You're positive no coffee?"

They sit at the round table. The fog adds a sense of unreality to the meeting, of secrecy, almost of conspiracy. Morgan is one of their own. This is why they aren't dragging him out of here in handcuffs. This is why, against all odds, they are giving him the benefit of the doubt. Emma almost hopes she's mistaken. But she knows she isn't.

"Why didn't you tell us you knew her?" she asks.

"I did."

"No, you told us . . ."

"I told you we answered a squeal two, three weeks . . ."

"June thirtieth," she says. "I called Vice half an hour ago, got the exact date."

"You told Lou about this, huh?"

"No, I talked to someone else up there. And I didn't mention your name, I just . . ."

"You shouldn't have done that. You have a tendency to be a lone wolf, Emma."

"Jimmy," Manzetti says, "how well did you know this girl?"

"I only saw her that one time. If you're trying to . . ."

"We've got your daughter's uniform in her apartment."

"I must've left it there. I probably went to talk to her on a follow-up, forgot Fiona's uniform there. That's probably what happened."

"So it *wasn't* just the one time."

"The one time and a follow-up, probably. This was an assault, you know, the disturbance at the XS. So I probably was doing a follow-up. In fact, I was wondering where that uniform disappeared to."

"You always carry your daughter's uniform with you on police business?" Emma asks.

354

"I was probably taking it to the tailor's or something."

"Jimmy, you're an experienced cop," Manzetti says. "If you were listening to this, would you buy it?"

"I know it sounds funny. But sometimes truth is . . ."

"We have you getting into a cab on Broadway and West Third . . .," Emma says.

"Come on, that was . . ."

". . . three, four blocks from where you live."

"That was Thorpe."

"We've got the cab dropping you off in front of the XS . . ."

"Thorpe."

"We'll bring the cabbie in, you know," Manzetti says. "He saw you up close, Jimmy. We'll bring back the other witnesses, too, give them a better look this time. We'll get our positive, Jimmy. You know we will."

"Unreliable," he says and turns to Emma and spreads his hands wide, and nods, seeking acknowledgment of a simple police fact: witnesses are notoriously unreliable.

"We'll take a bite impression, too," Manzetti says. "We're allowed to do that, Jimmy."

"Gee, no kidding?"

"We've also got DNA samples from the perp's semen . . ."

"Scientific experts never agree, ask O.J. about it."

"Point is, we've got a very good case here even without your daughter's clothes in the vic's possession."

"I didn't know you were *making* a case here. I thought this was just a conversation between fellow officers."

"What was the uniform doing there, Jimmy?" Emma asks.

"I already explained that," he says, and smiles, and starts to rise. "So if this little conversation is ended here . . ."

"Sit down, Jimmy."

"You giving me orders, Emma? I've been on the job almost twenty years now, who do you think you're ordering around? You know how many arrests I've made? Don't treat me like some fuckin criminal, okay? I *told* you how that uniform . . ."

"Were you seeing her, Jimmy?"

"Who?"

"Cathy Frese, who do you *think* we're talking about here? Were you seeing her?"

"I told you no. Listen, this is turning into an interrogation here, am I right? In which case, maybe you ought to arrest me and read me Miranda."

"You want Miranda? Fine!" Emma says. "You have the right to remain silent . . ."

"Cool it, Emma," Manzetti says.

"He wants Miranda, I'll give him Miranda. Anything you say may be . . ."

"Did you call Lois Ford last night?" Manzetti asks.

356

"No? Who the fuck is Lois Ford?"

"You know who she is. She's Heather Epstein's girlfriend. Did you call her at four in the . . .?"

"No. I never even met her. Why would I want to . . .?"

"We'll go to the phone company," Emma says. "Get a list of every phone call you . . ."

"Okay, I called her, okay? It's okay for *you* to be a lone wolf, right? But *I* make one lousy phone call on my own, to a person I believe is a *witness* . . ."

"Why didn't you tell me you'd called her?"

"I don't know what you mean."

"At breakfast this morning . . ."

"I was half asleep . . ."

"When I told you Thorpe called her . . ."

"I thought maybe he . . ."

"Why didn't you contradict me? Why didn't you say No, *I'm* the one who called her."

"Because I thought maybe *he'd* called her, too. You know, Emma, there's a logical explanation for everything in this world. There doesn't have to be a rapist behind every bush! Thorpe called a young girl for whatever perverted reasons of his own. *I* called a *witness* because I thought she might be able to tell me more about this person who was still a prime suspect in our case. All very logical, Emma. All perfectly under . . ."

"You always have phone sex with a witness?" Emma says.

"I did not have phone sex with Lois Ford."

357

"You know a girl named Cindy Mayes?" Emma asks.

"Cindy, Cindy," he says, and rolls his eyes toward the ceiling as if trying to remember. "Cindy Mayes, yes," he says, and taps his temple.

"Did *she* know you and Cathy were seeing each other?"

"I don't know what she knew or didn't know. And I *wasn't* seeing Cathy Frese. Except for that night of the disturbance and the follow-up in her apartment that one time. If that constitutes *seeing* her, then, yes, I was seeing her."

"Did Cindy know this?" Emma asks.

"I met Cindy only once in my entire lifetime, the night of the disturbance. I have no idea *what* she . . ."

"Did she spot you waiting for Cathy one night?"

"I never waited for Cathy."

"Recognize you as a Vice cop?"

"No, I really don't think so. Why would I wait for Cathy? I hardly knew her."

"Are you the one she's scared of?"

"Why should she be?"

"Because she knows you're the weirdo who waited downstairs for Cathy."

"Hey, weirdo, that's a strong word, Emma."

"It's her word, not mine."

"Strong word, weirdo."

"Well, how would *you* describe a man who dresses a whore in his daughter's clothes?"

"Does *what*?" he says, and actually laughs.

358

"It's not funny, Jimmy."

"Well, I never dressed anyone in Fiona's clothes."

"Wouldn't you call such a man a weirdo, Jimmy?"

"You know, Tony," he says, turning to him, "I'm just an honest cop here trying to do his job, I really don't have to take this from her. The job's tough enough without this petty bullshit. I may yell every now and then, yes, I may use the word fuck, I may fart, I may belch, I'm a cop, what does she expect from me, sonatas? But I would *never* use the word weirdo to describe myself. Or any other cop, for that matter."

Emma all but rolls her eyes. Morgan catches this.

"Oh, what is it, Emma?" he says. "Am I disappointing you? Would you like me to say I snatched every strand of hair from Cathy Frese's head, choked her to death, shoved my piece inside her, pulled the fucking trigger? Is that the *weirdo* Cindy described to you, *that* cunt? Well, I'm not him, you've got the wrong man here. I got a citation for bravery, you know that? Guy with a sawed-off shotgun, I dropped him in his fucking tracks! So, gee, I'm so terribly sorry I'm not handing you my head on a silver platter, but if you're going to seriously charge me with anything here, you'd better do it now. Otherwise, there's the door."

The room falls silent.

"Is that it, Jimmy?" Emma asks.

"That's it," he says. "No more questions. Find another patsy."

"Jimmy," she says, "what would . . .?"

"I said no more fuckin questions!"

"What would your daughter think if she knew you were dressing a whore in her clothes?"

"You'd have to prove that."

"Are *you* going to explain that to her, Jimmy?"

"There's nothing to explain."

"Daddy going to explain that to his little girl?"

"I'm a good father."

"Daddy going to take her on his knee and tell her he let a whore wear her skirt . . ."

"I didn't."

". . . her school blazer . . ."

"No."

"Her white cotton panties?"

"No, you're . . ."

"While he made love to her, Jimmy?"

"Hey! Careful!"

"How are you going to explain that to a thirteen-year-old girl?"

"This is my daughter you're talking about here, okay?"

"How are you going to tell Fiona you dressed a whore in her clothes and *fucked* her?"

The loft goes silent.

"Why'd you dress her in your daughter's clothes, Jimmy?"

He shakes his head.

"Jimmy?"

"I never . . ."

He stops himself.

"Never what?"

"Nothing."

"Never *what*, Jimmy!"

"Touched her."

His voice low.

"What?"

"I never did."

A whisper.

"What? I can't hear you."

He buries his face in his hands.

"Never," he says.

Emma waits.

"Never."

And all at once, he is sobbing.

He directs his confession . . .

But it isn't truly a confession.

. . . to Emma. He seems to be trying to explain . . .

No, not explain, actually.

He seems to be . . . well . . . apologizing. But it isn't even an apology. It's as if he's just chatting with her over a beer or a cup of coffee, trying to be charming, trying to be engaging, trying to demonstrate through his wit and his obvious qualities that he can't possibly be the kind of man he *himself* considers a monster. How can he possibly be this terrible person who *did* such things to a young girl? He is not that kind of person at all. He is James Fulton Morgan, son of an honest bricklayer in the Bronx, veteran of the Vietnamese War, holder of an N.Y.P.D. citation for bravery when he was still a patrolman in the Ninth and broke up a liquor store robbery where the perp was holding a fucking sawed-off shotgun on him!

He cannot help being flirtatious.

He isn't even *aware* that he's being flirtatious.

He is merely trying to convince the only woman in the room . . .

He seems to have forgotten Manzetti entirely . . .

. . . that he is really a nice guy worth knowing.

"The first time I met her," he says, "she was bleeding from the lip. He'd split her lip. There was a drunk up there who got insulted because . . . well, you know, Emma. Stanley, the big movie star from *Private Ryan* and *Sixth Sense*, I would've killed him if he'd still been there. I offered her my handkerchief. Clean white handkerchief, I always take a clean handkerchief when I leave the house in the morning. She took the handkerchief, dabbed at her lip with it. I gave her my handkerchief, Emma.

"She was . . . I don't know. Different. I must know, what, a thousand hookers? More. She didn't seem like a hooker. She was wearing this little white nightie, she looked like a kid who'd wandered into a whore house by accident, I wanted to read her a fuckin bedtime story, you know what I'm saying? Stood there dabbing at her lip. That pigeon-toed way of standing they have? Little girls? Fiona still stands that way sometimes. No panties, well, she *was* a whore, you know, I realized that, this *was* a whore house, after all, we were responding to a disturbance in a *whore* house, was what it was. Shaved little pussy.

362

A whore. They have no modesty. Standing there half-naked, dabbing at her lip with my handkerchief, describing the son of a bitch who'd hit her and this other girl, you met her, T.J., we talked to her yesterday. But Cathy didn't *look* like one, that was the thing of it. She looked like . . . I don't know. Well, you saw her, Emma, you were at the scene. Did she look like a hooker? I mean, she looked like a teenager, didn't she? Tell me the truth, didn't she?

"I took her aside—Lou was talking to the other girl, T.J.—and I told her if she was afraid the guy who hit her might be waiting downstairs or anything, Stanley, I'd be happy to escort her home. She said Oh, well, yes, gee, that's very nice of you, I *am* kind of shaken up, Detective, that's very nice of you to make such an offer, all that. You know how girls talk, her hands fluttering, all flushed kind of, just let me change, I'll meet you downstairs, okay?

"That's how it started. I sent Lou on his way, he's oblivious half the time, anyway, doesn't know *what* the hell's going on. This is now three, three-thirty in the morning, she comes down wearing blue jeans and a white T-shirt, she shoulda had a lollipop, I have to tell you. Cute as could be. Adorable. She took my arm. It was like we were both kids coming home late after a dance or something, I mean it, I felt I was still a kid growing up in the Bronx, she made me feel that way. I was still Jamie back then, in the Bronx, I didn't begin calling myself Jimmy till I joined the force. Jimmy's better for a cop, don't you think? Do you like the name Jimmy?" he asks Emma.

"It's a good name," she says.

"I think so. Lots of cops get brutalized by the job, you know, I'm happy that never happened to me. I wouldn't have been able to appreciate Cathy if that had happened to me. I mean, how many hookers have I met since I moved over to Vice? A thousand? It has to be at least a thousand. And yes, I've been tempted, yes, I'll admit that, I'm a human being, I've been tempted," sounding suddenly rabbinical, "some of these girls are very beautiful, you know. Well, take Cindy, for example, she's really a *very* beautiful girl, you have to wonder how some of these girls end up prostituting themselves. But, yes, I admit it, Emma, if you're in my line of work, you sometimes sample the sweets, I wouldn't be human if I hadn't been tempted, all those beautiful girls eager to oblige. But I never let the job brutalize me, I've always been Jimmy the Cop, same as when I was walking a beat. That's the thing. That's what made it possible for me to see Cathy as a human being and not some cheap whore peddling her ass.

"We went to bed together that very first night. She lives on Sixty-eighth, just off York, this little dump—well, you saw the apartment, Jesus. She was . . . I can't tell you what that first time with her was like. I'm divorced, you know—well, I told you all this, Emma, you know my whole life's history, I'm practically an open book. The point is, I've been with other women since the divorce, not only hookers, my

364

life doesn't revolve entirely around hookers, you know, in spite of my occupation, I'm a cop, okay? I'm a Vice cop. My job is to suppress vice in this city. I know my job, and I do my job, believe me. What I'm trying to say, though, is I've known other women—*straight* women—and none of them compared to what it was like with Cathy. None of them. What Cathy and I knew together . . .

"Emma, do you remember what it was like when you were a teenager? The first time you fell in love? That's what we had together. It was pure. Innocent. That's the only way I can describe it. Pure. I loved her, Emma. I truly guess I loved her. In fact, I can't think of anyone I ever loved more. Well, my daughter maybe. But aside from her, nobody. Do you understand what I'm saying?

"Last night, when I called Lois . . . I shouldn't have lied to you about that, Emma, that was stupid. I apologize for that. That showed a lack of respect. Of *course* you'd find out, did I think I was dealing with a person who didn't know her job? Forgive me for that, Emma. But the reason I called her . . . with Cathy gone . . . with no one to . . . I thought . . . I tried to . . . you see. Without Cathy, I was afraid I . . .

"Did you ever have the feeling something terrible was about to happen? Last night, laying there in bed . . . I had the feeling that with Cathy gone, something terrible might happen, I didn't know what. This wasn't the first time I called a girl for phone sex. I mean, well . . . I'm exposed to sex day and night, you know what I mean? So, yes, I've called girls and had sex with them on the phone, yes. Even though that's against the rules. And I admit calling Lois last night. But she wanted it as much as I did, nobody forced her to do what she did. You never have to force any of these young girls on the phone, they know more about sex than we do. You know what I mean?"

Sure, Emma thinks. It was consensual.

"They get younger and younger, the girls cruising the bars. I go to bars all over the city. One of the rules is no hookers, I can get hookers anytime I want, I just stop by and say Who wants me to padlock this place, and there are a dozen girls on their knees in a minute. That's one of my rules, no hookers. Which I broke, of course, the minute I started seeing Cathy. But she didn't look like a hooker, did she? Tell the truth. No phone sex, either, that's another rule. But I broke that one last night because . . . I don't know why I called her, I honestly don't. I just had the feeling something bad might happen this weekend. With Cathy gone, something terrible might happen."

What rules? Emma wonders.

"I used to meet her after work," he says. "Young girl on the street that hour of the night, hey, it's just not safe. Well, you know this city. I'm afraid myself sometimes, that hour of the night, and I pack a nine. This city is full of weirdoes, you know, Cindy was right to think it might've been some weirdo waiting downstairs. These girls get all kinds, believe me, they're wise beyond their years, these girls. You should've heard some of the stories Cathy told me, they'd curl your hair, the things men asked her to do. The things she had to do. She was hooking in Idaho, too, you know. Before she came to New York. You think *What?* Idaho? Hookers in *Idaho?* Well, there are more hookers in America than there are manicurists, believe me, I've been a Vice cop for a thousand years. That's my first rule. No hookers."

"What rules are you talking about, Jimmy?"

"I have these rules," he says. "No hookers, that's my first rule. No topless bars. No escort services. No phone sex. I have ten rules."

"Where'd you get these rules, Jimmy?"

"I made them up. To keep myself in line. Well, this job, you know. No pornography, no R-rated cable movies, no adult magazines, no singles newspapers—ten rules altogether. This world we live in, you need rules. You read the papers, there are twelve-year-old girls think nothing of giving blowjobs, they're like goodnight kisses to them. Read the newspapers, Emma, I'm not making this up. You see some of these young girls today . . ."

He shakes his head, lets the sentence trail.

"What, Jimmy?"

"No staring," he says, "that's another rule. I stare sometimes. It's a real problem. No staring is at the bottom of my list, but it's truly a problem. With me, it's a very real problem. These are very tempting times we live in, not that I'm trying to excuse myself. But I find myself staring a lot. At girls on the subway, at girls going home from school. I even stared at you, Emma, I'm sorry about that. Remember when you reached over the seat for your bag yesterday? I stared at you, I looked up your skirt, Emma, I'm sorry about that. But staring at girls is one thing, jerking off Lois Ford on the phone is one thing. Killing Cathy is another.

"I'm trying to tell you I *know* the kind of person I am, I'm aware of my shortcomings, I'm trying to do something about it. That's why I made up the rules. My mother had a lot of rules, too, when I was growing up. Rules are good for you. She was a gorgeous woman, my mother, red hair and green eyes . . . well, "Did Your Mother Come from Ireland," do you know the song? A gorgeous woman, but she had her rules, you know, oh boy, did she have her rules. She wasn't a tall woman by modern-day standards, my mother, but she gave an impression of height, well, what was she, five-six, five-seven, this was tall for women back then, wasn't it? Back then when I was still a little kid? My oldest memory . . . well, I'm not even sure it *was* a memory, maybe it was a dream, it sometimes *seems* like a dream, all of it seems like a fuckin dream."

I don't want to hear this, Emma thinks, and remembers what Morgan said when they were coming back to Manhattan on the Brooklyn Bridge.

Most of them were abused one way or another when they were kids, they got bad memories go back half a century, all of them sex-related.

368

"She was getting dressed for a party, and I was in her bedroom, watching. She always wore the most beautiful lingerie . . ."

I really don't want to hear this, she thinks. I don't care if your mother marched around the house naked, or your father beat you with a stick, or your sister entertained sailors while you watched, I do not care what trauma or traumas caused you to become the fucking rapist and killer you are today, I do not care at all. I do not care what caused Andrew to fuck the Swedish nanny, either, *if* he was fucking her, I do not care what caused him to fuck Felicia, whoever she was or may still be, I simply do not care what causes men to do the awful, hurtful things they do. So don't tell me about your mother, I do not care, I do not *care!*

"'I'm going to catch you, Jamie,'" she used to say, 'catch you, Jamie, catch you' . . ."

I don't want to know, Emma thinks.

"Tell me what happened," she says.

This is what you say to rape victims, she realizes. Tell me what happened.

"I'm not even sure," he says.

"Then tell me what you *think* happened."

He shakes his head.

"Tell me, okay?" she says. "Come on, Jimmy. Get it off your chest. Please. Tell me."

She holds her breath. Waits. Waits. Across the table, she can hear Manzetti's shallow breathing. Yellow fog presses in against the window panes. From the walls everywhere in the loft, the framed photographs of Fiona Morgan seem to be watching, listening attentively.

He nods.

She waits.

He keeps nodding.

"I was walking her home," he says. "She had her arm through mine . . ."

She has her arm through his, everything seems the same as always, nothing different . . . well, she's wearing a skirt. She usually wears jeans when she leaves work, but tonight—it's four in the morning, but it's still dark, and he considers it the nighttime, a dangerous time—tonight she's wearing a short skirt and a kind of loose blouse, no buttons, not a T-shirt, a tunic? No bra. She has very small breasts, you know. Very small. His daughter is more developed, to tell the truth, and she's only thirteen.

"It was very hot that night, do you remember how hot it was that night? The rain had stopped, a fog was rolling in. We walked through the fog, her arm through mine, everything seemed normal. I wasn't expecting anything out of the ordinary, everything seemed just the way it always was. I guess I asked her . . . no. I was about to say I asked her if she'd like to come to my place for the weekend, but I couldn't have because I knew Fiona would be there, I knew I had visitation this weekend. So it wasn't that. That wasn't how Fiona got in the conversation. I think what it was, actually, well . . . what I think happened was she told me straight out she'd changed the lock on her

370

door. Bam. Straight between the eyes. I changed the lock on my door, Jimmy . . ."

He thinks at first some john is maybe bothering her, following her home from the salon, something like that. He thinks she's asking him to help her with a problem she's having. Why'd you change the lock? he asks her. She tells him she changed the lock because she doesn't want to see him anymore. I don't want you to bother me anymore, she says. Don't come around anymore, she's telling him. I don't want you hanging around anymore. Don't wait for me outside anymore. I don't want you *touching* me anymore. I'm not your goddamn *daughter*.

"Well, I'll tell you, I honestly didn't know how *Fiona* had got in the conversation all of a sudden unless she was suggesting—well, I don't know *what* she was suggesting. I can tell you that ever since Fiona became a young lady, I've been completely circumspect. We're alone together a lot, and I know how impressionable young girls are, so I'm *very* careful about that, even though I find it strange that I used to wash her little bottom when she was a baby and now I have to watch my P's and Q's with her— well, they grow up, I guess. What I'm trying to tell you is I couldn't understand why Cathy was saying I don't want you *touching* me anymore, I'm not your goddamn *daughter*. What the hell was that supposed to mean? I've never laid a finger on her. *Never* touched her. Ever.

"This was very threatening, Emma. I don't know why. The idea of being locked *out*, of being told she didn't want to see me again, I found this very threatening. I'm a man who knows how to take care of himself, I've knocked many a cheap thief on his ass, but when she told me I was being locked out, she didn't want to *see* me again, didn't want me to *touch* her again, she wasn't my goddamn *daughter*, I found all this very threatening. Very upsetting. Because if I couldn't see Cathy anymore, if I didn't have *Cathy*, then . . . then . . . don't you see how threatening that could be? How upsetting? Not having Cathy there to . . . to . . .? What would I *do*? How would I manage to . . . to . . .?"

He shakes his head.

"Go on, Jimmy. Tell me what happened."

"I slapped her."

"Why?"

"I don't know why. She was scaring me. I grabbed her wrist. I said, I don't want to hear any more of that! I don't care *what* you want, you'll do what I *tell* you to do! She started screaming. I slapped her again . . ."

The fog is swirling everywhere around them as they struggle on the street corner. Someone is approaching, a black woman carrying a shopping bag. She stops dead on the sidewalk. Cathy is still screaming. He slaps her again, starts dragging her up the street. The black woman turns and runs. He drags Cathy by the wrist, tells her they're going home, never mind this shit . . .

"And no more about my daughter," he says, "you hear me?"

"Let go of me!"

"Keep my daughter out of your filthy mouth! Not another word about her!"

"Fine, just let go of me!"

"You hear me?"

"I hear you, goddamn it! You want to fuck your daughter, go fuck her. Just leave me . . ."

He smacks her again, harder this time. She begins screaming again as he drags her up the street and pulls her into a narrow alleyway between a sushi joint and a shoe repair shop. He hits her again, harder this time, his fist bunched, and she reels away from him, almost fainting. He grabs her again, by the hair this time, holding her up by the hair, punching her. She falls to her knees on the pavement. He unzips his fly. He grabs her by the hair again, meaning to pull her into his cock, onto his cock, but a clump of hair comes loose in his fist, and she screams again.

He grabs her by the throat.

"Be still," he says.

He does not want to kill her.

He tightens his hands on her neck.

"Be still."

He does not mean to kill her.

The scream in her throat tapers.

He lets her drop to the alleyway floor.

The fog sweeps in around them.

He falls to his knees beside her. He lifts her skirt and rips open her panties. Breathing harshly, sobbing, he throws himself upon her and sinks his teeth into her cheek and buries himself deep inside her.

The loft is utterly still.

Morgan sits staring at his hands on the kitchen table.

"Jimmy?" Emma says.

He looks up at her.

"Let's go now, okay? We have to go now."

"What about my daughter?" he says.

"What?"

"I'm supposed to get her again this weekend," he says.

CHAPTER
FIFTEEN

It is twenty minutes to eleven when she gets back to Chelsea. The fog hasn't yet lifted. She walks home from the subway station through thick layers of mist yellowed by automobile headlights. There are shadows in the mist. Muffled voices. As she lets herself into the house, she feels she is surrounded by restless ghosts.

It seems so still, the house.

These days, it seems so still.

She goes into the kitchen, grinds coffee, measures it into the coffee maker, pours in water enough for three cups. When Andrew used to live here, they made six cups of coffee every morning. She hits a button. A red light comes on.

It is seven minutes to eleven when the coffee is ready. She pours herself a cup. Sits by the kitchen windows, looking out at her shrouded garden. Sipping at her coffee, she thinks about Morgan again, remembers what he said about people like himself.

They think about sex every minute of the day, they can't stop thinking about it. Right now, right this minute, he's thinking about sex, I'll bet a million dollars on it. Running girls through his mind, memories of every girl he ever knew or hoped to know, turning them over in his mind. I know these creeps, believe me, I've been with Vice for almost a hundred years now. We better catch this guy soon, before he —

Before he *what?* she wonders.

She sips at her coffee, takes from her tote the list of phone numbers Thorpe called from his hotel room. Stares at the list for a long time. Listen, the hell with it, she thinks. He's in L.A., let *their* mothers worry. But she keeps staring at the list.

She goes to the counter, pours herself another cup of coffee, picks up the list again. Looks at her watch. Too early to call, anyway, she thinks. Well, she thinks, and sighs, and lifts the receiver, and dials the number in Topanga Canyon. The phone rings half a dozen times. She almost hangs up.

"Hello?" a man's voice says.

"Mr Thorpe?" she says.

"Yes?"

"Benjamin Thorpe?"

"Yes."

"We've been trying to reach you."

"Who's this?" he asks.

"Detective Boyle," she says. "N.Y.P.D. Where have you been, Mr Thorpe?"

"Is something wrong?" he asks.

"Nothing's wrong. Where have you been?"

"At the hospital," he says. "My mother-in-law had a heart attack."

"I'm sorry to hear that," Emma says.

376

"We just got home a few minutes ago." His voice breaks. "She passed away," he says.

"I'm sorry."

"Yes," he says.

She visualizes him nodding. She has heard him described so many times that she feels she actually knows him.

"Mr Thorpe," she says, "I'm calling as a friend."

"What did you say your name was?"

"Boyle. Emma Boyle. Detective / Second Grade Emma Boyle. Special Victims Squad. N.Y.P.D. You were the topic of some concern here in New York," she says.

"I'm not sure I . . ."

"Your Thursday morning comings and goings were under close scrutiny here," she says.

There is another silence on the line.

"You came close," she says. "Very close, Mr Thorpe."

"I don't know what you mean," he says.

"I think you know what I mean, Mr Thorpe."

There is another silence.

"Get some help," she says.

The silence lengthens.

"Mr Thorpe?"

"Yes?"

"Get some help. Do you hear me?"

He does not answer. She thinks for a moment she's lost him.

"Do you hear me, Mr Thorpe?" she says.

"I hear you," he says at last.

"Good," she says. "I'm sorry to have bothered you so early in the morning."

"No bother," he says, and hangs up.

She puts the receiver back on its cradle, nods, pours the last cup of coffee from the pot. Sipping it, savoring it, she wonders if she really should go up to Connecticut this weekend, shoot her mother-in-law, kidnap her own daughter. Shaking her head, smiling, she looks out at her garden. A fiery red azalea blossom seems to pop out of the mist.

She looks at her watch.

It is exactly eight A.M. in Los Angeles.

The fog is lifting.

The publishers hope that this large print book has brought you pleasurable reading. Each title is designed to make the text as easy to read as possible.

For further information on backlist or forthcoming titles please write or telephone:

In the British Isles and its territories, customers should contact:

ISIS Publishing Ltd
7 Centremead
Osney Mead
Oxford OX2 0ES
England
Telephone: (01865) 250 333 Fax: (01865) 790 358

In Australia and New Zealand, customers should contact:

Bolinda Publishing Pty Ltd
17 Mohr Street
Tullamarine Victoria 3043
Australia
Telephone: (03) 9338 0666 Fax: (03) 9335 1903
Toll Free Telephone: 1800 335 364
Toll Free Fax: 1800 671 4111

In New Zealand:
Toll Free Telephone: 0800 44 5788
Toll Free Fax: 0800 44 5789